DEVIL'S ROW

ALSO BY MATT SERAFINI

Feral

Under the Blade

Island Red

All-Night Terror (with Adam Cesare)

DEVIL'S ROW

MATT SERAFINI

Sign Up for Matt Serafini's
These Dark Woods Mailing List
at mattserafini.com and
receive an exclusive ebook

*"When justice is done it brings joy
to the righteous but terror to evildoers."*
— Proverbs 21:15

*"All concerns of men go wrong
when they wish to cure evil with evil."*
— Sophocles (The Sons of Aleus)

PROLOGUE

July 11, 1708
Outside the city of Oudenaarde, United Provinces

CLAUDE LAY SPRAWLED ON HIS back, his chest torn wide from a bayonet's savagery, shivering as the July sun taunted him with warmth he could not feel.

The fallen men around him sang death songs in discord: mortal groans and rattled cries offering to play him off life's stage.

And so soon? He was not yet seventeen and could only wonder now why he had not valued things more.

Not that anything back home was worth valuing. Long days of tending field, a father who spoke of nothing but cattle, an older brother determined to win the elder's graces. Blistered hands, bruised body, and bored mind. Hardly enough time to unwind from the daily repetition. Just a few short hours before bed to call his own.

It was no surprise that Claude only felt alive at night, when the cool grass rubbed his back and his eyes gazed the stars. He imagined other worlds and opportunities beyond this, wondered what they might offer. This wanderlust stayed buried, hidden from a father who hated that his younger son had chosen to be a dreamer instead of a laborer. At dinner, aged eyes bore into the side of Claude's face, contempt that burned hotter than summer sun, while brother regaled the table with tales of agricultural adventure. His enthusiasm was about father's placation, an act Claude could never find the ambition to compete against.

Passion for the family trade existed everywhere in the house, save for Claude's heart. He greeted each day with disdain and passed the time living inside his thoughts, performing designated tasks with hollow capability. Leaving home was his only chance. He had always known this to be the truth. Otherwise, life would slip past as it had for his parents and siblings. On occasion, he tried to picture himself in charge, scraping by with just enough food to eke out the winter. Raising destitute children as makeshift slaves to follow in his beleaguered footsteps. Weathering days that came and went with indifference, turning into seasons that passed as blithely as ships in the night, only to begin all over again.

A repulsive thought.

Today, the grass was at Claude's back once more, discarded weapons surrounding him. Fallen allies and enemies were mixed indiscriminately, as if the war still mattered to anyone here. The damnedest thought struck as he bled into the earth. Life *might* have been better back home after all. Carting crop surplus into town, hoping for enough coin to cover another season's upkeep felt like a better deal. It was not much, but it *was* living. Maybe that was preferable to this fool's crusade.

Or maybe he would not lie to himself and pretend the family business was suddenly worth anything to him now that he was dying.

Claude would have laughed at the irony if he had any strength left to do so.

Yesterday's march to Oudenaarde found the battalion

soaked in sweat and drained of morale. Soldiers wore apprehension as part of their uniforms. Shoddy masks of bravery tried hiding it, but the shared façade collapsed when you looked into their eyes. To Claude, it was like glaring into a mirror and seeing his unease reflected. A shared question from a hive mind: *Is this worth our lives?*

What did it matter to them? Did peasant farmers care who succeeded Charles II in Spain? This morning, they had faced an alliance of soldiers culled from all corners of Europe: the Holy Roman Empire, Great Britain, the Dutch Republic, Portugal, and the Duchy of Savoy. All because France had allied with Spain over matters he did not understand.

A cause that would probably never affect him.

Matters that had murdered him anyway.

Thoughts came slower as his body chilled. He recalled the false sense of hope being passed around camp last night: pats on the back, constipated nods of confidence, and stories of hijinks from back home. None of it brought a boost in morale, instead giving Claude a compelling notion to flee in the night.

The smart ones *had* fled, and probably still had their lives to show for it. Claude stayed because he had not liked the alternative. His father's eyes already judged him with severity. To come home a coward would provoke in him more scorn than he could stand.

He was paying for that stubbornness now.

All Claude could do was marvel over how long it took to die. A braver man might hold his fractured breath until the embrace of permanent sleep, or crawl toward the nearest weapon and inflict a more fatal injury. Anything was better than this protracted loss of consciousness.

The battlefield became less of one as time passed, turning into a mass graveyard. Only grim vestiges of warfare remained as the sun's glare finally lifted off his eyes, leaving his vision singed and nearly gone.

He wished his hearing would go as well. There were fewer voices now, but the ones that remained clung to hope of rescue by calling for help. Others prayed in ephemeral voices for hurried passing. It was much too late for that.

When the killing had started, Claude was confident that his musket abilities could keep his adversaries afar. Dragoon units crisscrossed the battlefield on horseback and kept the enemy distracted while his long-range gunfire picked them off like prowling coyotes back home.

It was only a matter of time before the enemy wised up and advanced, and Claude had been ready to meet that tactic head on. His scabbard dangled off his waist, waiting for the inevitability of close-quarters bloodshed. In a moment, chaos had engulfed the battlefield whole, forcing him to swallow notions of strategy in favor of frantic killing blows.

He had not seen the attack coming. A blade sliced through the carnage, drawn to his gut like a magnet. His killer had skidded through the pandemonium and lifted his rifle overhead with clenched fists, delivering a slice so wide that Claude felt his chest bone crack.

Then it was over. He was on the ground without realizing he had fallen. Instinct pulled his flintlock pistol from his holster and squeezed off its single shot. It struck the assassin through the bridge of his nose. A splat of blood stretched wide behind that head before jerking back and dropping from sight, leaving Claude to watch the skies and wait for the stars. One last dream, this of the heavens he prayed would take him.

The day traded deep blue for evening black. The air around him was stained by the smell of still-lingering gunpowder. Its residue marked his hands and clothes, and sullied the proximate bodies.

He wanted to move, but even that consideration was exhausting. While drowning in contemplation, the sky grew darker still, and more of the adjoining groans fell forever silent.

If he could survive the night, it was possible that he would be discovered once the armies came around to collect their dead.

The bayonet wound burned anew with that thought, squashing what little hope he dared to keep. This was an injury so fatal that he could not expect to survive it.

No, he was lost and death was only a matter of time. He would be somewhere else by morning.

That prompted him to pivot his head backward in the grass, compelled by the panicked notion that he would never again see a gibbous moon. That glorious harbinger of his open-ended evening dreams.

A cloaked figure walked toward him.

Through heavy eyes, it appeared to be a trick of the pale moonlight. However, it continued to advance, sidestepping strewn and damaged bodies on an undeterred path forward. The shapeless and shifting cloak strode with too much certainty for this person to be surveying bodies. It moved with a destination in mind.

Me.

Claude followed the shape with his eyes. It neared him and then circled. The figure paused at his feet in presumed study. Claude could not be certain if he opened his mouth to speak, or if he merely wished that he could.

Beneath the hood, shimmering eyes watched in silence.

He was not moving anymore. Had his body failed completely? The cloak rippled and spread like bat wings. A curvaceous form stepped free of it, long hair darker than the evening sky, a body whiter than the moon, and with breasts that bounced in time with her steps. Then her feet fell on either side of him.

She was a shadow now, a solid black monolith blotting out what remained of his vision.

"Please." His voice was gunpowder coarse. She knelt, her hair scuffing against his cheek while her lips curled around his earlobe, whispering for him to *shush*. Her breath was sticky and passionate; enough to ignite goose bumps across his fading flesh.

Her hands slid around his back. One caressed the base of his head while the other crept along his spine. She lifted him without regard for his injuries, taking him into a pitiless hold.

He grimaced with as much protest as he could offer. She did not seem to care, nor was she deterred when his opened chest spilled onto her. Instead, the sound of unmistakable arousal sputtered past her lips.

Her teeth clacked with the ferocity of a hammer falling on anvil, something anticipatory about the gesture, followed by the sound of breaking bones as her shifting skin lifted and fell— something beneath it trying to break out.

Claude's chin sat against her shoulder. Patches of thick hair grew from her flesh and scuffed his jaw. It was almost comfortable when compared to the uneven mound of dirt that had pressed against his neck for much of the day. Now that he was upright, he looked out across the battlefield.

There were others like her.

Monstrous shapes cradled the fallen, choosing bodies on either side of the skirmish with breath being the only apparent requisite. Some cloaks only now slithered from the darkness and closed in on their persons of interest.

He tried to say something, but red babble spilled down his chin and onto the animal's shoulder. Her voice was a deep-bellied growl.

She pushed him back into the grass, leaving him to stare at a visage that was no longer human. Yellow eyes swirled into huge bulbs that glowed hearth hot. A wolf's snout dropped into his face and delivered a gust of squalid air.

There was only time enough to cough. The string of eager saliva dabbed his neck and face before razor sharp jaws dove beneath his shoulder.

Claude was already so damaged he barely felt it. As the animal swallowed a piece of him with a satisfied huff, he could only close his eyes and imagine the sweet release he was about to experience.

It was not so bad after all.

NIGHT FALLS

October 30, 1709
Hungarian-Moldavian border

ELISABETH DID NOT SEE THEM until it was too late. They were there as soon as she opened her eyes.

Armed men pushed into the clearing. Their breaths heaved with the kind of excitement that sounded like fear to her eardrums. They might have trained for this moment, but could not so easily push away their trepidation. Doubt carried its own smell, and it was mounted on each of them.

Somehow, they had evaded her senses every step of the way. Even in this form, she had a wolf's hearing and smell. Somewhat muted while on human legs, but strong enough to prevent this kind of sneak attack. Usually. She only knew they were here now because they let it be known. How had they done it? That question alone made them formidable, but others dawned in rapid succession.

Who are they?
For how long have they followed us?
Finding her should have been impossible. She and Aetius

had scaled to the very top of this mountain ledge, close enough to the moon to shred it with her fingernails. No better hideaway for tired animals looking to leave the bloodshed behind.

Yet it had followed them here.

"We will call this *Nightfall*," Aetius had said of this peak, his thick hands clasped over her eyes as he led her through the brush not one week earlier.

She remembered the way her nostrils had cleared as the air thinned, a soothing feeling that set the world so far beneath them it became an instant memory. It was impossible to stop a lunatic grin from overtaking her lips as she stared at the sight of their future. "The evening descends upon us first up here," Aetius had said. "Fitting, because the night has always been ours."

The mountain's eastern and southern walls were impossible to scale. An impenetrable fortress crafted by centuries of erosion. Constructing an estate up here was going to be costly, though beneficial to what she wanted.

Isolation.

Once completed, their home was going to couch them here, away from everything. Nothing to do, save for the exploration of each other's curves in perfect solitude. Hidden from the rest of the world and relying only on each other.

Elisabeth could think of nothing she wanted more.

But those thoughts cracked and crumbled beneath reality, and the first crusader stepped into the clearing. Elisabeth smelled offcuts from the last week's worth of meals nesting in his coiled facial hair. Spoiled bits undetectable to human nostrils, but a rancid stink.

I know you, she thought, and growled at the realization.

He looked like a new man as he vaulted forward in a death charge, one possessed of confidence and rage. How long had it been? *Where* had it been? Elisabeth struggled to recall.

It was always going to happen like this, she knew. After terrorizing humanity for decades that blurred together like fever dreams, she would be a fool to expect anything less. The world hunted them as devils for their sins and sometimes that world was shockingly adept at killing.

Elisabeth scampered off the bedroll, caught between competing shrieks: the cliff side breeze howling at her back and a roaring battle cry that plowed toward her. It had been a while since fear was anything other than a memory, but she felt it now.

The assailant wore an off-white linen shirt cloistered beneath a dark doublet. A single lock of curly auburn hair jostled out from beneath his hood in the naked moonlight, dangling between fiery eyes. Black leather gloves climbed to his wrists and disappeared beneath silver vambraces that shelled his forearms. A matching sword sat in one hand, and he pulled a pistol from the holster with his other. Spot-ridden trousers were tucked into ankle-high boots spiked with silver toes.

He knew well what he hunted.

A silver pauldron clamped over his shoulder and kept the thick grey cloak in place. It billowed off his back, the whole getup daring her to find his vulnerability.

And yet, Elisabeth knew there was hope. Reaching this peak would have consumed whatever energy these men had. They looked disheveled in the moment, powered by adrenaline and little else. Less zealous hunters might have waited for daybreak and taken them then. This was to her advantage.

Elisabeth's bones broke beneath her human skin as the wolf awakened. Her lips curled into a battle snarl.

The soldiers, if they could be called that, hurled encouraging words into the sky. A rallying volley. Some voices were unmistakably British, meaning these boys were a long way from home, and had likely crossed the Holy Roman Empire to get here.

That was a month, maybe more, spent walking from Marburg to Ingolstadt, only to reach a chaotic land that would never bend its knee to the imperials they served.

This corner of the world had its own problems. Invaders to the north and east, armies clashing for little more than ego and leaving broken lands of death and destruction in their wake. In the debris of war, the darkness came crawling, looking to exploit the runoff of vulnerability. Elisabeth could not say precisely *what* inhabited the forests below, but there was very little humanity left out here. Violent men and malignant creatures had seen to that.

It was a perfect hideaway.

Or had been.

One of the men hovered at the clearing's edge, falling behind the charge. A teenager stuck in hesitation, with juddering motion that could not decide between charge or retreat.

Elisabeth sensed high tension among them. Doubt.

She also sensed the blood of her pups. It stained their blades and clothes. The army she had fostered off battlefield scraps had fallen once more, and the sudden anger she felt over this was unquenchable.

She urged her wolf to the surface, but the animal would not come fast enough. The hunters closed in around them and she braced for a fight.

One hundred years ago, I would have relished this.

A feather's tickle stroked her body. Raven-black furs enveloped her milky white flesh in tufts. Her eyes became inhuman orbs of ferocity that pulled the evening's obscure details into focus.

Aetius was already wolf. He puffed his chest and lifted onto the tips of his hinds. A howl rolled off his tongue and slid down the mountain, coasting over the tree beds far below—a rallying cry to any brethren in the area.

Strategic, but no one could reach them in time.

"Fan out and slay the abominations!" The familiar hunter cried.

Elisabeth's skull cracked and collapsed—an implosion that would have killed a human. Her cheekbones shattered. Her nose popped. The wolf's face pushed outward through the shapeless mess, revealing an angry animal that sang her displeasure through gnashed hunter's teeth.

The hunter skidded, as if encouraged by second thoughts. A puff of dirt kicked into the air between them as he took aim.

His weapon was impossibly fast. Three shots barked from the barrel, each accompanied by blasts of sparking light. Three silver pellets landed against her, striking her neck and chest with staggering force. The balls of her feet kissed naked air as the cliff nearly sent her tumbling. She prevented it by digging her hind nails into the dirt.

Four men converged and readied their weapons with killing strides.

She felt Aetius' body tense with impending battle. The brown wolf took point and moved to meet them head-on, shielding her from the bulk of combat. A sliver of barely recognizable affection passed between them, followed by a battle roar so forceful the trees nearly toppled against its gust.

Elisabeth struggled to catch her breath behind the stinging gunshots. The pain was nothing worse than a surface pinprick, but the silver closed her throat and lungs like the worst kind of allergy. Aetius would not have to worry about that. He would be dead if their ammunition pierced him.

She hoped they had squandered most of it on her army of pups. A comfortless, yet practical thought as the silver pellets poisoned her bloodstream. Her breathing became a labored struggle while her nostrils burned.

Time to get out in front of the action. She trotted up

beside Aetius to draw their fire. Once those guns clicked empty, they would not have the opportunity to reload.

The male wolf growled in protest, outraged by this tenacity. Elisabeth would have scoffed at his useless display of chivalry if there were time, pushing forward, knowing full well she was the faster beast.

Another shot fired and then another. Elisabeth was nearly upon the familiar one when a silver pellet crashed through her chest. If the new wound brought fresh pain, she was already too numb to feel it.

Other men had guns too. A series of sparks ignited the clearing in whitish-yellow. Aetius allowed her to become the center of attention, understanding his fatal vulnerability to these weapons. He trotted around the clearing's outer circle to ensure they could not hit a moving target while another shot pegged her through the loin. In the flashing sky, her coat was wet with blood.

The guns were at last empty, and the fight was fair.

She lunged for the familiar one, but the crusader ducked beneath her reach and tumbled through the dirt. She hoped Aetius would be there to scoop him up and tear his head off. No time to check as the others divided their focus between the two wolves.

Aetius' jaws closed around the arm of an attacker and snapped the bone clear. It was not the familiar one, but any dead man would do when there were this many to choose from.

The others glanced at their fallen companion, and Elisabeth used this pause to drop her mouth low. With a lunge, her razor smile raked across an exposed neckline. The throat offered a wet crunch as she tore it free and swallowed it whole. No time to savor the juices spilling down her gullet.

Two maimed and dying men dropped to now-sodden earth, and Elisabeth tasted the earliest hints of victory through the blood. Repelling them was easier than expected, and Nightfall would soon be housed upon their shallow graves.

Neither wolf had noticed the three additional men advancing from the forest behind them. Elisabeth turned in time to catch a glimpse of bloodied wolf pelts sliding off their shoulders, understanding at once how they had evaded their pointed wolf senses.

Cunning.

They would have marched the mountain path single file, for it was too narrow to do anything else, masking their stink in the blood and fur of wolves.

That made her angrier.

Elisabeth pushed her midnight mane against the back of her lover. Instinct allowed a hasty survey of the arena as the crusaders closed a semi-circle around them. Two of them went on bended knees as their trembling hands readied crossbows. A third sprung forward, slashing his sword through the night.

Her reflexes anticipated this and parried without effort.

Aetius' powerful joints bent for maximum spring in his pounce. He cleared the distance to the swordsman before Elisabeth could, toppling him in a flurry of angry claws.

A marksman's arrow whizzed past, a shot successful in attracting Aetius' attention. He soared from the gurgling corpse and toppled the two bowmen with outstretched talons, nails smashing through both their faces with a thunder crack. The thrashing bodies needed an extra moment to realize their brains had been destroyed before falling limp around embedded killing nails.

Elisabeth focused on the remaining men as Aetius struggled to retract his paws from broken faces. She flashed her teeth and snarled one final warning. Leave now, she tried to tell them, because maybe then they would be spared.

They would never be that, but they were certainly free to think it.

Her warning prompted caution in the killers, their own mortality never so obvious. The situation boiled to an impasse. The hunters looked reluctant to move against the black wolf. They watched both animals as Aetius wrestled his arms free from the smashed faces, leaving his victims broken and spilling blood over campfire ash.

Fresh blood was an aroma that got Elisabeth salivating. Thick strands of drool rushed down the rivet at the center of her tongue. Bloody spittle dangled off her jaws. She could not wait to feast.

It was two versus three now. This fight was against madmen who surely believed themselves instruments of God, and that stoked Elisabeth's motivation further. In this age of *enlightened* thinking, when skepticism and atheism rose against the church's reach, this mindset, blind devotion, was both archaic and bothersome.

Elisabeth wished she could return to her human guise long enough to tell them that their *Lord and Savior* had abandoned them. Knowledge that would not matter to converted men. And they would never consider the words flung from the mouth of a *foul thing* such as herself. Their destructive ignorance was entrenched and made them worthy victims.

Her eyes bounced between them, searching out signs of weakness. The softest among them was to be kept alive for torment and the familiar man would die, his time long past. Only he did not look ready to go. He stood ahead of the others, shoulders rising and falling in excitement. She sensed stimulation, unfettered resolve, perhaps, while eyeing the silver blade in his fist. A weapon poised to strike at just the right moment.

He's scared. The pressure eats him and he threatens to buckle beneath it.

She tasted it from here—a sticky sweet stain on her huffing tongue. She wanted that delectable treat and shuffled her paws forward in order to claim it. His fear delighted what remained of Elisabeth's humanity. Misguided men like him were commonplace, and had been since her turning.

Nevertheless, they always died the same, with last-minute prayers to deaf, heavenly ears. Frantic cries that only incentivized her aggression. Gruesome bloodletting was almost never enough because her hatred for them was like nothing else.

God's love was a lie propagated by savvy clergymen for political gain. She supposed they would discover this nugget on their own soon, and that would have to be satisfaction enough. Elisabeth admired humanity's willingness to exploit the goodwill of its own, and thought that nonbelievers were smart to turn their backs on such philosophies. God held no love for miscreants like these. How could he when so many atrocities were executed *"in the name of Christ,"* including one that saw a young girl hauled away from her ailing mother.

That distant and foggy memory echoed like an old war wound, becoming another motivator in this fight. Her claws raked the earth for traction, readying a death charge.

A pike exploded through the front of her chest.

White-hot pain hit her in a violent spasm. Her back arched and she cried out as the blade obliterated her rib cage. A geyser of blood vaulted through the air, coating the frock coats of the front-facing killers.

Her breathing collapsed and her knees gave out. She hurtled toward the dirt.

Above and behind, the pike jostled upward with a grunt that prevented her fall. Her claws fell away from the slick blade jutting from between her breasts. Her body regressed into human form and her hands continued to slip off the wet silver, making anything beyond a fleeting grip hopeless.

An armor-encrusted arm looped around her neck and hoisted her out of horizontal free fall. The pike jiggled from side to side and widened the wound while increasing the pain.

All she could do was scream.

"Here is how you die, filthy whore. Like the mongrel you are."

The pike tore straight down through her innards until the blade bounced off her pelvic bone and knifed back up, cutting a larger swath through her organs. A silver shark's fin sliding through a bucket of chum. It fell out her back and clattered. She dropped with it.

Her vision blurred. Disbelieving fingers grabbed at the vertical slit that ran down her length.

"Take her head!" A voice called from above.

Elisabeth dug her fingers into the dirt and closed them, pulling along like a dying dog.

The men exchanged cruel laughter as a boot heel swung between her legs, but she was too numb to feel anything more than the general landing. Hands took her shoulders and spun her. Bloody hunks of earth flew past her lips in a cough while another boot stomped straight down onto her face and broke her nose with a crack.

"Back to hell, bitch!" The broadsword sliced through the air and hacked the side of her face. Her jaw exploded, sending tiny bone fragments flying. Nearly blind, she used the balls of her feet to push against the ground. A pile of flesh and bones moving on instinct, to nowhere in particular.

She heard Aetius in the distance, cries buried beneath a cluster of hacking swords. One final shred of attention lingering long enough to register somewhere in her dissipated mind, then it was as lost as every other thought.

Elisabeth slugged on, her head dragging. Cloudy eyesight caught a glimpse of wolfen limbs flailing as blood streams shot high into the night. For a moment, it looked like they had stained the moon.

An image that signaled an end to the dream of Nightfall, for there was no way of getting to him.

And no way to escape.

Only thing left was to die. Succumb to these wounds and meet Aetius in the beyond. Anything was better than this. Two hundred years ago, she might have thanked these men for breaking her curse, but without him—

Queen Alina expected her huntress to perform certain duties. Duties that Elisabeth had once savored: bearing daughters and sons for the queen's kingdom. Not through her loins, but through her bite.

Time spent in the arms of her lover had fostered resentment for that role, a position to which she had no desire to return. Dying with Aetius meant leaving Alina's world with a guilt-free conscience. It was not rebellion if you were dead. And at this point, dying would be just fine.

Except that you cannot.

Elisabeth pushed her legs up and down and slid across the clearing like a slug. A few remaining embers from tonight's fire popped in the pit beside their bedrolls. Hours ago, she had made love there and then lapsed into a confident sleep, certain that nothing could hurt them.

The gash down her chest, the bullets lodged inside her organs, and her splintered jawline begged to differ.

She could not see the cliff side in the dark with failing eyesight, but knew she needed to reach it. Her would-be killer called out from somewhere above, an airy taunt that sent her scurrying.

Think about the rage.

It was a welcome distraction from the pain and she embraced it. Driving anger that recalled those *rehabilitative* nights spent in an Inquisition prison two centuries earlier. She had wanted nothing more than to break out and destroy those who had gleefully violated her. That hatred flooded back as if it had never left.

Elisabeth's retreat took her between two rocks and her hands coiled around the cliff. The night winds rustled her hair as she attempted a deep breath, catching only a tired wheeze of relief. Beneath her was the only clear path up and down the mountain. An arduous walk even without fatal injuries and eager murderers on her heels.

Far below, the watery ravine was little more than a blur.

A wolf's whimper came from somewhere behind, severed by a blunt chop. Aetius was gone and the night was quiet.

Then hurried feet dashed toward her.

They probably thought this was justice.

"Kill her before she drops!" The scream was desperate.

"Kill her?" That voice belonged to the stealthy one who had run her through. "I'll take that bloody cunt for a victory fuck…always wanted to screw one of these things."

Elisabeth pushed off over the edge and slid down the sheer rock wall. The drop chewed her already mutilated face before discarding her onto the familiar dirt path, knocking free what little wind her lungs carried. No time to recover. She crawled to the precipice and rolled off.

Then she was falling.

The wind chapped her during the plummet. She hit the water so hard that she was certain she had missed the lake entirely and splattered on the rock basin beside it. Her arms cracked back, dangling like noodles. She drifted atop cool water, her head slipping beneath the surface while her body teetered on the brink of functionality.

She slipped beneath the lake and drifted to the bottom. Her back raked across the rocky floor while her eyes fluttered.

Drown now and Aetius died for nothing.

Elisabeth could not truly drown. Such was her *gift*. But no varcolac could recover in duress, so she struggled to her side and kept watery groans pent as she fought to reach the surface. At last, her head broke the water and she sucked the open air as best she could.

Her hands slipped through the wet dirt while she tried to climb onto shore. The mud felt oddly soothing and cool on her torn body and broken face. Despite the ragdoll tumble from the heavens, she remained intact.

She had to get up and keep moving, but there was no chance of that happening. The killers had not come this far to leave her fate to chance. No, the familiar one would find her and finish the job.

She had only delayed the inevitable.

It would take them the rest of the night to descend the mountain. It took a varcolac more time than that to recover from less injury. Still, if she could regain just enough strength to slip away.

To do that, she needed to sleep.

So she did.

○

The animal's roar rolled off the mountain and blasted across the treetops like a ferocious wind gust. A growl that sent the area's living things scattering.

But Codrin was not alive.

He lifted his head off the cavern floor and squinted. His skin felt like dry leather, tight and constricting, while his vision registered vague shapes. Cloudy shadows that sprawled across the floor around him. His ears functioned considerably better, and that is what brought him from slumber.

His stomach rumbled. Something crawled on top of his head. He scratched it and wound up scraping away two strips of corroded flesh along with a tuft of wispy white hair.

"How frustrating," he said.

Voices were almost never used down here. His words became an echo that aroused the others. Soon they were in the throes of early waking, too. From somewhere behind him, the creature whose name he did not know might have stirred in its chamber.

Codrin's heart would have pounded had it worked. He called this fiend *strigoi viu* because he did not know another word that accurately described it. If the witch heard their awakening, it or *she* would be the one determining their course of action. Her needs fulfilled before all others.

That could not happen this time.

Codrin's task was finding blood for the clan and this was as close as he had ever been. The land was in strife, entirely vulnerable. The Devil's Row moniker had been nothing if not earned over these last few seasons, making human beings as scarce as afternoon rainfall. As such, Codrin's people had gone unfed for so long their strength was sapped, barely strong enough to rise with the moon, let alone infiltrate what few unsuspecting villages remained.

The clan had positioned several sentries throughout the land, each with orders identical to Codrin's. But that howl was close by. The fates had decided he was to be the hero.

"Rise," he told the slumbered as they stretched across

the cool cavern floor. They had chosen this outpost on the witch's invitation. It was mostly safe, and the temperature this far below ground was the same in summer and winter. Long slumbers were easier and more comfortable. Closer to the feeling brought by soil sleep.

The others might have protested Codrin's arrangement with the witch had they known about it. The price of asylum had been their three weakest bodies, paid immediately upon arrival. She took them as soon as they slept, and in exchange, gifted them with safety for as long as it was required.

Even witches worried about the scarcity of victims in times of unrest.

"Why do you awaken us?"

Codrin studied the face of the one who asked—a woman whose name he did not recall. His disdainful glare receded some as he was stunned by the cruelty with which age had treated her. Her face was gaunt, as if someone had stretched a thin sheet over a skeleton. Her lips were without color and pellucid flesh looked like it might tear upon touch.

"There are travelers nearby," he whispered.

The woman got off her knees, joints cracking as she fumbled for her cloak. Her body was as skeletal as her face. Chest recessed, with jutting ribs, sagged breasts, and contracted hips. She slipped the fabric over her scraggly figure and dropped to the ground, palms pressed against the cavern floor.

So deep was their sleep that to be pulled from it was often disorienting.

She coughed twice, both times much too loud, and said, "I do not see what we are supposed to do about travelers."

Codrin decided he did not like her. "Careful," he said. "This will require us to work together."

Around them, four others rose, each resembling graveyard

cadavers. They staggered and groaned. Old bones could barely support what little weight remained on them.

Codrin would never admit she was right, but agreed all the same. How were they supposed to drink in this condition? The witch would wake them on occasion, feeding them whatever drops did not fill her phials. Meager offerings that kept them cognizant and little else. In order for his task to be successful, they were going to need more strength than those driblets afforded.

He slipped his cloak around his bony shoulders, pulling the hood up and over his scabby head. The girl stood nose-to-nose with him now. Her mustard eyes were narrow and when she opened her mouth to speak, fangs pinched through her lower lip. They were so dry he expected puffs of dust to shoot through the punctures.

"I do…"

He silenced her before she could talk and then started past, moving up the winding incline that carried them through the cavern's stomach and into the forest above. He would not wait for the others. They were followers and would do precisely that.

The girl kept pace like an eager stray while the rest ambled far behind in casual pursuit.

When the top was reached, Codrin stopped and threw his hands on either side of the stone opening. He stuck his neck out to savor the night sky, tasting flesh, crisp and juicy, on the tip of his tongue. An enjoyable delicacy when he had the luxury, even if it was a precursor to what mattered most.

The blood.

They were here for the blood, of course, and on behalf of an entire village. Withdrawal dulled his senses, *their* senses, rendering them a cabal of inefficient predators. The ability to hunt was never truly gone, but it would not come easy after the passage of so much time.

He closed his eyes out of habit and the forest came alive around him. Jittery cicadas danced beneath leaves, restless Dalmatian pelicans shuffled in an overflowing nest above, and far beyond everything, a wolf danced with the men trying to kill it.

With the path clear in his mind, Codrin started into the wilderness when her fingers clasped around his shoulder, yanking him so hard he might have toppled.

"Where are we expected to follow you?"

"Can't you hear it?" It was impossible to mask his impatience. That she would rather sew apprehension made her dangerous. Not only to his men, but also the village. No one should witness this fractured leadership. The others were as desperate as him, and no telling how they would react if they thought her plan was better.

"I hear *you,*" she said. "We are too spent to go rushing off like this."

"Better that we waste away?"

"We can never truly *waste away.*"

"We are not getting any stronger. What will happen if we go another season without sustenance? That witch will put us in those cages when she gets desperate enough. You want that?"

"She would never…"

"Listen." Codrin eyed the rest of the men who now joined them at the bottleneck. "There is food out there." He took the girl's decayed hand in his and eased her into the undergrowth. "Smell it."

She closed her eyes and took a long, greedy whiff. Around them, the cloaked men filed out and did the same.

"We can have it," he said. "The wolf. The men. We will be heroes. Saviors."

She was nodding now.

Codrin sensed trepidation on her mind. On all their minds.

They were right to feel it. Home was a distant memory, so alien now that the cave's belly almost felt more like it. Combating a field mouse in this condition was an uphill battle, and if they waited any longer, they would not be able to best one of those, either. Success this night was going to take time and require cunning.

Nevertheless, he intended to deliver, and would reassure his men of that. When they returned, everyone would be indebted to Codrin. Perhaps then he would find respect among the elders and be allowed entry into their inner circle.

It was about time they listened to his ideas for assured survival.

More growls tumbled down that mountainside. A rush of blood drifted through the air like wet morning mist. The others were not so weak they could not smell it, too. Somewhere up there, it had been shed.

He looked at the girl and caught a glimpse of concession in her eyes. She would not admit he was right, but possessed the good sense to understand what needed doing. That was something.

"Shall we go," he said, and started into the trees.

"We shall," she said and the rest of them followed.

MEN OF ORDER

SEBASTIAN MILES HAD WATCHED THE girl spiral to her death. Nearly an hour later, he remained somewhat horrified by the brutal way in which she had gone out. He thought of this while his breath returned and his pulsing heart slowed.

At last, it was done.

He stood inside the clearing with the other men, not a word passed between them. Two months ago, they were fifteen strong and packing enough silver ammunition to genocide every monster in this region.

Four remained. A legion of those creatures had been slaughtered between there and here, though Sebastian was not about to sleep any better because of it.

He doubled over, sucking air and thinking about the madness along the way. Could he truly return to hunting London lowlifes? Would he ever sleep again knowing what was *really* out there?

His *leader*, Garrick, stacked the bodies in the clearing's center. He tended to the dead men first and then piled the wolf's severed appendages on top.

His *apprentice*, Timothy, made his way to the clearing's

edge and sat as far away from the bloodbath as he dared venture. The boy's blunderbuss rifle was tucked beneath his arm while his nose hovered over yellowed and worn book pages. His eyes bore through the words, as if this madness could be explained away by philosophy.

Sebastian felt for him. Truly. The kid had not signed on for this hunt. It had gone far beyond thief-taking. Their usual business was raw and bloody, but predictable. Desperate men could be counted on to act desperately. Always.

Sebastian wished to be back home—his dive loft above the Piccadilly Tavern on the corner of Croft and Thorne. You had to step over a pile of shivering jemmys just to get in the door, and the fumes of spilt rye wafted up through the creaking floorboards so often that the wood was warped and smelled like you could get drunk just by licking it. You might even hear a whore's moans in the alley if some lucky sod had enough coin to float a tumble.

Nostalgia aside, Sebastian could make due with homesickness. The guilt he felt was for dragging the kid along. He walked across the clearing, still gasping for air in the wake of the assault. They were victors, sure, but this did not feel like cause for celebration. His mind glimpsed the mutilated wolf woman tumbling over the edge once more, the bloodiest and most broken body he had ever seen, and his heart suffered a sting of pity for the beast. She deserved extinction, but not like that.

The late October air was thin up here, a welcome respite from the sweltering heat that had greeted them throughout the first leg of their journey. Sebastian tugged the loose linen shirt beneath his frock coat as he walked, pools of sweat gathering beneath his arms and across his steel-grey chest.

The other surviving men had recovered much faster. He did not like admitting it, but age had long since slowed him.

S'ok, he thought. *I'll never have to work again after this ride.*

His hand tapped the gin flask that dangled off his belt. As parched as he was, as much as he needed a sip of home, his thoughts returned to the first of their fallen, Evan.

The fate of his oldest friend and fellow thief-taker had been sealed before the commencement of this blood hunt. By men desperate enough to err on the side of unpredictability. Men who had done more than run. Men who had decided to circle back through the night and slit the throats of their pursuers.

Evan's throat was as far as they got, his struggle rousing Sebastian and Timothy from already unsound campfire sleep. The killers were out-gunned and, without the element of surprise, revealed themselves as cowards who would quickly flee a straight fight.

The ensuing hunt lasted for two days, hot pursuit that turned colder than steel to the throat. As signs of gnawed grass became commonplace, it was Timothy who realized they were following horses without riders. Fleeing killers would not have allowed so many breaks, and it became clear they had abandoned their animals in a last-ditch evasion effort.

Sebastian had them reverse direction and follow sporadic tracks back to a main road, to a badly damaged travel coach that had spilled into a gully off a dirt path.

Neither man had been in a merciful mood then, executing the unarmed killers—who had already murdered the wagon travelers—to avenge their fallen friend.

Their weapons were still swirling with smoke when Garrick and his mercenary army found them. The witch-finder, or whatever the hell he fancied himself, had been impressed with their abilities and brutality, offering the chance for them to put their skills to the test.

"This battle will make you rich…if you survive it," he had said.

If only they could have known.

But the past is for reference and not residence. Sebastian decided there was no point in dwelling there. Both he and the boy had made their choices then, and stood on the brink of a brighter future because of them.

Assuming you can forget the things you've seen.

Sebastian thought he had earned enough gin money that forgetting would not be a problem.

"It's over," he said, announcing himself to Timothy as he circled around to face the avid reader. In the clearing, Garrick worked on converting the stacked bodies into a flaming pyre.

Timothy was glued to the pages, eyes rummaging them, as if searching for hidden meaning between the lines. The kid had reluctantly grown to accept that life was more than oft-quoted creeds found in scholarly pages, but that never stopped him from taking comfort there.

"The end of law is not to abolish or restrain, but to preserve and enlarge freedom. For in all the states of created beings capable of law, where there is no law, there is no freedom."

This oration prompted a groan in Sebastian. Every word was codswallop to his ears. No place for it out here. Garrick was too occupied at the moment to pay any attention to Timothy and his books, and for that Sebastian was thankful. He was much too tired to mediate another disagreement between the two.

Garrick hated when Timothy quoted John Locke, and Timothy hated that Garrick knew who John Locke was. One habit the kid had yet to kick was assuming that everyone in his path was an uncultured sloth.

"Once we catch the wolf woman, pup," Garrick would say each time Timothy challenged him, "convince her that what she really needs is a hellspawn government."

Sebastian agreed with the witch-finder in secret. He could

never tell Timothy that, nor would he chide the boy for rejecting their cynicism. It got to everyone sooner or later, and there was no reason the kid should have to deal with it prematurely. The longer you thought you could make a difference out here was reason enough to get out of bed some days.

Timothy's breaking point was inevitable. It would come once he saw, first hand, that the solution to lawlessness was more than the simple establishment of order. Sometimes bad men and vicious monsters needed their brains blown out to keep the world spinning.

Months after the retaliation for Evan's killing, the kid continued to struggle to accept his cold-blooded actions. Retribution was a reflex that could not always be suppressed. And where Sebastian accepted this, Timothy could not. Regret plagued him on their easternmost journey to hunt the Raven, retreating into his books, surfacing only when he was required to perform the tasks he now abhorred.

Timothy Hackett was a changing man in these wilds, and his eyes reflected a person at ideological odds with himself.

"All that's left for us is to claim that reward," Sebastian said.

Behind them, Garrick and Ritter finished stacking bodies. They spoke inaudibly, and Sebastian had no desire to know what of. The job was finished where he was concerned.

They were strangers in a strange land. A place far removed from the comfort of decaying London. The old city was not much these days, but it was home and he knew how to traverse it. When families hired him to find the thief or killer that had wronged them, Sebastian did so in a matter of hours—usually. His web of lowlifes kept their eyes wide and their ears open. The information they would gleam was often enough for him to bring his target to justice in time for morning bacon.

Petty crimes were glossed over to attack the worst of it.

Sebastian slept well by that coda most days. If a lord or lady had to get fleeced out of some pocket riches so that he could bring a rapist to justice, so be it.

Out here was a different story, though. No barmen to consult, no corner pickpockets to grease. It was fair game, kill or be killed, and that was a real pisser.

Once the bodies were stacked and ready to burn, Garrick called them over for a huddle. He offered a few comfortless words, and then asked if anyone had anything to say about the departed. A ring of silence passed around them.

The witch-finder shrugged and lit a match to set the corpses ablaze.

It was always the same. A thoughtless prayer spoken over a shallow grave. They pretended to mourn, but relief was their reality. Glad to have been spared to fight another day. No one seemed especially proud to think that way, but it was a silent understanding in Garrick's dwindling army.

Sebastian watched the bonfire with unease. Hard to shake the feeling he could have easily been among that pile, or any of others just like it along the way.

Because they had followed the raven-haired wolf, no one knew her real name, and her army across the Holy Roman Empire, losing most of their men during battle at an isolated border estate called Freywald.

Freywald had been a small village surrounded by pastures and meadows on the Hungary border, the only place that had not yet become a haven for the varcolac plague.

A place where its inhabitants were too scared to leave their homes at night, lorded by an agricultural estate that had almost completely withered, unable to keep its population healthy or safe. With supply lines dried for good, a few desperate souls had ventured for help and were never seen again.

From the stories told, Garrick had sensed Freywald was a trap, theorizing that Raven had abandoned her army there. Everyone felt the gaze of hungry eyes watching from the forest and suspected it would not be long before the enemy called.

The battle came eagerly on the first night and everyone who could swing a sword was tasked with fighting.

The wolves had poured from the trees in every direction—a clever onslaught that prevented them from fortifying the perimeter. Areas with high defenses were quickly flanked. The fight raged until dawn and without interval. The sun was high but the wolves kept attacking, a torrent of teeth and claws that demolished almost all living things.

Victory was narrow, delivered barely, and at the price of Freywald's existence. The streets were left devastated, the population eradicated, and Garrick took to examining wolf carcasses with increasingly bugged eyes.

"She's not here," he screamed. "The Raven is gone!" Half their men were dead and Freywald was one night away from becoming a ghost town, but Garrick was only getting started.

He demanded the head of the raven-haired bitch, and ordered the handful of injured wolves be brought to the sprawling estate house on the hill, where the witch-finder was holed up, forbidding anyone else to progress beyond the entry hall.

Sebastian and Timothy tended to their own dead in the village below while tortured screams haunted the hilltop for days.

When Sebastian was finally allowed entrance, he learned that wolves harbored an allergy to silver. That exposing them to the metal could be motivating. His glimpse inside the hilltop home revealed an estate of horrors: spilt entrails, disembodied heads, and mercy pleas from the lips of former enemies. Their mouths had been jammed up with silver coins so that their facial features were swollen and bloated.

At the center of it all, the witch-finder stood wearing only a pair of linen shorts. His molded physique was covered in splatter, and yet the dark ink of several tattoos came through. He wore symbols as others wore jewelry.

"I have it," he had said. "Her."

Extracted information sent them galloping east at a breakneck dash through an area controlled by the Habsburgs. They resupplied in a village called Pest before storming onward into the Transylvanian mountains and beyond.

To this place. And last night's battle.

The bodies were on their way to a crisp and Garrick had broken off from the group. He stood against the cliff and peered out across the cool sable sky.

"We have to get down there," he said. "Raven is hurt, but she will recover."

"Can't wait to find her," Ritter said, rubbing his hands together as though his mind had hatched a devious scheme.

"Ah, yes," Garrick said. His words popped as he made a small circle around the man who had sliced open the she-wolf. "You are determined to stick your prick inside her, yes?"

Ritter's smile was black and rotted. "Best quality whore I've ever glanced…don't care if she is gutted and shot. If she draws breath, I'm screwing her 'til she don't." He looked to Sebastian and Timothy with a perverted plea for support.

"A rousing set of values," Garrick said.

Ritter's face hardened against the firelight. "I followed you this far, Garrick. Listened to every miserable order you gave… including those that got my brothers killed. If I want to have a slice of that cunny…"

Garrick drew his six-shooter and fired. The gun sparked and through a haze of gun smoke, Ritter stumbled back with a splat. Their companion in the broadest sense only toppled while the hunter holstered his gun and turned back to watch the open sky.

"Morality is always the first thing to go," he said with complete composure.

Sebastian thought back to the bloody aftermath inside the Freywald estate and wondered how Garrick could make that statement, then decided to bite his tongue. They were nearly through this.

Timothy, however, could not bite his. "These men lost theirs a long time ago," he said, "before this journey."

"Everyone has a choice, pup. Even Ritter had one."

"When the only world you know is one where men in power take what they wish from those who have nothing, what can you expect?"

Garrick scoffed. "Just ready yourselves. We're leaving."

Sebastian reloaded his single-shot flintlocks. He carried two in holsters set against the small of his back. Once, he had asked Garrick where to obtain a weapon that fired six shots without reloading.

"Magic, as far as you know."

They regrouped and collected everything of use from the satchels of their fallen company. Garrick looted Ritter's body of everything before flinging the corpse onto the roaring flame. He did not bother to ask if anyone had anything comforting to say.

Timothy was at the start of the mountain path, looking down into the water far below. Sebastian peered over and nudged his shoulder.

"What are you doing with your share of the bounty, kid?"

Timothy's eyes were glassy. "Haven't given it any thought."

"We both know you're university-bound. No more trawling the night looking for dragsmen, aye?"

"How can I face that place now? How do I advocate for

civilized ideals in the wake of the things I've done?"

"No one needs to know the things you've done, any more than they need to know you once had great pox on your cock…"

"Because of a whore that *you* had me lie with."

"You got an injection for that…cleared right up," Sebastian said.

"After a month."

"Well, when do I get to hear the end of it?"

"Never."

Something approaching a fond smile sat at the corners of Timothy's mouth. When he saw that Sebastian had noticed, he turned away to mask the levity.

"I would hate to see you punish yourself simply because you think you've compromised your ideals. No one makes it through life without doing that. It's all in how you make up for it."

"I get it," Timothy said, "but each killing gets easier."

"And each has been justified, but that doesn't mean you gotta like it."

"Good, because I don't. The echelons of university deserve better men than I." He fished the battered copy of *Two Treatises* out of his satchel and waved it around. "I saw myself in this world once…but no more."

"Don't act like you're beneath them now, kid. Before your time, Evan and I chased down an academic who'd been drugging and pegging his students. He took the position so he could slither up next to impressionable minds and violate them. You're still a scholar, now more than ever."

Garrick wedged his way in between them and motioned for them to follow. "Listen to Sebastian, because you're certainly no killer."

They fanned out single file and started down the mountain.

"Thank God for that," Timothy said. "I'd rather stand

in front of a bunch of hungry minds and advocate science and reason over this, witch-finder."

"Call me witch-finder once more, and I'll leave you burning atop that pyre with Ritter."

Sebastian's hand curled around the hilt of his pistol. Bickering was not uncommon for these two. But the threats were new.

"Why would I refrain from calling you what you are?" Timothy said. "You take orders from the church. Execute those who are kissed by Satan…"

"What makes you certain that I take orders from the church?"

"You spoke once of your familiarity with Vatican City. Why else would a murderer like you know that place…witch-finder?"

The kid's goading put Sebastian on the defensive.

"You ever see a witch-finder do anything other than burn peasant girls at the stake? Or look for third nipples on the chests of vagrants? I ask, because I have not."

"You're no better than they are, then. Killing men in cold blood. Throwing lives away like game pieces."

"You can do better?"

"Couldn't do worse," Timothy said.

"No man's knowledge can go beyond his experience," Garrick said. "Sound familiar? Or do you only preach Locke when it can be used to condemn our *incivility*?"

The kid rolled his eyes and continued walking.

"Silence from here," Garrick said after some time. "Finding Raven is all that matters."

Sebastian used a rag from Ritter's shirt to wipe wolf's blood off his silver blade. Not even the mightiest creature could have survived the damage they had doled, let alone that fall.

Garrick needed to know for sure, which meant one last follow.

I can do this.

He grabbed for his flask and took a generous swig of London gin, closed his eyes, and let it set fire to his throat.

A taste of the home he longed for.

○

Elisabeth bled out in the mud, dreaming. A recent memory filled her thoughts with warmth as her body shivered in shock.

She stepped outside the manor house into late August air. The sun was bright enough to wrinkle her brow and she squinted through it. Aetius trotted by her side, keeping the form he felt most comfortable wearing. The wolf lapped her naked thighs and panted as she walked.

Across the bridge and down the hill, her pups trounced what remained of the village populace. This was their most recent conquest. Her ears flexed to enjoy every last raucous and lusty grunt from her most eager children: those wide-awake and unsated in the morning light.

Elisabeth's muscles burned and her head ached. This was the regimen that followed regression. She was used to it now, but only because there was no other choice.

Aetius, on the other hand, seemed to think he had one. His rebellion meant keeping the wolf around for as long as possible.

It annoyed her on days like this.

She ruffled the fur between his ears and encouraged his change. The wolf stuffed his muzzle into her curvaceous bottom, and his nostrils puffed. She swatted him away with faster reflexes.

"Not now," she growled.

The wolf rose onto his haunches and offered a glimpse of

visible excitement that matched the familiar look in his eyes. She was uninterested in going again so soon. The lake called her name and she hurried toward it, ignoring the wolf's defeated whimper.

Elisabeth did not mind her lover's unbridled lust. Their union was free of matrimony, and they took other partners as the mood struck. Neither one cared for cuckolded feelings, however, usually taking lovers while in the presence of one another.

In last evening's raid, her pups had been over-eager, as children often were. Elisabeth had allowed them to attack while she stayed back with Aetius to savor the carnivorous fruits of her labor.

The pups had been clumsy and unfocused. They wounded many but killed none. Because Elisabeth did not want their outfit swollen to unmanageable numbers, she swept in with Aetius to ensure the victims succumbed to their wounds.

Then they cherry picked a few captives to enjoy. Aetius found a young peasant girl whose flower had never been plucked. Elisabeth settled on a strapping young solider whose loins burned bright for her, despite witnessing his wife's violation and disembowelment only moments earlier. That he was still able to perform sexually delighted her so—his morality and grief shred so fast that he could not have had any to begin with. Yet, it was not nearly as much fun as savoring Aetius' jealousy as she forced him to sit back and watch.

Fucking a plaything was never truly about pleasures of the flesh. That kind of thrill had waned long ago. This was about leverage. Driving Aetius out of his mind with desire was one way of maintaining their bond.

And, she supposed, her control.

Teasing Aetius in such ways kept his eyes alive with awe and wonder. Maybe it hurt him to see her bouncing up and down in the lap of a human wretch, but it was the sort of hurt that became necessary after a century of unadulterated love. It stoked his fires, and once the soldier had been well spent, lacquered in sweat and resting by the hearth, certain that his life would begin anew among his conquerors, the fun really began.

It started with the change. Claws broke through her fingertips and she used them to slice the plaything's stomach. His intestines spilled past the gashes like boiled linguine, and they feasted on his innards before Aetius seized her in violent, pent-up passion.

Everything up to then had been foreplay.

All of this while the virgin prisoner sat captive, marinating inside her own fear-turned-insanity. The sole witness to satanic depravity, she screamed until her voice stretched hoarse and disappeared. When she stopped being fun, she became the main course at evening's end. Innocent blood being so much sweeter, they took their time devouring her in order to savor it.

Elisabeth felt nothing but tedium this morning as she waded into the lake with a bar of soap in hand. She scrubbed crusted blood off her body and watched the wolf run circles on the beach. He dropped into the dirt and rested his snout across his front paws. Shifting eyes stared with disappointment, annoyed that she had changed back so soon.

She polished her body until her skin was soft and fresh. Satisfied, she plodded from the water, angry that Aetius could not fetch a towel.

When they got back to the estate, the antechamber's marble flooring felt cool on her feet. Broken bones and human gristle lined the great hall's floors, a repulsive sight on a full stomach. Soon the smell would be too foul for her human nostrils and they would be on their way.

The wolf trotted across the hall to the picked-over meat and wrestled a bone from a shoulder socket. His jaws clamped down and his paws steadied his hold long enough to snare the lingering beef.

Elisabeth watched him with swirling fondness and annoyance.

The wolf caught her eyes and froze mid-bite, confused. His whimper indicated that he missed his huntress and was lost without her. After all this time, she knew how to read the animal.

When he continued his gluttonous feast, her attention drifted around the room to the displayed paintings. The décor was repulsive.

"Look," she said. It was a conversation she wanted to have with human Aetius, the stupid wolf only able to understand basic sentiments. "It is all so trite."

She spoke in particular of an oil-on-panel piece that depicted Paris of Troy alongside three nude women. If the story was to be believed, and she hated that it once had been, then he was *gifted* with Helen by the supposed goddess of love, Venus. Apparently, Paris had chosen Venus as the most beautiful of three sisters, and the celestial being was so flattered by what a human thought, she had handed him a woman to demonstrate her appreciation.

Vile.

Why should a woman of power give a damn what any mortal says of her allure? Because it was a story cooked up by long-swollen and pathetic men.

That piece hung beside another rancid work called *Lucretia.* This one showed a moon-faced woman, her tiny breasts popping from her gown. She held a dagger at her own chest. Lucretia had been raped by a Roman king and was so overcome by shame that she was about to stab herself to death.

Elisabeth gnawed the inside of her cheek while studying these depictions of women as victims and objects only. She had created pieces superior to this filth, and would again.

Compelled now to walk through the rest of the manor, she examined all the artwork and was depressed to discover what passed for taste in this barren part of the world.

When she came back downstairs, she smacked the large wolf upside the head. "I am not going to spend my days speaking to myself."

Aetius dropped to the floor and groaned. His thick coat of fur was soon swallowed by bulging arms of hardened flesh, and his wolf's dome receded to become the face of the man she loved.

She fell on all fours and forced her tongue inside his mouth. "That is much better," she said.

"I could fuck you again right now. The way you tease this animal is a burden no one should bear."

Elisabeth smiled. "I have not begun to tease you." Her laughter was cruel. He was going to have to do a lot better than spoiled pillow talk.

She took a seat on the lord baron's throne, an elevated and unremarkable chair that, she imagined, was used to hear the whines of the peasantry. Worries of the day that included damaged crops, spreading smallpox, and whatever else passed for problems here. She rustled against the stone backing, but there was no getting comfortable.

"I grow weary of this," she said.

"Then you've reached a decision?"

"I wish to leave this, all of it, behind."

"Our pups will not make it out here."

"That had better be a jape. Do *we* require training now? The pups will sate themselves as they see fit. This was never about my tutelage."

"But the queen…"

"…will find another huntress. These are not responsibilities specific to me. Are you worried about the queen, or do you mistrust my judgment?"

"I have never trusted anyone more."

"Once a soldier always a soldier, is that it? The Rome you served is no more." Elisabeth outstretched her arms. "And this empire is one in name only. Far to the east and nothing like the one you used to know."

"My loyalty is to you."

Elisabeth cocked an eyebrow and studied him. His eyes remained soft and adoring. She kicked out her foot and stroked his thigh with the tips of her toes, scraping back and forth while a smile stretched across her lips.

"I am sorry, my love." And she was. Her frustration had nothing to do with him. It was not right to lash out because she was miserable. Most days, she loved his choice to remain inside his true skin. It was proof that his loyalty to their kind went beyond a need for instant gratification.

Aetius slipped a robe around his shoulders and kissed her forehead. She reached for his head and held it, keeping his lips pressed against her skin for a long while, closing her eyes to savor him.

Contented growls rumbled in the distance. "They are only now realizing their potential. The queen's need for chaos will be well met by them."

"I know you." Aetius closed his gigantic hands around her bare shoulders, squeezing away the last of her changing pains. She moaned in approval. "You want to do more in this life than simply exist."

"Pleasures of the flesh are as stale as day-old bread when there is nothing to sustain them."

"You were not complaining last night," he said and closed his wet mouth around her neck.

She batted him away and launched off the throne, wrapping a cloak around her naked form. "I spent my youngest days as a wolf in Rome. Painting, sculpting, creating…without those outlets, I would never have been able to accept what I became."

"One day, I shall thank Fane for siring you. If he hadn't rescued you from persecution…"

"*Rescued* is an interesting word." She could not tear her eyes away from the nearby picture. Christ's crucifixion as depicted through a crude scrawl of pen and ink. The sight made her grimace, and prompted similar recollections.

Elisabeth's hands balled into fists as she bounced up and down on her toes. "The men who took me from my village chose to make a very public display of my…*blasphemous* ways. There, Fane *rescued* me, sure. From one group of monsters to another."

Becoming varcolac had been disorienting and terrifying. One of the queen's oldest lieutenants, Anton Fane, had planted his curse inside of her, begging only that she serve by his side. Dark urges grew and spread like an infection, despite every effort to rid them. She declined Fane's long-term invitation to rule, gravitating instead toward the city of Rome. She hoped it would receive her artistry and provide the escape she needed.

Her mind had been garbled confusion then. She subjugated the darkest thoughts by depicting on canvas the things she had done, along with the impulses that encouraged those actions. Her work was seen as a harsh rejection of the Christian movement, so radical that almost no one wanted anything to do with it. It brought scorn where she had expected praise.

More than two lifetimes separated those memories from where she now stood.

Aetius hugged her, this time without sexual imposition. He whispered supportive assurances in her ear that suggested he knew what she was feeling. Understood why she would feel compelled to settle down.

"That's what this is about, yes?"

"Settling down?" She did not consider it *settling.* "I am tired of living for chaos. Why not find a place of our own?"

She never mentioned this before because Aetius had never stopped being a soldier. This would mean abandoning all that he was.

"Say where, my love. And it shall be built." His speech was genuine, his heartbeat natural. As far as she could tell, his enthusiasm was sincere.

That made her smile.

Then laugh.

If it were so easy, she would have floated this suggestion long ago.

"I have never considered where to live…"

"Consider it now." Aetius pushed her against the wall, knocking the crucifixion picture to the floor where it was better off. His kiss was gentle and went no further. "Once you reach a decision, I will see that you get there."

"And you have no problem with this, at all?"

"The more I consider it, the happier I believe it will make me."

"It would mean leaving these pups…"

"Like you said, we are not tutors, and there is considerable wealth in these lands for us to sack. Once we have taken it, I will get you a palace."

The possibilities turned in Elisabeth's head and she giggled like a girl with a childhood crush.

The Mediterranean was her first choice. The weather there was beautiful, the food varied and plentiful, but what of Paris? It was, after all, the cradle of modern culture. Those there were likely embrace her work without ostracizing her refusal to pander to the church.

"I will consider the options, my love. Now tell the pups to get ready. We've got a lot of ground to cover."

It was a nice thought of better days. It continued to turn in her mind as mud seeped into her mouth from the corners of her smile. Elisabeth sank deeper into it as she continued bleeding out at the mountain's base.

○

They were nearly down the mountain when Garrick's hand flew into the air and halted the trek.

Instinct had always been one of Sebastian's strengths. He reached for his pistol while curling his free hand around the basket-hilted blade, lifting it a hair from its sheath.

No way of knowing what made Garrick so cautious, but there was no reason to discount him now. He had brought them this far.

Barely.

Morning chipped away the night, leaving the sky a lighter shade of dark. The forward path was dense with trees that would block out the daybreak as soon as they traveled ahead.

If Raven was near the lake, she would be easier to find. They had to assume she was resourceful, and thus would have slipped into the forest for evasion.

Sebastian hoped she was not that smart or able, provided she was alive at all.

Garrick's hand continued to hold them in place, his head turning to try and catch some distant noise in his eardrums. If the she-wolf was alive, she would have smelled their descent long ago, so the hunter's foreboding was over something else.

"There." Garrick's voice was flimsy.

The mountain's base was swallowed by the tree line, and the path through the forest before them was streaked with blood. The men armed themselves at the sight, stepping with caution over spilt intestines that stretched across the forest floor like uncoiled snakes.

A horse carcass lay beyond some trees, its underbelly gashed and pulled so wide the animal's remaining anatomy was in clear view.

Further along came the severed head of another.

"Someone wants to keep us here," Garrick said.

"How can she be alive?" Panic traced Timothy's words.

Garrick shot him a look so angry that Timothy swallowed any additional gripes. The hunter ground his jaw and grabbed a fistful of the kid's frock, yanking him close.

"Give us up again and you'll think Ritter got off easy." He pushed the kid back and said nothing more.

Sebastian felt numb while staring at his animal's remains. Temper, named for his tumultuous attitude, had served him well, carried him long and never quit when it mattered. As such, he ate as well as his master, and whenever a town offered the service, Sebastian paid to have him groomed and comforted.

An animal's respect was often mutual, and much too difficult to acquire.

He was going to kill the one responsible for this.

Garrick ordered a change in direction to a trail that took them toward the lake. As they reached the beach, the water looked like rippling crystal beneath the rising sun.

Timothy and Sebastian went to work on finding a trail, but there was nothing beyond a few animal hoof prints, those that got thirsty in the night and came here to drink.

Garrick walked along the mud and his boots suctioned with every step.

"She's here," he said. "I feel her…"

"Possible that she drowned, ya?" Timothy said.

"That's right, pup. Thank you for volunteering for a swim so you can answer that question. Sebastian and I will circle around the lake and look for tracks while we await your conclusion."

Timothy looked defeated, but they had agreed up front to follow Garrick's command to the letter for as long as they remained in his employ.

The kid pulled his clothes free while Sebastian searched the trees around the lake and Garrick headed down the muddied beachfront.

If only they could have been more efficient last night, they would have been in the throes of a celebratory hangover now.

Sebastian paused in front of a downed log and dropped to one knee. It was scuffed by drying mud from the sole of a boot. Not much, but all there was to go on. The girl had gone over the edge nude, meaning that someone else had come this way, and recently.

The outermost crust of mud was still moist.

A few steps away he found another half-print in the dirt. He sidestepped the track and ducked below low-hanging branches to find another. This one was a full-on boot print pointed in the direction they had just come.

Someone carried her off.

Sebastian hurried back to the waterfront where the kid was only now diving beneath the surface. Best to let him search so they could rule out the notion that Raven had drowned. He wanted to be wrong about the tracks, anyway.

Timothy reappeared and brushed wet, straggly hair from his face. When he noticed Sebastian watching he shook his head, then gasped for air and slipped back under.

She was not there. Someone had ridden to her rescue just in time, slaughtering their horses so they could not follow.

Sebastian waited for the kid to come up for air once more so he could get him out of the water. Garrick was further along the shore, by the rocks, waving his arms back and forth. The silver vambraces on his wrists caught the sun as he motioned for their attention.

Timothy reappeared with a deep gasp and Sebastian waved him out. The kid used his cloak to dry off before reaching for his shirt that was now the color of London pig shit.

They reached Garrick, who wore a face of panic as his eyes danced around the surrounding trees.

"I should have seen it," he said. "When we attacked last night, one of those creatures howled at the moon…a cry for help."

"How do you know?" Even now, Timothy had to challenge.

"Because it's being answered."

A figure wrapped in a red robe glided out from behind some trees—its face hidden by the hood covering its eyes.

Timothy lifted his blunderbuss but Garrick whispered for him to stop.

"There is more than just one," he said.

Sebastian turned to discover his own hunter's instincts had been correct. Two more bodies approached from the beach. Each robe was a dark stain of crimson. Black rope belts cinched their waists. Their steps were Sunday calm, garish appearances unnerving. Three more appeared and converged on their party from the tree line.

Theirs were the tracks he had seen.

He reached for one of his pistols.

"Don't do it," Garrick said. "We'll not be shooting our way out of this."

"I'll be damned if I'm surrendering," Sebastian growled and took aim.

"The only way we'll survive this day is if we do exactly that," Garrick said and tossed his weapon to the ground.

Sebastian could not believe what he was seeing, but watched the hunter lift his arms to the sky and step away from the others, allowing for the thief-takers to make their own decisions.

The hunter intended to live through this.

Timothy's face dared to hope that Sebastian had an escape plan. Some type of strategy the kid had not yet considered. Sebastian did not relish submission, and hated to disappoint his understudy even more, but sometimes there was nothing to be done.

If giving up meant there was a chance of escaping down the line, what choice did they have?

"Put it down," Sebastian said and threw his weapon beside Garrick's.

O

There was commotion beyond Elisabeth's eyelids, bustle that aroused her consciousness. Her eyes fluttered. She coughed sand off her tongue and rubbed her throbbing head.

A broken piece of tree ebbed against her skull. Her shoulders remained submerged in the lake, and one side of her face was caked in beach mud.

How had they missed her?

Her skull protested any kind of heavy thinking and her muscles were lit with regression's fire. Beneath the water, her fingers traced the length of last night's fatal wound. It was already closing, the most inconsequential of scars now.

Wandering fingers found her jaw, pushing her mouth

around in a circle to assess the damage. The bleeding had stopped, leaving an open scab on the clean side of her face. She rolled onto her back and crabbed out of the water, arching as the sun's glare stung her watery eyes.

Breathing was hard, moving harder.

In this state, she doubted she could take the rest of them. She massaged her temples until the throbbing rescinded just a notch. Was it possible they believed her dead?

They have to know I live.

Elisabeth pointed her nose at the sky and attempted to sniff them out. This cursory exploration of terrain offered nothing that suggested they were any closer. It was the squalid graveyard odor that interested her as it fastened itself inside her nostrils.

She heard a groan in the distance, an unmistakable expression of pain.

It took all her energy to sit up in the muddy basin, steadying herself on the palms of her hands. The mud attempted to swallow her fingers as she focused.

Another moan ghosted across the lake, bringing next the sound of shuffling feet.

In spite of everything that happened, Elisabeth smiled.

Those fools left me for dead.

Their presumption must have been that she would succumb to the damage. Laziness that would be their undoing. How could the familiar one be so careless? Had not he the desire to see this through?

"No," she muttered. Her voice was a gravel-laden rasp that barely registered as human. "He is not that stupid." Best not to presume anything. Just because she did not sense them did not mean they were gone. Humans were resourceful animals. Their survival instinct knew no limit.

They were able to kill Aetius.

Thoughts of him came back, each one bringing emotional shudders. Her head jerked and she wretched all over the beach. Tears welled at the bottom of her eyes but she would not wipe them. To mask these emotions, to pretend they were nonexistent, would be an insult to him. Reveling in misery was the only way she could grieve.

He deserved that, at least.

Life did not feel worth living without him.

On that mountaintop last night, entwined and dripping with sweat, they had discussed their future. Nightfall, their own kingdom on high. A life of solitude. It was the first time since childhood life felt rife with possibility.

If only she had fought harder to defend it.

Instead, she had been arrogant. The assault was a blur, but Elisabeth could not stop scrutinizing her actions. Had she wanted to see Aetius fight to defend her honor? It had not been a conscious decision, but she wondered about it anyway.

Self-loathing was more powerful than the unending sobs, all of it together a very human gesture of weakness. One she would not fight, but resented all the same.

Her arms curled around her knees and she buried her face between her thighs as the tears fell.

She was alone now.

And angry.

○

They were forced to march, surrounded on all sides by red cloaks.

The forest brush was thick enough to scrape their cheeks and rake their heads. Their captors would not speak a word. They had confiscated their weapons through silent gestures before closing in around them, ebbing them along.

Sebastian and Garrick exchanged glances. Looks of the *how in the name of Christ are we getting out of this* variety. The hunter seemed unsure and Sebastian's confidence was only slightly higher.

It was a hostile walk. They were shoved if their pace slacked, then cracked across the back of the head if it happened again.

The six cloaks wore their hoods low enough to conceal their faces. Even their exposed chins were draped in shadow. Chapped leather gloves covered their hands and steel daggers were tucked into their belt ropes.

At least one was a broad. Sebastian had taken a balled fist to the face for staring too long at the sunken jawline and almost attractive, pale lips. Even her antagonistic grunts were feminine. Almost pleasant.

I've been out here too long.

The pace became grueling, the three of them forced to keep step with their aggressors. They moved hurriedly for reasons Sebastian could not guess.

Timothy groaned but kept on, even once his feet began scuffing the ground with fatigue. The kid and the witch-finder were younger men, but the point of exhaustion had long since passed them all.

Still they went, with wobbly legs, dry mouths, and droopy eyelids. The sun's intermittent rays poked through the treetops. Sebastian's forehead was damp and his fingers tingled.

This is a death march, had been his first thought, but if the cloaks had wanted them dead they could have done it at the lake. No, they were being driven toward a specific destination. If Garrick was right, and these captors had answered the varcolac's cry for help, the three of them would be answering for their crimes very soon.

"We must stop." The woman's voice sounded slight.

The red cloak on point froze at the sound of it. His half-glance back seemed stunned that it was one of his own who had violated the treatise of silence.

She did not wait for permission, reaching out to touch Sebastian's shoulder, easing his stride. He did not protest, having been struck by that very hand earlier. She stepped close, revealing thin strands of yellow-grey hair bunched at the back of her hood. Her lips curled and the tips of two pointed teeth stuck out from the top gum line.

"This is a waste of time," the leader said.

"Dearest Codrin," she said. "Are you in such a hurry to make a name for yourself that you would be this rash? A waste would be if this man dies before we make it home."

"I want them exhausted." Codrin's voice matched her weakness.

"You think them livestock. Don't be a fool…"

Codrin turned and his hood pulled with the sudden movement, offering a glimpse of the man beneath it. Only he did not look like a living man. His skin was grey and sunken, with hollow sockets for eyes that only hinted at life. His chapped and discolored flesh seemed more natural in the company of buzzing flies and bending maggots.

Garrick, who was closest, recoiled at the sight.

"Never condescend to me." Codrin said.

"Then be smarter." She offered this simply, as if it were the only possible response. "They are no good to us dead."

Codrin's laugh was more of a hiss. "These men are professionals." He took a handful of Garrick's robe and rubbed the fabric between his fingers. "They have survived worse than us."

"It is not him I worry for," she said. Her fingers were

wrapped around Sebastian's wrist. "This one will die if we push him further."

"You'll say anything to get your way."

"I do not care who delivers them. I only care that their blood is pure. This one's heart cannot hold at this pace. If he dies here, then he will be an empty husk by the time we supply him."

Codrin looked to the sky as the October sun disappeared behind a puff of storm clouds. In a moment, fresh rainwater came rolling down off the greenery overhead. Garrick and the kid did not wait for an invitation, sticking out their tongues to catch as much of it as possible.

Sebastian followed their lead.

"This is the time for us to move *faster*." Codrin pointed to the sky.

"You know best, oh wise leader. And will you receive a hero's welcome once they hear that you delivered two when there could have been three?"

"Very well." Codrin threw his hands up in frustration. His laughter was the sound of someone coming unhinged. "Let us stop. Rest. Become a fellowship. We'll swap stories of upbringings and hear of family hardships back home. Who among us packed a cauldron so we can boil stew on the fire?"

The woman released her grip on Sebastian and stepped away. She folded her arms across the front of her cloak and looked off through the forest. A sullen victory.

"Since we are…*resting*, I might as well ask," Codrin said, looking at the witch-finder. "Your weapons are curious. Where did you get them?"

"Had them commissioned," Garrick said, devoid of his usual wit. "By a wizard of the divine, no less." His emblematic sarcasm had arrived with the delay of only a few words.

"Commissioned," Codrin laughed. "I believe that part.

These are unique. Silver ammunition, silver blades…almost as if you are hunting something specific."

"Rabbits," Garrick said, "a blight to be exterminated. Did you know those hoppity fuckers encourage the spread of savage cats and foxes wherever they go? See, those predators come crawling to hunt the twitchy simpletons, and wind up sticking around to prowl local wildlife. With rabbits, everything around them pays the price. Destructive to the native animals of any land."

"Well-read, and with rapier wit," Codrin said. "How lucky for us."

"Wit? I do this out of concern. A true nature's man, honestly. If encouraging predators was all those creatures did, I might give rabbits a pass. But that's really just the start of their evil. Little pricks suck down seedlings like Londoners swallow gin, you follow? Get too many of those bastards in one area and watch your local trees and shrubs wither and die. You ask what I hunt and I'm telling you. Someone's got to stop those things before there's nothing left."

"Amusing," Codrin said, "but your tenacity holds no purpose with us. We hunt the same thing, you know. We took your horses, yes, but only because we needed their blood. That carried us a little further along so that we could take you. In happier times, I would've passed you over for a taste of varcolac."

"If it's wolf you hunt, you glanced over one back there in favor of taking us."

The pale man looked ashamed, like a dog without claws. "In this…condition, there is little we could do against one."

"She is sliced groin to sternum. Her wounds are fatal."

The woman cloak turned. "If she is sliced open, then she is of no use to us. You fools bled her dry and could not finish her still? And now you hope for us to kill her?"

Garrick's smile spread wide. "I hoped you might."

"Enough." Codrin placed his hands on either side of Sebastian's face, against his cheeks. He leaned in close and the stench of decay followed. Sebastian knew this type of smell from delivering rotted and sun-drenched bounties to paying customers. Never from a *living* creature. "You are well enough to continue, yes?"

Sebastian fixed his gaze so his eyes gave an amenable answer to that question.

Codrin looked at the woman next. Her face wore a scowl.

"Unless *you* wish to sit here with him while he gets a few winks, we've wasted enough time."

She began walking and the red cloaks shuffled with her, leaving Codrin usurped and standing with his shoulders slumped.

The forest path carried them until the day was spent. At last, they reached a clearing and found greenery stretching wide in every direction. The rain had stopped somewhere along the way, leaving the air breezy and raw as the sun pulsed from behind one last tuft of grey clouds.

The cloaks stopped at the forest's edge. Their captives swayed in the confined space between them. A valley sat across the way, and when Sebastian squinted, he saw roofs reaching up out of it. Getting there would consume the rest of the daylight and beyond.

Their final destination.

The opportunity to rest lasted only a moment, and Sebastian's legs wobbled. The cloaks urged them into the clearing with a few cautious steps, the way a person waded carefully into cold water. The grass was slicked from the pouring, and their boots left obvious footprints in the mud puddles.

Each step made it easier for Raven to find them, provided she was alive. The sun slid out from behind the straggler clouds and dried their slow steps.

Garrick made the move so fast that even Sebastian was startled by the hunter's speed. He lunged for the female cloak, who had taken point on the march. He yanked the hood off her head and pulled her arm back, swiveling his body and hurling her to the ground. She snarled and tumbled into the grass, frantically reaching for her hood.

Smoke rose off her body as her skin cracked like eggs on a buttery griddle. Her grey hair wilted and her pale skin blackened.

Then she burst into flames.

"Get them," Garrick screamed, already moving onto the next.

Timothy was faster than Sebastian, pulling the hood off the rear guard and sending him down with a kick to the knee. The flame engulfed his cloak as if it had been doused in whale oil.

Sebastian lunged for one, but his target was faster. The cloak's dagger ripped through his shoulder and twisted. Blood bubbled outward with force that matched his scream. His attacker's tongue dangled; yellow eyes widened with greed.

Timothy came rushing. He tackled the blademan and yanked his hood away, rolling free as the killer ignited.

The two remaining cloaks scrambled off in the direction they had come.

There was no time for Sebastian to stop and consider the blade jutting from his shoulder, or the blood sliding down his shirt. He went fumbling for the sack that housed their confiscated belongings, and tugged Garrick's six-shooter free of the musty fabric. He sighted Codrin's retreating cloak at the end of the gun barrel.

He squeezed off two shots, and then a third and a fourth for good measure. Each hit their targets, but the cloaks barely stumbled over the impact. They kept moving until the tree line swallowed them whole.

"Forget them," Garrick said between huge breaths. "If we're not somewhere else before nightfall, more will come." He plucked the blade from Sebastian's shoulder and tossed it aside, offering a few encouraging slaps on his cheek. "They'll smell you faster than a thirteen-year-old girl at red tide."

"The hell were they?" Timothy fished his blunderbuss out of the sack and looked across the way like a bloodhound.

"You know exactly what they are, pup."

Sebastian motioned to the far off rooftops. It hurt to lift his injured shoulder and he cupped a palm down over it. "Is that where they were taking us?"

"Seems so," Garrick said. "This land is under perpetual siege. The Ottomans from the east occupy it, but the Russian Empire swoops down from the north to try its luck for nothing beyond a desire for expansion. Villages like that suffer the most. Probably nothing left save for those bloodfeeders."

"What then?" Timothy said. "Go back for Raven?"

"No. There's no telling what else answered the wolf's call," Garrick said. "We had the element of surprise and squandered it. It'll be years before I can get that close again."

"We've left an obvious trail from the lake," Sebastian said. "If the wolf intends to find us, she will."

"And if those red cloaks come back with friends…"

Garrick nodded. He chewed his bottom lip. "Follow me," he said. "We'll need to find shelter before dark."

Weary sighs circled them.

They fell in behind the hunter and headed east, away from the village.

◯

It was almost dark before Elisabeth moved.

She had fallen back into mud cool enough to soothe her irritated flesh. Her body ached even as the scars receded.

The physical ones, at least.

Tears had sapped most of her energy. A cathartic outpouring of emotion. Today she had only wanted self-pity, but other urges began to rise in her as the sun disappeared behind the mountain, producing the beautiful foreboding of dusk.

What needed to be done could no longer be ignored. Only reticence kept her in place. Leaving here meant that Aetius was really gone, and she was not ready to accept that.

Elisabeth did not wish to say goodbye, because like her mother before, it meant that his memory would fade over time. He had sacrificed his life so that she could escape. The idea that she would one day lose the details of his face, forget the muscled lines of his body, and never again taste his lips, brought crippling dejection.

She looked at the dimming sky with watery eyes and wondered, *where am I supposed to go from here?*

Of course, she knew. Knew that certain things were expected of a huntress—even one with a waning sense of duty.

This cloak of night brought none of the expected calm and comfort; only advantage. Unlike humans, her eyes did not fail in the shadows.

Elisabeth hoisted herself and shook the atrophy from her muscles. The lake was a mass of dark and shifting water. It lapped clean her blood-caked thighs and cooled her sweaty form. A dip beneath the surface jolted her mind from the shackles of self-pity, rejuvenating her with a sense of purpose.

This was Aetius' parting gift. *Life.* It must not be squandered on brooding. Love and sorrow were for humans—distractions from the doldrums of their brief and pointless existence. A side of them that Elisabeth wished she could jettison. Because she was more than that.

The varcolac were so much more.

She cleansed herself in the water as best she could, wishing for a bar of soap. She had often found them stockpiled throughout the Holy Roman Empire's estates while the villages lived in filth and squalor. The cruelty and oppression of it was amusing, even if she could not understand why so many of the repressed allowed it.

She stepped from the lake and felt good. There was temptation to return to the queen—Alina's soft spot for the first huntress was such that she would be welcomed with open arms and legs. But that was far from the type of ecstasy she craved.

Elisabeth lifted her nose and searched the air for *them*. Every human's scent was unique, and the familiar man's was one she would never forget. Arrogance personified. The smell drifted to her and her heart drubbed with rage.

They had been here, but she knew that already. Worse, the graveyard stench was heavier now. Her nose wrinkled at it. The only way to sort through these conflicting odors was to reach higher ground. The idea of seeing that campsite once more stung worse than any injury, but it was the only way.

It would mean one last chance to say goodbye.

Ascension up the narrow and winding path was slow. It afforded her prey the opportunity to further distance themselves, though it mattered not. The wolf would make up the distance once it came time for the chase. She imagined them enjoying a victory celebration of loose whores and dribbling mead.

Let them think they won. If they did not see her coming, her vengeance would be sweeter still. She would kill them and lay waste to every hospitable village along the way.

Throughout the years, Elisabeth had trained her ears to ignore the forest's constant sounds. Most animals stepped light and the ones that did not, such as bears, were distinct enough to disregard. Man sounded obvious, moving with graceless steps. Finding them was never terribly challenging.

There was nothing out of the ordinary in her ears tonight, but as she climbed the mountain, the rancid whiff of decayed flesh grew until she felt like vomiting.

Scorched animal pelts hit her nose so hard she coughed reflexively. Her feet were callused and sore by the time she reached the former sight of Nightfall, but she ignored the pain. As soon as she allowed the wolf in, it would be gone within minutes.

Two cloaked figures sat beside the remnants of her dream, ghostly reminders of it. Dual pairs of yellow eyes pierced the night, though faces were obscured beneath hoods.

"Forgive us," one spoke. He rose and took a knee. "We did not realize what had happened until we reached this peak. You grieve. Is it for this one?"

These parasites were of no interest. Theirs was an image so far removed from the queen they were merely demons in human form, and their rotted presence only annoyed her. She pictured them scampering up here in the hopes of finding a fresh body to suck from. Imagined them sifting through the fire-kissed remains with disappointment.

"Speak quickly, vampire."

The brazen one got off his knee, and the other followed with hesitant steps.

"Codrin," he said. When it was clear that Elisabeth was nonplussed by his name, his words became hurried. "We heeded the wolf's call and found the ones who injured you." The vampire's yellow eyes dropped to the embers. "The ones who murdered him."

"Where?"

Silence. Their sunken faces awash with defeat. Their lips flicked open and shut, as if the proper words could not be formed.

It was obvious why.

"You lost them," she said and felt like crossing a hand over her breasts when she noticed them leering. She would not give them the satisfaction of shame, however.

"Our elder ordered us to return with them…"

"Them specifically? Or any scraps that you can muster? From the look of it, you two are nothing more than dried-out rinds."

This prompted the shameless vampire to stop and re-shuffle his words. "You have to understand, we are a starved people. Many have not tasted blood in a year…maybe more."

"Tell me where they are." Elisabeth cared more for the prosperity of wild lynxes than parasite plight.

"They slaughtered four of us…*we* barely escaped."

"You do not know where they have gone?"

"No, but we wish to ally with you. To find them and avenge those who were taken."

If they had delivered the familiar one as a gesture of goodwill, she might have rewarded their deed. But a malnourished elder somewhere figured he could siphon fatigued men in order to feed his followers. She knew it was not their intent to interfere in this, but they had, and it was infuriating.

Elisabeth closed the distance between them. The vampires only stared at her curves as she approached. They yearned, despite being depleted. What little blood remained in their systems flowed to their loins and dictated their thoughts.

Another insult.

"I am faster on my own," Elisabeth said. It was clear the loud one did not intend to leave the topic at that. He started to speak once more, and so she did what needed doing. She punched his silent partner in the chest. His rib cage exploded around her fist as she burrowed through his innards and took his heart against her palm. Her nails wrapped around the muscle, squeezing from it what few drops of life remained.

The creature dangled off her limb, impaled. When she retracted her arm, the shriveled heart looked like a prune in her hand. She pitched it straight into the air like a fox toss and her victim watched helplessly for a moment before keeling over.

The other refused to run. He fell again to one knee, babbling about allegiances.

Too late, greedy creature.

She threw her palm down over his bald and rotted skull, raking her fingers over his head. Dead skin coiled beneath her nails like carved wood.

The vampire whelped, but fought to repress the display of weakness.

"Why did you leave me on the beach, vampire? You could have had me as easily as a game bird."

"We are hungry…"

"You said that." Her voice rose over his. "And I do not care."

"We knew that we could never take a varcolac…not in our condition."

"Is that the only reason?"

"Yes."

"Would you feed on me…given the opportunity?"

The vampire's yellow eyes narrowed, leery of the question. "We would. *Your* blood is stronger than man's. Strong enough to bring my people back in full."

"You would try drinking from the huntress?" Elisabeth's features darkened in succession with her thoughts. She released his head and the vampire grabbed her arms without a hint of strength. His hands slipped from her wrists and dropped limp when he realized his pleas would not work.

The creature cried. An arousing display of fealty that made her feel powerful once more. Her bloodlust rekindled.

The wolf's change started on faster than she might have liked. Her hands swelled, throbbing as thick claws pushed through the tips of her cracked and shedding fingernails. She did not want this yet. Her bubbling throat and shifting muscles ached, though the wolf came no closer to the surface.

She lashed at the vampire's neck with frustrated confusion. The parasite's yellow eyes bulged as his head came loose, dangling off his shoulders like a hood. A weak stream of blood sputtered and, thinking that her point was made, she left him writhing.

There was no reason to put him out of his misery. Without blood, he could not regenerate with any serious pace and the sun would eventually rise to finish the job.

His body flopped around inconsequentially as Elisabeth walked to the cliff and inhaled. The familiar one's smell hung there, the way an extinguished fire lingers above the hearth. She sensed anxiety on their bodies—a smell more prevalent than perspiration. They would be all the more difficult to track because their defenses were high. Surely they would be expecting her to hunt them. But they were further provoked by clumsy vampires and their desperation to feed.

They moved fast. In retreat.

"You fools," she said with balled fists. The sight of the almost-decapitated vampire seizing in the dirt brought no gratification. She stepped over him in a hurry to catch her enemies. The cowards. How many more lives would they wreck along the way? How many more families would they obliterate by stealing daughters away from their ailing mothers in the name of good and God?

And yet, you did nothing to prevent their crusades when you had the power and ability to do so.

"Shut up," Elisabeth said, hostile to the contradictory thought.

You raised an army of wolves, and for what? Rather than do battle with them, you sought to terrorize homes similar to the ones your enemy ransacked. You both destroy lives, innocent lives. You are *no better than they.*

"My army was for the queen," she screamed. Justification she said, but did not believe. Elisabeth pretended her intentions were noble, insisting to herself that she had raised that army as one final pledge of devotion to Queen Alina. Truth was, it was all she could do to walk away from the role of huntress without enervating guilt.

And even that had not worked.

Elisabeth knew her thoughts were spot on. She was evil and was never meant to be happy.

Aetius' remains were strewn across the spent fire. His flesh was so charred that his limbs resembled scorched logs. It had not been enough for the hunters to slay him. This ritualistic cleansing, mutilation before burning, had been done to ensure he never rose again. Short of covering him in salted earth, they had taken every last measure.

She knelt and gasped over his blackened skull. His teeth had been bashed out, leaving jagged pieces of dentin behind. She sifted through the ashes and collected the undamaged ones in her hand, closing her fist around the longest pair of killing teeth she could find.

How many lives had ended because of these? How many times had his ravenous bite pierced her flesh in passion? A menagerie of pleasure mixed with searing pain that felt as though her virginity was being taken again and again. She was never more alive than in those moments. When his wolf was inside her, filling her with girth she could barely grope.

That is when the pleasure truly began.

She circled the mountaintop like the animal she could be, sniffing the slender air and teasing the animal to her surface.

Reaching them would be simple. Killing them, harder.

Blue eyes lifted toward the moon as the tremors took her.

"Change me," she whispered. The pearly object up there held no genuine sway over the wolf, but the animal was often encouraged and enticed by the darkness it promised. Her arms stretched and reached for it. Dark hair lifted off her slender appendages and her hands became pointed once more. She dropped and landed on her knees. The pain surged, but that one final push never came. Then she was left watching her mane recede back into her skin. Her human lungs sucked desperately for air that was hard to get.

Becoming wolf had never been more painful, the turning and regression falling on her at once. None of the benefits, but all of the bodily pain. Even her very first transformation had been easier.

Aetius' fangs were clamped in her hand. She dropped them in the dirt. Despite her discomfort, she took the time to push them down into the soil and place a noticeable stone over it.

The wolf would come no further than this, it seemed. Elisabeth crossed her arms and rubbed her shoulders. Squinting into the forest below, she thought she saw the flicker of torchlight well in the distance. It forced her thick lips into a perverted smile.

Without the animal's speed, she would have to work to catch them. She slipped into the dead vampire's cloak, wondering why the wolf had chosen this moment to be shy.

The answer came from the back of her head, as if the wolf sensed her curiosity. Her mind flashed back to last night's hail of silver gunfire and blades, suggesting the animal had recoiled from the onslaught of those implements. They could not kill her, no, but the agony they brought was pure, debilitating.

Her head ached from the almost-change, feeling like she had just swallowed nine flagons of spiced wine. A spiked pain throbbed behind her eyes. Her legs rocked as she tried to stand.

In this moment, the familiar one stood more of a chance than she might have liked.

Elisabeth crossed an arm over her bruised rib cage and shuffled on, hoping she could find a way to surprise him still.

THE MOUNTAIN PASS

GARRICK STOPPED LONG ENOUGH TO light the lantern. The vampires had killed their horses, but never thought to demolish their equipment. Only one lamp had survived their violent emancipation, but it was all they needed.

The inside of the light used a round burner and circular wick, allowing the flame to be stoked by a steady gust of air. It intensified the light source and encased them within a cylindrical orange perimeter.

"You're easy enough to spot beneath the sun with all that silver," Timothy said. "Why not make things easier for our enemies at night as well?"

"Keep japing. It's all very helpful as we try to navigate out of here," Garrick said.

Sebastian's shoulder ached beneath the makeshift bandage. The last thing he needed was this bickering. Maybe those who died back in Freywald had been the lucky ones after all.

"Let's just extinguish this," Garrick said and dangled the lantern against the kid's nose, "and walk around with our arms outstretched. I am certain we can feel our way to safety."

"Dammit," Sebastian whispered, so tired his words were

nearly impotent. "Shut your mouths and stay sharp."

Timothy started to huff a response but Garrick shoved him the moment his lips parted. "You're a know-it-all. You think you could've saved the lives of the men we lost, right?" He paused for dramatic effect. As soon as Timothy opened his mouth to speak, the hunter was already talking over him. "I'm not relinquishing command. You agreed to my leadership and *nothing* has changed. As for your concern? The varcolac hear as well as they see and smell. Your endless yapping tilts the scales as much as this light does."

"Don't tell me you're fine with this?" Timothy said, looking now to Sebastian for backup.

"Shut it, kid." Sebastian's feet scraped the forest bed as he rushed off to catch the hunter and the retreating light.

Timothy believed himself better than this line of work, and that was the root of the problem. That he was correct certainly did not help. The kid earned a living at thief-taking because London afforded no better options. The city never recovered from the sprawling fire that had consumed much of it. Sebastian delighted in making the kid, and his like-minded academic brethren, feel guilty about that. The fire's origin was a topic of debate, but many believed the catalyst was a bonfire loaded with rebellious texts and scrolls.

The very ones Timothy clung to for guidance.

London liked to say the fire was John Locke's fault. Timothy countered with the argument that the city got what it deserved for rejecting Locke's pleas for societal betterment. To Sebastian, blame did not matter. He preferred to deal with the aftereffects. Plagues far worse than the bubonic one. Thievery was the epidemic no one spoke of, and it forged the need for his profession.

The difference between Timothy and Sebastian was

simple. The old man had been happy to assume the role whereas Timothy saw it as a stepping-stone to something better.

"Where are you leading us?" Timothy said once he was caught up to the light. It was a more practical question, at least.

Sebastian could almost hear Garrick's eyes roll from the front of the party.

"Away," he said.

"Away? Your determination to kill Raven has left you, then?"

"No, but my motivation to continue with the two of you has."

It was Sebastian's turn to take offense. He walked side-by-side with Garrick, despite his raw shoulder wound gnawing away at his able body. "Don't be a bloody half-wit. You've no right to blame us for what happened on that mountain. We did as you said. It was the kid and I who brought the big wolf down and killed him proper. Your quarrel was with Ritter…"

"Aye," Timothy said. "And you shot him dead. So what's the problem?"

"The problem is that Raven will be ready the next time I set out to kill her."

"There is every possibility in the world that she is dead," Sebastian said. "Those injuries…"

"…will heal. The varcolac do not wither and die like we do."

"We are in retreat then?" Timothy sounded relieved.

Garrick said nothing. Their march punctuated by breaking branches and rustling animals moving outside their drum of light.

"You have fulfilled your roles," he said after an arduous length of silence. "We head for the nearest city where I will arrange for you both to be paid. That way, pup can go on pretending he's changing the world by reading books that tell him how to think."

Sebastian was glad for this news, but the incompleteness of the job left him unfulfilled. This was the first time he would be paid for failing.

Behind him, Timothy chewed his thumbnail, which he did when at his most pensive. "If Raven *is* alive," he said, "she may come for us, yes?"

"Of course. That is why we hurry. If she reaches full strength, we won't stand a chance. The element of surprise is no longer with us and she will take more than our lives for all the ways we have wronged her."

"How do we stand our ground when we are on *hers*?" Timothy asked.

"We make for the city of Constanta on the Black Sea. The Order of Osiris has an outpost there. Not even Raven will follow us beyond those walls."

"Is that what you call yourselves?" Sebastian said.

"It is, and I will tell you no more."

"After all the secrecy," Sebastian said. "I'm surprised to hear you mention it so casually is all."

Garrick quickened his gait, leaving the thief-takers trailing at the edge of the lantern light.

A blocky shape grew from the shadows in the distance. In the past, when their unit had been at full strength, Garrick would have ordered them to fan out and ready their muskets while taking a perimeter around it. As they got closer and the light brought it more detail, they found a singed and broken foundation of wood.

Sebastian's hand curled around the flintlock's handle. The sinister nature of the scene was too obvious for an ambush, but he would not leave things to chance.

They passed the cooked structure and found another, and then another. An entire village put to flame, leaving smoldered ruins that the forest would soon swallow like curling body hair covering a scar.

"Where are those who lived here?" Sebastian asked.

"Red hoods, most likely," Garrick said. "Fed off this village for as long as they could and then put it to torch to hide what happened."

"Where are the bodies then," Timothy said, peering into a doorway.

Theirs was the only sound as they traveled a dirty path between two destroyed homes.

"Not even animals tread here," Sebastian said. The foliage growing around them was completely unmolested.

"And if they were left for dead, why don't I see any remains?" Timothy poked his head into a nearby building with shattered windows. "Not a one."

"For once, I agree with you," Garrick said. "It's best we continue on. There's nothing here that can be salvaged."

They made their way through what remained of the village, hurrying as though its oppressive silence could somehow hurt them.

Once they were free of it, Garrick dipped his lantern to the ground to highlight curious tracks that tamped down through overgrowth. A trail headed away from here that could only have been made by wheels.

"The bodies were carted out," he said.

"A wagon," Sebastian said. "Someone loaded whatever could be salvaged and headed out. These tracks are sunken...a pile of bodies would weigh that much."

"So could basic thievery," Timothy said.

"You saw ruined bed frames and dressers back there, kid. What you didn't see was bodies."

"The vampires were looking for bodies," Garrick said. "We know that much."

"They wouldn't find them if they were buried," Timothy said.

"A burial." Garrick slapped his thigh. "This place is ravaged. Russians and Ottomans clashing over the right to call this land theirs. You might be a problem solver in the classroom, but the civility you know does not extend out here. No one's burying the dead when the living are being slaughtered."

"What then?" Timothy said, voice rising to challenge.

"Bloody bodies are a treat for vampires," Garrick said. "If the red hoods found nothing here, someone else took them."

Sebastian had heard stories about men who drank from others, but always from the mouths of tavern lushingtons, and only once their brains were at their soggiest. After months of tracking humans who became wolves, he could barely accept *that* notion.

Now this.

This was not a journey so much as a heated nightmare: A world where people burst into flames from sunlight while wolfmen roamed the gloom.

They followed the wagon trail single file, each of them weapon-held, marching for so long Sebastian kept expecting to see the breaking sun at any moment.

"We may be able to fortify here," Garrick said of a rock formation at the trail's end. It was a mine adit fortified by thick wood propped overhead to provide access inward. Wagon tracks led off to the right, alongside the mountain.

Even if they hid for the night, daybreak did not guarantee safety. Though at least they stood more of a chance when they could see their surroundings beyond a limited cone of lantern orange.

Garrick stepped into the adit and his gun hand waved for them to follow. It was swallowed then by encroaching dark. Sebastian went next, and Timothy brought up the rear. The ground offered a gradual slope, their boots kicking up a flurry of cave dust that stung their eyes.

The air was cool but humidity dogged them all the way down. Sebastian's collar was drenched and itching, completely soaked through.

"Look," Garrick said. The lantern light showed a row of extinguished torches lining the path, each bolted into the earthen walls by metal sconces.

Sebastian mopped his forehead with the back of his hand. His skin was slippery, a rising fever extracting the last of his strength.

The mine spiraled down along the cave wall and they hugged it with caution. Loll too much to the far side and the drop would prove fatal.

Sebastian wanted help, but his stubbornness and dignity prevented the request. Asking for assistance was an admission of weakness. He could not be this ailed by a simple dagger. Not when he had suffered so much worse over the years.

Yet, he could not stop thinking about the inevitable. Was his time at an end? Maybe not today, but soon? And what to show for it? A legacy of memories, truly. Whichever ones Timothy chose to carry. There would be no one else to tell his story, and the world would continue on as though he never lived.

The chamber echoed as it carried them below. In Sebastian's sweaty haze, he became convinced they were marching straight into hell. That dying here could be for the best. He would be in the company of others, at least. It bested the lonely alternative: Croaking back home while the Piccadilly Tavern patrons were none-the-wiser. They would not give a piss until his rotting body stank worse than the vomit-lined floors.

They'll tell my story night-after-night in drunken jest. 'Poor sod upstairs shit himself when his heart gave out…we found him spilt across the floor with his knickers beneath his muddy arse.'

My legacy.

Sebastian's steps became shambles. His shoulder throbbed again, irritated by the flow of sweat. His eyes rolled as the thoughts behind them swam in the sounds of a hazy lullaby that was both inviting and familiar.

Something mum used to sing?

Awareness was gone, replaced only by the growing melody that floated up through the darkness and soothed his ears like cool velvet draped across a sun-chapped neck, massaging his mind until it was the only thing in there.

Only the pacifying sound of that voice.

A serenade for his mortality.

Garrick stopped and Sebastian felt Timothy's arms take gentle hold of him, encouraging his halt. The hunter peered over the ledge into the dark fog.

"What is that?" Timothy said.

Garrick was unable to mask his bafflement. "Singing."

What followed next cast them all in stunned silence.

The sound of laughter echoed below.

○

"Wake up."

Elisabeth awoke with a gasp, wondering for a moment where she was.

That's right…

She arranged herself into a sitting position and adjusted the rancid red cloak so that it once more covered the length of her body. She had looted both vampires of everything that might be useful, knowing this terrain would be unforgiving on a human being. The seared and loose boots that enclosed her feet were rough and over-spaced, but as she wiggled her toes, she remained grateful that she did not have to continue on bare feet.

Getting down that mountain had taken more than just time. Her body had only recently pulled itself back together, and she unbottled every last drop of strength in order to reach the forest and keep moving. Her enemies were out here somewhere, but her human legs flared as if to say she would not be catching them tonight.

Once she reconciled that setback, she gathered a few downed branches and arranged them into a crude framework, drawing on what little she recalled from her childhood in Iasi.

She and her cousin, Sanda, had once built a hideaway when they were girls no older than eight. They had retreated into the forest to hide, two children determined to skirt responsibilities of laundry and house tending for as long as they could. That time away felt like it had spanned an entire summer, but was probably only a day or two. Time had absolutely no meaning to the carefree.

Elisabeth allowed a fond smile to creep into her face as she reflected on that. Using the spare cloak she had taken atop Nightfall, a breezy hole punctured through one side where she had punched the vampire's heart free, she was able to mimic what Sanda and she had done then: build a narrow shelter to escape the elements. It was not enough to make her forget the warmth of her wolf's mane, but it kept the wind off her while she stole some shivery sleep.

"Wake up," the voice repeated.

Elisabeth crawled into the dark air to find who had awakened her. As vulnerable as she felt, her human from retained some of the wolf's perceptions. That at least made it easy to spot the woman standing between two trees.

A mane of golden curls glowed, despite the onyx black night. A brilliant and familiar sight, it prompted Elisabeth to bow her head and avert her stare.

"My queen," she said.

"No. Look upon me with companionship." Alina stood encased in gold and black armor that preserved her champagne-glass figure. It instilled regality and authority, despite her contradictory words.

As such, Elisabeth did not feel comfortable looking. She could not recall the last time she had been in the presence of Her Grace. This reunion should have been ceremonious. Under different circumstances, it would have so much more. Tonight, however, the informality of it felt like insubordination.

"Stop it, huntress." The queen's voice was disarming. She stepped to Elisabeth and the earth trembled around her boot falls. This was more than a woman standing here. It was a force of nature. Darkness. Trails of despair rippled behind her like a cape. Alina brought famine, debauchery, and disaster to every corner of the world. It came in many different ways, but was almost always because of her.

"I have failed everyone," Elisabeth said. Emotion consumed her. She despised herself for showing Alina her throat. The huntress should never be weak, and though she was in the process of abandoning that life, it was impossible to abstain from her sense of duty while looking into Her Majesty's sparkling opal eyes.

Alina sought to assuage that swirling sense of pity. "I am here for you. Not the other way around. Do not say what you think you should. Speak to me as a friend."

The queen's fingers reached out and slid across Elisabeth's jawline scars, her tongue clicking with pity as she turned the battered head left and then right, lifting Elisabeth's chin high to survey the damage dealt to her favorite soldier.

Elisabeth's tensions eased at the touch.

"That's better," Alina said, wearing a consolatory look. "I cannot imagine what you've been though." Her hands slid onto Elisabeth's shoulders and gave a gentle shake—a slight effort to snap her back to her senses, or at least assess the possibility of that happening. "The wolf is hurt. She bore the brunt of the punishment so that you would not have to."

Elisabeth could only nod. Giving herself over to the animal should have been a reflex, something done without thought. Even now, she encouraged the beast to take control of her body, but the wolf no longer listened. If not for the lingering abilities that stayed with her as a human: sight and hearing, along with a marked uptick in strength, she would have sworn the creature had abandoned her entirely. Elisabeth's every effort to reach the beast was fruitless, those thoughts resonating like a single raindrop falling on the ocean.

Did the wolf even know she called for her?

"You cannot push her like this," Alina said. "The wolf must feel comfortable inside you once more. Your body heals but your mind is fractured. You could have died back there, and you've allowed that to change you. Scare you."

I wish I was dead.

Alina eased Elisabeth into her arms, sensing her misery. Her ivory touch traced down her back, becoming a sweltering and muscular embrace.

"You never need to feel shame, Elisabeth, and I do not wish for you to regret the gift I've given you. I could not live with myself if I knew you resented me."

"Never." The answer was immediate, reflexive, leaving Elisabeth to wonder if she had even meant it.

"Return with me now, then."

Elisabeth stuttered, but the queen was not interested in refusal. Alina's lips fell on her at once, her tongue striking like a snake. Their mouths interlocked and Elisabeth felt her need for vengeance wavering beneath this persistence.

The queen preyed on vulnerability, so this was no surprise. Gentle kisses quenched Elisabeth's thirst for companionship. Their tongues rolled, slowly at first, but then much harder, as familiarity returned to this passion.

Elisabeth thought she must have smelled worse than a city trash heap, having been out here for so long. Last thing she wanted was anyone standing this close to her, queen or not.

Alina's mouth retreated long enough to offer a breathless whisper. "Remember the siege of Paris?" She chuckled and tipped her forehead to Elisabeth's.

Oh, how she remembered. A countryside of razed earth and burning windmills, replete with a hysteric populace. Food, a scarcity. They had feasted off that fear, taking flesh as they pleased and turning others into lunatic madmen over the flimsiest promises of survival. That was, of course, until the conflict reached a regrettable, anticlimactic finish. Thousands of people wilted and died from starvation, almost at once. Paris, a metropolis of misery, had become a cathedral of silence overnight. Together, Alina and Elisabeth had admired Henry IV's brutality, his willingness to serve death by the hundreds of thousands so that his claim to the throne could no longer be contested.

The horrors visited upon the innocent throughout that siege were numerous, but Henry of Navarre got his crown in the end. There was a lesson about the calculus of war in there, and Elisabeth came away from it understanding that a million losses were acceptable if it meant standing victorious.

She did not think she agreed with that anymore. At least, she did not want to. One more night with Aetius was preferable to all of the destruction she had visited upon these lands. What did she have to show for any of that? All of the urges she had felt like sating, and the lives ruined because of them. Just footnotes now. And the price she had paid for them had been too high in the end.

"How I miss you, huntress," Alina said. Her lips pulled away leaving a thread of shared spittle between them.

The queen's hands slid to Elisabeth's hips and lifted the frayed cloak in balled fists. It shimmied up over her thighs until Alina's hands clasped around her bottom, squeezing fingers over soft flesh and purring in admiration.

"Please," Elisabeth said. "Do not…"

"Tell me why."

"I cannot lose myself in you. I want to…more than anything else, I *need* it. But the ones who killed Aetius are out there."

"We will orchestrate their deaths from behind Castle Daciana's walls."

The castle offered the safety Elisabeth craved, carrying her far away from the realities that faced her now. The thought of curling up at the foot of Alina's throne was a powerful lure. It was a room of pure splendor; the earliest prophet remained crucified there to this day, clinging to life, sustained by an eternal supply of blood trickling from his severed genitals.

Alina had enjoyed this tableau so much, that she had rendered him a permanent fixture there centuries earlier. He revels in the debauchery of her kingdom, a witness to nightly orgies and bloodbaths, cackling with madness every now and again at the sight of the most blasphemous accomplishments.

Elisabeth wanted to hear that cracked voice once more. It was more welcoming than a homecoming feast, and Alina stood here offering a way out.

"I know you loved Aetius," the queen said. "As did I, but…"

"I need to bathe in their blood," Elisabeth said, "and I

have to do it myself." Plotting the familiar one's destruction from Castle Daciana was too impersonal for what these men deserved.

"I had to try," Alina said. "I wish my huntress would come back."

"I'm not sure she ever will be back," Elisabeth said. "Once I kill them all…"

Alina pushed a finger to her lips and dragged it back and forth like a paintbrush.

Elisabeth resisted the urge to swallow it. The mixed appetites of hunger and lust were baffling, and she blamed her animal instincts for the competition. Anger and desire were pent inside, and she would not allow herself to experience the latter. She would kill every person in this world before dishonoring Aetius like that.

"If you choose to do this alone," Alina said. "You will truly be alone. The wolf cannot return to you until you're at peace with yourself. With what you are."

"I no longer know what I am."

"You've always known, girl. You were only all too happy to forget."

"How many little girls have I orphaned? Were their screams any different than my own all those years ago?"

"Stop thinking you had this coming. And do not equate yourself with the butchers who attacked you. They are human cowards, lashing out at us because they can never be as great. If you remember the siege of Paris, then you know this. They think nothing of harming their own kind over the pettiest of squabbles. You? You're better than that. We all are. We don't hurt each other, for one thing. So never apologize for what you do. This is your world, not theirs."

"Does not feel like my world." Elisabeth rubbed her belly where the pike had sliced her.

"Even with the gift of invulnerability, you are not unstoppable."

"So I've learned," Elisabeth said.

Alina lifted the dulled blade off the ground beside Elisabeth's feet, looked it over, and handed it back with glaring disapproval.

"I salvaged this off the vampires," Elisabeth said. "I do not need anything more."

"Make them suffer, then." Alina said.

Elisabeth smiled through the tears as the queen turned to walk. She watched her dissolve into the night.

"I will do more than that," she growled.

The wolf was quiet, wherever she was.

◯

They stood against the face of darkness and listened to the voice that spoke to them from the bowels of the mine.

"Why have you come?"

"Passing through," Garrick said.

Sebastian hung between the other two men, their arms hooked beneath his shoulders. His breathing was shallow and growing worse with every moment he remained upright. They chose their steps carefully, shuffling through the cooling shadows as the bottom neared.

It did not matter how cold it got, Sebastian's head was scorched and sweaty. He could feel the speaker beneath them thinking Garrick's response over.

"I figured," it said. "No one dares come this far otherwise."

"We do not mean you any harm," Garrick said.

"That assurance has no meaning to me or any native. Not anymore. You are not from these parts. I can tell as much without setting eyes on you."

"Please," Timothy said. "Do not fear us."

"If it was fear I felt, you would have succumbed to my defenses." An eruption of yellow light shot upward and arced over their heads like small meteor trails. "Which I have just disarmed. If you intend to come all the way down, do it now. I will set these again as soon as you enter my home."

The wall sconce just beneath them ignited with newfound fire that sent shadows rummaging. They walked toward it and then headed for the next one, using them as markers to navigate the void. The ground leveled out and the darkness ahead stirred, assuming the shape of a small woman.

"Relax," she said. "This is my sanctuary, and you are welcome in it until I say otherwise."

"Our friend is hurt," Timothy said. "Can you do anything?"

Her answer was a soft purr.

"We have to put him down," Garrick said.

The woman was opposite the freshly lit torches, moving through the darkness, performing a task Sebastian was only vaguely aware of. Then the center of the room boomed with fire and their host stood beyond a roaring pit of flame.

"Please," she said, her timbre rising over the blaze's excited pops and hisses. "Come."

They followed the petite, almost elven-sized creature as she kept in front. Only a thin piece of loincloth decorated her slender frame, and the bottom curves of her derriere poked out from beneath the cut.

Sebastian remained man enough to ogle, thinking there were worse ways to die than in the presence of a woman like this.

She ducked beneath a flap of patchy fabric that led into a man-carved tunnel, to a room decorated with a damp rug and a dresser topped by lit candles. A corner bed called to him.

"Put him there." Her voice was soft and her accent unlike any Sebastian could place.

He fell onto the mattress. It was like dropping into a pile of fresh-plucked feathers.

A small and soft hand tapped his cheek. He opened wide to find a beautiful face in his: exotic eyes, a mixture of coral blue and summer green, thick and sharp cheeks, a wide mouth of large teeth. Sebastian felt as though he had died and this was his angel.

Never had a woman of such beauty given him anything more than a sack of coins. And that was only for retrieving stolen property. This one was at the bottom of a salt mine.

Still think you're not hallucinating?

"Let's get you out of that shirt," she said and eased him up, lifting the fabric off his stomach. He screamed when she tried moving his injured shoulder and so she reached for a blade and cut free the linen.

She wrestled it off his torso and Sebastian saw the undersides of her small, beautiful breasts.

"I'll clean his wounds." She grabbed a bucket off the ground and gave it to Garrick. "If you would, please go back the way you came, you will find a small spring beneath the exit. Fill this."

Timothy stood against the wall looking helpless, the blunderbuss bandied across his chest.

Garrick returned with the water and she took it at once, sitting on the bed so that her naked thigh brushed against Sebastian's torso. It felt impossibly smooth. She took his flask and popped it open, emptying its contents straight onto the bloody shoulder wound.

Sebastian's teeth gnashed, but she was faster, clamping a hand over his mouth and leaning in. She smelled of sandalwood oil, and her brownish-blonde hair tickled his mouth like fresh blades of grass.

"You mustn't," she said. "I'm certain you know what else is out there."

The pain roared, though he wanted nothing more than to feel her touch all over his body. This treatment was worth twenty stab wounds, easy.

She daubed Sebastian with fresh water, wiping crusted blood off him. Her touch was soothing, even as she redressed the wound. Once she was finished, she patted his chest and flashed a smile warmer than his delirium.

"I'll be back to check on you, as soon as I see about feeding your friends."

"I think we'll stay here just a while longer." Timothy crossed the room and checked over Sebastian's bandages, flaunting his mistrust of her hospitality.

"As you wish." She smiled and slid into the seat across the way, crossing her legs and showing off muscular thighs that flexed in just the right way to captivate the room. "It's not often anyone finds their way down here."

"Do they ever?" Garrick said. "This is a mine, is it not?"

"It's also the safest place in Moldavia. The soldiers aren't going to come down here, and there's hardly anyone else left to worry about."

"Hence the traps," Garrick said.

"Hence the traps," she agreed.

"Are you from the village nearby?" Timothy asked.

"Yes. *Prah.*" The name rolled off her tongue. "It was destroyed last summer when the Russians tried seizing this corner of Moldavia out from Ottoman control. Most of my people died, but a few of us escaped into the trees and made it here. I was the only one without fatal injury. As such, I am the only one who still lives."

"It must be lonely," Garrick said.

"It is safe."

"You can leave with us," Timothy said.

The woman looked to Sebastian and laughed. "I think I am better off taking my chances here." Then she stood and waved a *come-hither* finger at them as she exited the room. "Come, please. I have plenty of stew and some mead. I will tend to your friend while the two of you relax."

Garrick and Timothy looked reluctant to leave, but Sebastian nodded his approval. Truthfully, he was looking forward to being tended to. Conversation in the next chamber was jovial but quick, and he was relieved to see her return soon. She stood in the doorway, watching in silence.

Sebastian stared at the seductive outline, unable to think of anything but the things he wanted to do to this woman.

"I opened my finest mead for them," she said. "They are well occupied and that will, I hope, allow us the necessary time to get to know one another."

"I haven't had the pleasure of your name."

"Tulcea," she said and crossed the room with a motion that resembled a slither. "Believe it or not, this might be the first good night of sleep I've had in a year." She brushed the loincloth straps away from her shoulders and slipped from it, disappearing into the shadows before he had a chance to admire her body.

Sebastian watched the darkness with more intensity than he thought possible. He spotted her at the foot of the bed, the outline of her chest rising and falling. He felt her eyes trained on him, and the heat dripping off her was more inviting than any campfire.

"H-had I known you were here," he said, flubbing his words and becoming a stammering fool. "I-I would've made a pilgrimage to this mine. A lady such as yourself should be afforded a hundred restful nights."

"So silver-tongued." She did not laugh though, coming around the bed so the light caught her face. Her eyes sparkled with mischief, and her tiny breasts stood firm, nipples hardened by the mine's open air. He was not ashamed to admire her small but polished torso. She was patted in dirt, as to be expected from someone living at the bottom of a cave.

Her gaze matched his then, and her mouth became an inciting grin. What confidence!

Tulcea dragged the chair bedside. She sat and smiled as she caught his eyes studying her contoured legs, and what was between them. She did not speak, only reached into the water bucket for the soaked cloth.

She pressed it to his head and he groaned beneath the refreshment.

"What business brings you here? Your dress is very regal and you feel...*different*. Capable. A trait that has long departed these lands."

Contentious voices carried in from the main chamber. Garrick and Timothy, dueling ideologues. Worse now, because their argument was tempered with alcohol. He hoped their blather would leave them passed out so there might be peace and quiet for once.

It would afford him some well-earned alone time with this beauty.

"We were looking for someone," he said.

Tulcea studied him. By candlelight, her features were warm and inviting. More than generosity, she showed interest. Her lips parted to reveal a dazzling smile.

She was a thing of beauty and looking upon her got his heart racing.

"Do not be afraid," she said, selling the assurance with a bat of her eyelashes.

"What would I possibly fear?"

"Me," she said and stood. Her features vanished as she blew out the candles. Light steps slinked across the room and tugged the fabric roll over the room's entrance. It dropped down to the floor, blotting out the hall's faint candle glow.

"Show me what kind of warrior you are."

In a moment, Tulcea got onto the bed and hovered. It was dark, but his eyes soon adjusted so that he could savor her slender figure. Her feet slipped against the sides of his thighs and a cool shiver spread through him.

Injured shoulder and flu be damned, he needed to have this woman. There would be plenty of time to heal later. His spirit had been wounded for far longer, and Tulcea offered it the purest remedy.

What mattered tonight was her caress. Those curves. Her taste.

She dropped then, her meager frame writhing atop him. She suckled at the tip of his chin with a playful snicker and her nails, long enough to leave hot, white trails of passion beneath them, raked his sides—euphoric sensations unlike anything. His thoughts were adrift in this moment, and there was no regard for anything beyond it. Maybe he would stay here and take her as a wife.

"Don't get ahead of yourself," she said with a giggle.

Sebastian might have considered that comment under different circumstances. Tonight it was easier to close his eyes and moan beneath her cleansing touch. How she had peered into his thoughts and plucked one of them out was a mystery for another day. Or maybe it was influenza fiddling with his perceptions once more.

A hand slipped beneath the band of his trousers and he grew against her touch. Then she snapped her fingers free, laughing at the tease. They were damp and for that he felt a swell of shame. A sliver of light shone on her face from a source he could not find. It illuminated her mouth, a smile that cast this moment in splendor.

That's right, she hissed, somehow in his head once more. He questioned it now, though his thoughts drowned in desire.

I am yours.

The room was lit again, faint at first, but then glowing hotter. Tulcea spun so that Sebastian got a lavish view of her femininity. She was on all fours, glancing over her shoulder through dark and damp blonde hair.

"Taste me," she whispered. "Wherever you want."

The urge to lick her clean propelled him forward. Candlelight—or whatever it was—bounced off her posterior. His heart raced and his hands shook as he clasped palms over jiggling flesh. Hard to believe this was happening.

"Lick me," she snarled, her demand devoid of patience.

If Sebastian's body still ached, adrenaline did not allow him to feel it. He dove at the altar of flesh, angling so that he could taste everything.

His tongue ran along her legs, prolonging the moment so to tease them both. Her soft skin pleased his mouth, and eager hands explored her shape, massaging her rounded cheeks and tracing her thighs before trailing down to her ankles.

There were curved talons where her feet should have been. The slightest touch sliced his fingertips open.

Sebastian screamed and recoiled, scampering to the bed's corner. Bird-like feet clasped together in an effort to hasten his retreat. Her head pivoted to face him while her body remained in a forward-facing position on all fours.

In between dangling stands of greasy hair, her eyes were emblazoned like hot coal.

The room stunk of vinegar now. Her body cracked and aligned naturally beneath her immobile and glaring head. Green liquid spattered against her thighs and spilled down her muscles with sticky consistency.

She launched up and managed to get above him, her legs somehow twice as long. Sebastian crawled between her in an attempt to escape, as the purulent fluid smacked the sides of his face and lips. He winced and got a mouthful of her juices, filling his throat with runny, chunky liquid that tasted like pub vomit.

He could not do anything but puke it back, falling off the bed and gagging for any taste beyond the one littering his tongue.

A witch's laughter boomed, so loud and unpleasant that Sebastian would have covered his ears if he were not so desperate to scrub his mouth. He rose from the puddle of runny fluids, hacking up into his arm. His pistols were on the floor wrapped in his littered clothes. He grabbed for the gun and jammed its barrel into Tulcea's bloodied face.

She found this gesture hilarious, crowing as she became the shadows. There was only the sound of her breathing then, rough and labored.

Garrick came through the doorway in that instant, tearing away the obstructing flap. There was light now, and Sebastian gasped when he found the woman tucked into the farthest corner between bed and wall. Her jaw distended almost to the floor, dripping with green mucus while her liver-spotted flesh looked like spoiled beef. The pruned hag grumbled at the unwelcome exposure.

"Enough!" The hunter cried and lifted his blade. She might have shrieked in the instant before it broke through her skull, but the hit was followed by a crunch that shot all the way up the mine. The witch dropped like a sack of wet garbage and the hunter seized her wispy white hair, dragging her with his fist.

Sebastian did not miss a beat, taking her by the curled feet, aware of the shoulder pain but ignoring it in favor of removing this blight. They hurried into the mine's entry chamber. Timothy was sprawled across the floor, a wooden goblet of spilt wine beside him.

They swung the body to and from a few times to gather momentum before tossing her atop the roaring flame.

She sprung to life then, thrashing and screaming as the hungry fire accepted her. Her hands closed around hot embers that caused her palms to hiss as she struggled to escape.

Garrick lifted his gun and sunk two shots into her skull.

All was quiet then, save for the trailing sizzles of roasted witch. Sebastian dropped onto the bench slab, drained once more, hacking mucus in an effort to forever cleanse his throat of the poison.

The smell of cooked flesh and the taste of foul bodily fluids were trapped inside his head. He pinched his nose and lifted a smoked torch from its sconce, relighting it over the shriveling corpse. He wanted as much light as possible in here.

"Bloody hell," he said.

"Best you don't question it." Garrick's words were spoken with experience. It was easy to forget his trade sometimes. He had seen this kind of thing before.

Timothy's stomach rose and fell. Sebastian was glad to find him alive.

"He's fine," Garrick said. "There was never any danger for him."

"What was in that drink?"

"Nothing foul, just mead. It was the song she sang upon our entrance that impacted each of us differently. Put him to sleep, awakened your need for cunny."

It was humiliating for Sebastian to think about how close he had come to whatever that thing had intended to do to him.

Instead of dwelling on that thought, he asked how Garrick had been able to avoid her lure altogether.

"Marks of Osiris. A life of servitude has to have a few perks."

Sebastian recalled the host of foreign symbols inked and carved across his torso that he had glimpsed at Freywald.

Timothy stirred. In the firelight, his face was that of a constipated drunk.

"Sorcery had a go at you, pup," Garrick said. "Though I am positive you will think it an empty stomach or a light head."

The kid did not respond. Sebastian knew him well enough to recognize his confusion. "We cannot make camp down here," he said.

Garrick waved that statement down with his hand. "This is the safest place for us to stay. The creatures that call this land home are not likely to come anywhere near here…varcolac included. These witches can drum up power over anything. They spend blood and flesh like currency."

"Excuse me?" Timothy said.

"Blood magic. The *strigoi viu* are a type of witch that uses blood and flesh to extend their lives and bend the laws of physics. It's the only thing that matters to them. Markets all over the world are in place for these things to trade in specific bloods. Vampires, varcolac, demons…each have different potencies…different uses."

"You know this *how*?" Timothy was on his feet but looked brittle.

"BECAUSE I USED TO COLLECT HER FUCKING TAXES." Garrick's scream had all the patience of an unfit mother's.

The kid's silence only grew more befuddled.

"You stupid gash," Garrick said. "Just how would you expect that I know?"

As Sebastian braced himself for another round of heightened tensions and sarcastic responses, his companions went silent. Garrick pulled his hood down and ran a hand through his curly red hair. Once the anger had faded from his cheeks, he cupped a palm over Timothy's shoulder and waited for the kid to flash an assuring nod.

It was the most concern the hunter had ever shown him.

They sat for a long time watching the witch burn, her withered body coated with black char.

"We did imprison one once," Garrick said. "Thing was behind a rash of child killings in Athens. Snatching victims without common bond, peasants and royals both. Seven children gone before the city turned to the order. We are an indisputable necessity, pup, whether you like it or not. I arrived there on the eve of the eighth disappearance." Garrick paused for a moment and his face wrinkled. Sebastian was glad to see that something, anything, was capable of getting to him. "Wasn't long before I stumbled across a baby's tiny intestines spread out inside the Acropolis."

"Such evil," Timothy muttered. He caught himself as soon as he said it and closed his mouth. He had not intended to speak it aloud.

Garrick seemed content to ignore him this once. "I do not think the discovery was accidental, for the creature was waiting for me. When I caught up to her, it, whatever, in the underground, it did not look human, or even real. I cannot describe what I saw then, only that the green and red ink scrawled across my back protected me in the basin of that hellhole just as it did tonight. The monster wanted my blood…and more. To it, a warrior's blood has value. I took her alive, but it was only by the grace of luck that it happened that way. An allergy to my blade and the elixir it wore struck her through the heart, reversing whatever demon's blood she had ingested. Much like this hag, the façade fell away, leaving a faded old woman. Transporting her was not easy, but the Vatican City has means to contain any evil."

"You studied her?" Timothy perked up at the implication.

"Aye. She was the first one in captivity. That meant she was of interest. What we found was that her dedication to dark magic was more addictive than an opium high…something she couldn't live without. I don't recall how long we had her. Felt like days before one of the night watchers, three floors up, mind you, cut herself on an iron gate. That drop, hardly enough for the guard to notice, was all it took. It slithered its way to the witch, enabling her to assume another form. With it, she was able to deceive her way to freedom. Four of my brothers and sisters were dead before anyone knew things were amiss. I cut her down with this blade and regretted ever bringing her back. The order was less upset, favoring information over destruction. Who cares that we suffered losses when the knowledge she gave us was so valuable?"

"And you continue to serve such a righteous lot," Timothy said.

"I serve so children like you do not have to."

"Another of your failures, then."

"Do not think *this* is serving. You are surviving. Once we reach Constanta, you will go on with your life, yeah? Trying to forget the terrible things you saw. Eventually, that will happen, you realize. Once you've taken comfort in the arms of the right woman, sewn your seed inside of her, this…*life*…will be little more than an unpleasant memory for you. For me, however, it will continue as reality."

Sebastian drowned out their bickering by wandering back to Tulcea's room. He continued to ache, but it felt good to be able to move around at his own pace. He examined her quarters by torchlight while Garrick's words dogged him. Not the story about the Acropolis witch, but rather Timothy's eventual fate. A wife and children was an optimistic outcome, considering their current lot, and if it happened to come true, he wanted to stick around long enough to see it.

The witch's room was a mess. There was nothing sensual in here now that her magic had worn off. That creature, the *strigoi viu,* had sworn an apparent oath to squalor. Spoilt bed sheets were stained every shade of dark and light. Bloody droplets pocked the floor. They led back into the corridor and down the hall, away from the main chamber.

Sebastian followed it and Garrick picked up on his curiosity almost instantly, telling the youngest of them to stay put and shout if anyone else came down through the entrance.

For once, Timothy did not contest.

A wooden cart encrusted in brown blood sat in the connecting chamber. Splatter streaks stretched across the thin hay bed, darker than oil by torchlight. There had to be another entrance if Tulcea had gotten this thing down here.

"There could be more of them," Sebastian said, ashamed of the terror in his voice.

"These things do not dwell in hard-to-reach places because they are itching to join a social circle."

Sebastian dragged the torch to a rickety table of severed limbs. Torn and grayed appendages sat alongside blood-caked blades and glass phials brimming with a spectrum of colorful liquids.

Their missing villagers.

A row of cages lined the outlying wall. Two young men and a woman, each imprisoned separately. They glanced up from on scraped and dirty knees. Lifting their heads looked to consume all the strength they had left. Each was nude and their bodies wore open scabs.

"Look for a key," Sebastian said. "We've got to get them out."

Garrick had him by the arm, shaking his head in firm refusal. His six- shooter tapped the barrel of Sebastian's flintlock, a *you know what has to be done* gesture.

Sebastian hated the implication. These prisoners were young. None looked older than Timothy. Just kids. Emaciated kids. An outfit of tight and sunken flesh separated them from their skeletons. They rustled at the noise of intruders, though it was doubtful any of them could see.

Vision went when starvation took hold. Back home, he watched a hundred starving families battle for twenty loaves of stale bread in the alleyways of darkest London. Those too weak to fight curled up on the sidewalk and simply wasted away.

"Help us." The voice was wafer frail.

Of course they would help. The thief-taker's oath was to defend those who could not fend for themselves. That battle had now extended into a world previously unknown to him, but witches and vampires died the same as men. The rules of this game were unchanged.

The cages were locked, and Sebastian searched amidst the dungeon's grisly remnants for a key.

"You are wasting your time." Garrick stood in the center of the cavern with his arms folded. "There is but one way to help these Godless bastards."

The prisoners refused to pay him any mind, focusing a chorus of hoarse pleas on Sebastian.

"She must have had it on her," he said in a frustrated sigh.

"Yeah, where? Between her legs or up her arse? Did you taste brass when you ran your tongue across her taint?"

"These are not our enemies."

Garrick sighed and walked to the cages. He shot the

nearest prisoner through the eye. The teenage boy's head lurched and the back of his skull cracked, splattering his final thoughts all over the wall behind him.

The girl in the next cell began to growl, and Sebastian saw the onset of glowing yellow eyes mixed and swirling with whatever her natural eye color was.

"*Your* girlfriend was bleeding these creatures," Garrick said.

The young girl's face twisted and pointed ears took shape.

Beside her, the boy's expression was curious. His eyes were pained as he clasped his hands over his mouth.

"It is no wonder Tulcea incapacitated the two of you with ease," Garrick said. "She is working off the blood of demons."

The cells no longer housed teenagers. A hulking animal paced back and forth in the limited space where the girl had been. The boy on the far end hissed through extended fangs.

"Take your gun and put that beast down," Garrick said as he eased the torch from Sebastian's hand. He took the fire and slipped it between two of the bars, stabbing the boy who was too weak to resist, his only defense a meek wave of his arms to stave off the flame.

Garrick was undeterred, thrusting it forward like a spear and leaving dark stains on the skeletal flesh. The boy's skin chapped as the torch hit him again and again. He slipped down off the wall so his back was on the floor, and then his hair caught fire.

Sebastian watched the vampire burn, but he stopped processing everything and lapsed further into a daze. He was only vaguely aware that he held in his hand the means to kill a varcolac. Despite everything he had seen since late August, he could not get used to the sight of these shifting creatures.

The reality was that they shared this world with devils. He found perverse comfort in that thought, because there had to be angels as well, surely. How could there be one without the other?

As certain as he was, he could not bring himself to ask Garrick for confirmation.

If the answer is no…

Sebastian crossed himself and took aim, deciding he did not like where his thoughts were leading him. His eyes held against those evil orbs dangling beyond the bars. A prayer tumbled from his mouth, but her howling stifled it and startled him into taking the shot early. The bullet crashed through the animal's snout, a wellspring of blood pouring from her blown-out nostrils.

The wolf regressed, leaving a naked girl shriveled in death.

"Well done, thief-taker. This may not feel like a victory, but she is free to walk the beyond at last."

"There is no victory here," Sebastian said and lowered the smoke-swirled barrel.

"You are alive. Let that be all you need."

"I was barely that."

"The hag was not your fault."

"What a fool I was."

"The fairer sex is alluring, and that's before you weave magic into it. You'd have an easier time getting the Whigs and Tories to see eye-to-eye than resisting her."

The witch-finder would say no more. He went about searching the chamber for anything of use.

Sebastian left him to scavenge. When he returned to the large chamber, Timothy was huddled over one of his books, staring through the pages once more. When badly shaken, the kid needed scholastic reinforcement like Sebastian demanded gin.

Sebastian said nothing. He dropped onto the bench, eager to put the day away. His shoulder continued to hurt, and he cleaned it with water from the wellspring before redressing it with rags cut from his doublet.

Soon he would be back in London, drowning in all the gin he could drink. Ridding the streets of a criminal element he could understand. You did not wind up with a hard on when you chased down a pickpocket.

"What are we reading tonight, pup?" Garrick's fireside arrival was marked by boisterous condescension. "Tell me a bedtime story."

For a long while, the kid stayed silent and Sebastian thought that was for the best. However, he was excitable like any young pup. Never content to sit idle and suffer goading. Timothy cleared his throat and Sebastian rolled his eyes behind his lids.

"This is philosophy," the kid barked. "There's no story to tell."

"Explain it to me anyway. What do you take away from all that?"

"That religious texts are artificial and primitive. That we have to move beyond superstition and favor reason."

"That doesn't sound like Locke or Hobbes to me. One favored religious tolerance, the other argued that a unified religion best served the state."

"Exactly. Their strongest concepts are still mired in superstition. What hope is there when even the smartest among us look to appease the man in the sky? And I still cannot believe that you know them. Have studied them."

"I think myself well read, you know. Enough of my life has been lived on the road, and so the warm comfort of books *is* known to me."

"And yet you seem to understand very little."

"Yeah? Well, someday, when there is time, we must waste more energy debating their philosophies, neither of which will ever come to pass. I wish I had the luxury of sitting around all day advocating idealistic nonsense. The world will never be what you want, you know."

"Never try to make it better, then? That's your solution? Sounds like your order should forget about everything it does if that's the case. And, so you know, that viewpoint did not sound like Locke or Hobbes because it's not. It's me."

"Of course it is. So profound. Will you tell me next that the sky is blue?"

"Slag off."

"No, by all means, let's talk about your viewpoint. Do you feel comfortable with that conclusion in the light of all we've seen? When a woman turns into wolf? When creatures that thirst for blood hunt us? Why must you go on pretending that things are precisely as they were before you took on this march? What good is life if you do not adapt to it?"

There was silence then, and Sebastian realized that he was hanging on every word, resisting sleep because of it. Maybe he did not want to ask Garrick if there were forces of good beyond this world, but he desired an answer all the same.

"Anyway," Garrick said as Timothy sat in stumped silence. "You'll get no argument from me. Because of the church, man is no longer interested in self-sufficiency. He'd rather ask the heavens to solve his problems, no matter how obtuse. *'God, let me find something with which to wipe my arse,'* that sort of shite."

"I'm having a hard time understanding you then," Timothy said. "Before we joined, I would've said that religion keeps man distracted from the realities of his life. What you just said. Because let's face it, the existence of God cannot be proven, and those who make baseless claims on the contrary belong in a sanitarium."

"And now?" Garrick's tone smacked of inevitability. "Does it have to be one or the other? Too much tobacco will kill you, so should we never smoke it? Isn't it possible to have a little faith without looking to the sky for every inconvenience?"

The air in the chamber was confused. Timothy tried speaking, stopping and starting a few times, but succeeded only in making frustrated huffs.

"Your contempt for me is why, exactly?" Garrick said. "Because I contradict your subscriptions? Make it hard for you to pigeonhole me?"

"Your hostility is unbecoming and…"

"As is yours." Garrick countered before the kid could finish. "Let's agree that our arrogance is mutually off-putting. Do you know what you really need?"

"For this to end."

There was more conversation, but Sebastian ceased following it. Sleep overtook him and he dreamt of Tulcea. There, she was youthful once more. Frayed blonde hair, the way he imagined she would look after a night of furious passion. Dull red lips parted to reveal a forked tongue. Jade eyes sparkled and her irises were half-moons: An exotic creature crawling to him on all fours, a clucking sound from the back of her throat that sounded like mocking laughter.

But he did not care. His heart ached in his chest as she neared. Her body glistened with exotic oil that taunted his senses and made him want to lick her flesh.

She called out but her words were muted. Her tongue curled and tapped the edge of her lip. He wanted to feel it working across him, easing his nerves as he became a slave to her whims.

His hand reached for her, stretching until his fingers scuffed the soft flesh of her belly.

Above them, in the world beyond this one, the tête-à-tête between his companions was reignited, their argument thunderous. Tulcea broke away from him with a tear like a bandage ripped from the skin.

Sebastian jolted and nearly rolled off the bench.

"As you can see, this tale of woe is so powerful that even our old friend decided he could not sleep through it."

The hunter continued without waiting for Sebastian's reaction. Through the fire, Timothy's concentration had never looked more intense. He was interested in what Garrick had to say, perhaps for the first time ever. There did not appear to be much disagreement here, though the sound of voices echoing in this open chamber had been more than enough to wake him.

"The first time I saw the Raven," Garrick said. "I was alone and inexperienced. The order does not send us into the fray untried, so for my first assignment, they sent me to your neck of the woods. A cliff-side inn on the coast of Rhossili." Garrick's tone regressed into its usual mockery. "Ocean blue waves breaking on unmolested sienna beaches...quite the sight if you can muster a damn for that sort of thing. The sun climbed so high there that it slicked the clay-colored sand with blinding glare. Beauty that makes you believe everything is going to work out just right. Deceiving."

Sebastian sat up, mirroring Timothy's interest.

"A month passes. I spend it watching every soul who takes a bed on their way to the village of Scurlage. Scrutinized those who hurried past even more, but they turned out to be the ones without the coin to spare. There wasn't a highwayman in sight to disrupt the tranquility. I dare say that Sebastian would have been bored."

"I'd give half my pay for a piece of boredom like that now."

Garrick did not acknowledge the comment. "You want to pretend the world is a nice place, pup, this is the kind of hamlet you need to settle down in. No easier place for you to put your back to life's problems, to curl up in your texts and imagine the world as it *should* be. No one's going to come along and call you an asshole for thinking like that there."

"If you think I'm running from reality," Timothy said.

Garrick shushed him with a reflexive turn of his head. Things went quiet and he continued. "A more seasoned man than I would've seen it. Fucking hell, I should have at least *sensed* it. But my blade was dry then, and well, you and I might've been better friends at the time. All I knew was what my books had taught me.

"I passed evenings in the dining hall, nursing my ale while hoping for an interesting ear to bend. I liked the nights when that didn't happen better. Girl behind the counter, the innkeeper's daughter, had taken a shining to me. A beautiful sight, truly. Blonde hair to her arse, and teats that swelled up out of her garment. She batted eyes at me every afternoon and asked me to regale her with tales of high adventure. I had none, but that didn't stop me from talking. When the order takes you, you spend your first years familiarizing yourself with a curriculum of texts, some of them common and others obscure. I plagiarized every outré tale I could recall, positioning myself at the center of each. She adored me more with every passing lie until the temptation was too great. We spent that first night in the cellar storeroom, fucking like the filthy bunnies I hate so much. She left me exhausted and spent on a pile of hay, slinking back to tend desk when the morning came 'round. Had another go the next night. This time, she was bold enough to knock on my door. On the evenings when we did nothing, I threw my ear to the patrons and gleamed all I could from their travelers' tales. I would catch her watching me from the corner of the room, hungry eyes undressing me. Men in brothels do not objectify whores with as much lust as she held in those gazes.

"I do not think any of you are surprised to hear that she grew attached, and asked to accompany me upon departure. The order would sentence me to death for less, so it was never a possibility. Even if it were, considering the amount of lies I had told, there was no chance of keeping my stories straight. Our classical romance would wilt before we made it out of that horrible country…no offense."

Sebastian reached for his flask and shook it. Only a few swallows remained. The fever endured but he could not resist this. In all of their months on the road, the hunter had never spoken this much.

He's scared.

That made Sebastian scared. He took a swig and felt the warmth spread across his chest as he sat and listened.

"On an especially quiet night, we were about to go for a toss when a horse-drawn carriage clopped near. Before I could register what a peculiar hour for arrival it was, a man covered head-to-toe in black gentleman's dress entered and requested the most lavish accommodations possible. He then requested supper and took a seat in the thickest shadows, finding a spot where the lantern did not reach.

"Miriam brought him a bloody slab of prime rib that dribbled onto the hay-covered floor. I sat across the way and watched him eat it with bare hands. Once he was finished, he merely folded his hands and stared. I never saw his face, but there was an instance where the moonlight, perhaps reflecting off a rising wave, hit him with just enough glow for me to see his jutting cheeks and parted lips.

"He was smiling. Grinning as if he could do nothing more. I will admit, pup, that even you would have taken action before I did. So dull was I that I simply rose, dominated by gnawing unease. I wanted nothing more than to sleep, to be rid of that feeling."

"How could you not know?" Timothy said. "Even if you were as dull as you say, you have your instinct."

That may have provoked a smile from Garrick. His face

was as difficult to see as the well-dressed man's in his story, but his features seemed to lighten, even in the shadows.

"It's been my cross to bear," Garrick said. "I settled into the confines of my room, eager to let the day's ingestion of wine send me off. Just before dawn, there was a soft knock against my door, and a feminine voice calling me *stranger*. I cracked it to find soft, blue eyes meeting me in its crevice. I had never seen her before and I did not get the chance to say anything. Because she pushed in just enough to touch my wrist and whisper, *everyone is dead*.

"I followed as she led me into the hall. Every door up there had been opened. The guests lay butchered in their beds. Slashed throats, a pitchfork rammed through, pinning others where they slept. I knew at once the well-dressed man was responsible, and that I was going to have to kill him. I unsheathed my blade and started downstairs to find Miriam. A part of me realized that she was dead, though I was not yet jaded enough to leave it to chance.

"When I was nearly down the steps, the woman took me by the shoulder and whirled me around. The sky outside was just blue enough for me to see her face. She would've been stunning if not for the blood that lay across her mouth. She spoke again with such triumph and delight that I realized it was my own put-upon bravado that had doomed the inn. *Will you vanquish us like you killed the djinn?* she asked in mockery."

"Djinn?" Timothy said.

"One of the many tales I offered Miriam. She must have been spreading my stories to some of her friends in Scurlage. It was this *heroism* that brought devils to investigate. I heard a pop from the darkened serving room, and Miriam's head ran across the floor, bumping against the foot of the stairs, her eyes staring up at me with blame. I jumped over it and my boots skidded on the blood trail behind her. The well-dressed man lurched from the corner, obscured but *still* smiling.

"I knew then that she must've thought I would save her. That two monsters were of no consequence to a *warrior* such as me. Stories of my triumphs only provoked their cruelty.

"I did the only thing that came natural to me in that moment. Despite all of the training that had conditioned me to do otherwise, despite the silver blade in my sheath that could've killed them both, I ran. I ran outside, toward their horse and buggy. The sun was only then rising and I knew there was not time enough to retrieve my own animal from the stables. My retreat was hasty and wolves converged from all sides, trotting after me, determined to punish my braggadocio.

"They never got me. It was Miriam, her father, and their customers who had been made to pay for my transgressions. I swore that I was going to kill her. Years of research, deducting potential eyewitness accounts from every corner of this continent. I knew I would find her again one day, and it was not until those Spaniards started a war with the empire that she came out of hiding. Stories surfaced that she was a boogeyman on the battlefields, turning wounded men into demons just like her. Those tales spread until I could no longer ignore them. It was another year of hunting in her vicinity before I could get closer still. And the rest, you know."

It did not seem like a natural place to end the conversation, but there was nothing left to be said. The kid stretched back and nodded off first, and Sebastian took his cue shortly after. He heard Garrick stirring for some time, probably trying to bury those awful memories once more.

When morning came, they gathered their things and rinsed off in the basin. Garrick went off to loot the rear chamber of all glass phials, throwing a handful into the fire. Next went the books bound in dried human flesh, volumes of spells written in a tongue no one could understand.

Timothy had suggested they keep them to decipher, but

the hunter refused. "If we do not make it back, these cannot fall into the wrong hands. We may not know how to decrypt them, but we cannot take the chance that someone else might."

The whole and quartered bodies went next to the fire.

Once done, they followed the wagon tracks through the rear chamber out into the forest. The land that stood before them was dark, but Sebastian was glad to be out of the mine.

He wanted to think that the worst was over now that Constanta was just a few short days away. He remained hopeful as best he could, but those prospects were dashed each time he closed his eyes.

For he saw Tulcea there. And she wanted him to go to sleep so that she could have him again.

He pushed the image from his mind and continued walking.

THE CONSTANT WOLF

PART OF THE WOLF REMAINED with her always, even when the animal hid.

Elisabeth was grateful for that, as it was her only means of hunting while on human legs. The creature's vision and hearing were incomparable. They kept her human eyes and ears constantly fine-tuned.

If she could not navigate the forest as a wolf, this was better than nothing.

Hunter's musk swirled in the air, swallowed by the mine's entrance. No mistaking where they had gone. Concentrated heat stemmed from the depths—raw desire rising like mist. One, if not more of them, was in heat. Elisabeth chewed her lip as she considered this. They had never been lost in each other's flesh. If they had, their scents would have been entwined before now.

Whatever was down there with them dispelled her investigative curiosity.

It is something that can kill me, she thought. *Or worse.*

Her reluctance to go where she needed to surprised her. She had been certain she no longer cared about living, just as long as the assassins paid for their trespasses, but her attitude was not as cavalier as she had once thought. The creature in the mine commanded the same magic that Alina wielded. Elisabeth sensed various wards and charms nearby, rifts between this world and the one beyond it, defenses marking this territory as occupied while keeping opponents at bay.

If dying was the worst thing that could happen to Elisabeth, she might have considered the intrusion worth the risk.

But witches did more than kill. They took your body and mind if they wanted, and harvested your flesh and soul if they did not. No amount of vengeance was worth chancing that.

Elisabeth picked up on a strand of particularly cool air, a crisp gust hovering outside the drafty adit. There had to be another way in, and she walked off to find it.

Her trip around the mountain lasted nearly as long as the evening.

Because Alina had interrupted her sleep, Elisabeth's desire for rest superseded her penchant for revenge—at least while the familiar one and his companions were entombed with the witch. There was nothing to do but wait, and her body required rest. True, they might never make it out of there, but she would not underestimate them, either. She would be waiting at the exit, rooting for their emergence. Her fingers flexed around the dagger while her mind drifted through blood fantasies. Her eyelids were on weights that drew down over her vision. Her march became a barely conscious shamble on jelly legs.

If this sorceress is even half as powerful as the queen, they will die, robbing me of my purpose.

Her past experiences colored these thoughts. When Elisabeth was a pup, she had watched one of their own, a wolf with the same gift of invulnerability, get pulled apart by such sorcery. Alina's magic had not protected the young man, a fledgling called Ben, from being unraveled like sweater string until only his innards remained in a roadside pile of mush.

She and Ben had set upon a lone traveler in search of a quick kill, just as pup wolves might stalk rabbit ahead of a pack hunt. They were oblivious to this prey's cursed aura, sensing only an easy meal. As wolves, they closed in on the walker and discovered he had been ready, whirling to greet them with a face that looked to have been stripped from his skull and then reapplied with hasty patchwork.

His own flesh, or what he wore as his own, was crassly stitched across his cheeks, chin, and forehead, pieces of varied color that created a jarring puzzle pattern.

A hand shot up in front of his face, fingers wiggling toward the sky. His tips were stretched and pointed, coils of skin peeled away from the appendages like a potato. The bone beneath looked swollen, inhuman. When he opened his mouth, a wide eye somehow glared at them from the back of his throat.

Ben locked in step, his body convulsed. Blood seeped from seams she could not see until his fury pelt began to peel. And then fray off in larger strips. In the time it took Elisabeth to turn her head, Ben had become the floor of a butcher's shop.

"We rub our backs in search of wings we never had," the traveler had said. *"For I reached into the sky and found nothing there but clouds."* His laughter rolled over Elisabeth's startled screams, instilling in her a sense of fear rarely experienced.

She retreated with a wolf's gallop, his words following forever in her ears as fatigue grew and she dared not stop, scampering across the hillside with all the desperation of a wounded animal. It had taken most of the night to outrun his tongue, which seemed to hover between her ears even as the sun had begun to stretch wide in the overhead sky.

Even now her heart pounded as she remembered this.

So she moved parallel along the outside of the mine,

following the mountain path and holding her breath so not to disturb the creature that nested there. Elisabeth could think only of her growing discomfort being this close to one who held that power.

Why did I refuse Alina's offer?

She had not been tempted by the queen, but her invitation was *something*. Being alone in the wilderness only cultivated her despair.

It was difficult to think about Alina now. Rather than dwell on what could have been, Elisabeth tortured herself over what had been lost. A few weeks ago, Aetius had the most wonderful surprise for her. She tried to bask in those memories while she moved, forgetting about the magic and thinking about the way his voice had sounded then.

"Do you know how beautiful you look in the moon?" he had asked.

"My natural habitat." Her expression remained cold then. A layman would have thought the compliment lost on her, but it was nice to hear, even if she would never admit it.

"*Our* natural habitat." Aetius slipped a powerful arm around her buttocks and squeezed until the sensation stimulated her.

She moaned in surprise and dropped her mouth, refusing to indulge his lust. "You *do* get all worked up after a slaughter."

Aetius took her in his arms and forced her back against the carriage wheels. Protruding spokes were uncomfortable and she wiggled for freedom, his strength keeping her pinned. His arms were like bulging tree stumps pressed against her shoulders as his mouth slathered her neckline with wet kisses.

Her mood was cold and disinterested, but she allowed him to continue without resistance. Elisabeth liked that Aetius cared enough about her to take what he wanted. She saw it as a seed planted. And that seed would grow into astonishing pleasure the next time she allowed him inside her.

The sloppy kisses soon grew tiresome and she shoved him with a dominant growl. When she felt like being conquered, she would foster the illusion that he was in charge. That was a delicate balance, though, because men were no fun once they had been emasculated.

Aetius grinned, amused by her aggression.

"Once we are on the road," she said, "perhaps we shall pass the time however *you* see fit."

They loaded one of the carriages with burlap sacks that brimmed with looted riches. It was a shame that her pups had gone to war in Freywald to buy them the time to slip off like this. Whatever happened there would take attention off this robbery. The body count would be catastrophic, and plebeian superstition would reign supreme. They would blame God, wonder if they were being punished for something they had no control over, and spend the rest of their lives atoning in misery.

Aetius pulled open the door on the second carriage and groped Elisabeth again as he lifted her up and inside.

Their escape had been planned and plotted: Ramp up the children and see their journey to voracious creatures made complete. Freywald was to be their final test. Many would not survive, but those who did would be forged into hardened predators that would stake their claims in the evening shadows.

It was also their opportunity to make a clean break. She had deprived her frustrated lover of fleshy pleasures throughout the last month of meticulous planning. Six estates sacked, wealth removed with precision, but every bit of their attention in between heists had been focused on the pups. Raising their confidence and then fortifying their capabilities.

She had felt guilty about withholding her body, but got off

on Aetius' desperation: The hopefulness that flashed whenever she bounced her hips, or happened to glance his way with a hint of suggestion in her eye. Aetius was starved, nearly crazed, and could think of nothing else.

Elisabeth liked that. So much that she had allowed him to bathe her one evening. As she rose from the piping hot and spiced water, her eyes caught his bulge. Weakness penetrated her. The constant wolf sitting in subconscious darkness urged her to take that gratification, instinct driving her to it. The need to be sated grew like her lover's cock.

But Elisabeth would not.

It was more fun this way, especially as his anger and frustration increased. To wield that much power over someone was not something she took lightly.

You are mine, she thought while watching him climb into the carriage. He slipped an arm around her shoulder, an innocent gesture that became a firm caress. His muscles eased hers after two months of road-weary tension.

She shut her eyes and placed her head on his shoulder. His lips fell over them, kissing her lids with gentle puckers.

She turned upward and placed two small kisses on his neck, and then savored the silence.

Outside, two of their cubs feasted on a banquet of drivers and passengers—two children they had come to like above all others. Those who could be trusted in matters beyond satisfying their animal instincts: Claude and Jean. Both fine additions to Alina's unsanctioned army.

Elisabeth and Aetius enjoyed eating mixed company: Withered buggy drivers and the wealthy lords and ladies traveling beneath them. The quality of their flesh and innards ranged, but that made every meal fun as well as gratifying.

With their bellies full, they had regressed and cooled off in the roadside lake, turning Claude and Jean loose on the leftovers.

The cubs were only now finishing their meals and returning to the road as naked young men covered in blood that was somehow blacker than the evening sky around them.

Elisabeth made it a point to turn the other way, ignoring their flopping manhoods. Not out of respect for Aetius, but to deny them the satisfaction.

They will lie and say they had me anyway.

The young ones dressed in whichever spare clothes could be scavenged from the luggage boxes. Then they climbed atop the wagons and started them off.

Her army was behind them, part of her past, and she was glad for it. Elisabeth was never much for following orders, and even less for giving them. The cubs were Alina's now, servants of chaos. It was better that way. If they happened to live as long as she, they would have their own opportunities to grow tired of such things.

Elisabeth had considered sacking more estates, including Freywald, but stashed her bloodlust for the sake of the pups. They would not have any fun out here if there remained no one to terrorize.

"Will you miss it?" Aetius asked after the carriages had been rolling for some time.

"I never wanted to be a leader," she said. That was true. She knew it was probably different for him, a Roman centurion taken by wolf bite during a barbarian hunt. The sole survivor of that attack, he had crawled on his knees back to a legion encampment, forever changed by the animal's kiss.

For a creature like that, one who fought in the Midnight War alongside Alina and the first vestiges of varcolac, battling a Church-led inquisition so secretive it had been stricken from history books, it was easier to understand why a life of regimen was a difficult habit to kick.

Elisabeth could not understand, however, why he was not more compelled to settle down beside her. That bothered her when she allowed her mind to dwell on it.

"You know," she said and traced the lines of his hardened stomach with two of her fingers. "I could not ask you to leave everything you value behind."

"There is one thing I value." Aetius put a gentle finger on her cheek and lifted it to his mouth with a soft press.

"Why do I sense disappointment in you, then?"

"We killed many and turned a few. Our legacy is intact for the immediate future, and the queen inherits a faithful army of pups on behalf of us. They will serve her every word gratefully. As long as my future holds you, what else do I care? Why would I be disappointed?"

She cocked an eyebrow and shuffled across the coach to the opposite seat, studying his face for an answer to that rather cryptic statement. When she could not find one, she asked, "What do you mean?"

"I mean whatever is to come of us, huntress."

"And what *will* come of us? Build a home and live out our days while the world changes a hundred times?"

"That thought had occurred to me."

The carriage continued along the winding mountain pass that broke them free of the 'Holy Roman Empire' as she considered this. The huntress was an idea, as predictable as any over-performed duty. If she had the ability to age, she would have written it off as a young woman's game. Even now, the conceit remained accurate. Those in other corners of the world wielded the mantle just as well.

But they were not the first.

As if that mattered. It was a distinction without pride. All it said of Elisabeth was that she had been at this a long time. All it said was that Elisabeth had more reason to want to step away.

Aetius took her foot and placed it in his lap, rubbing the sole. "I have a surprise for you."

She did not answer, only tilted her head back to enjoy his caress.

"Once we are back home, Claude will depart us to carry out a very special assignment."

A wide grin spread across her face. She did love surprises and there were so few of them these days.

He lifted her toes to his mouth and kissed each one before closing his lips around them, sucking. It made her giggle and she tugged it free, offering a playful kick to his chin.

Elisabeth could not fight her swollen smile. She dogged him for details but he would say nothing more. Her grin curved, making her cheeks pop. Her tongue fell out in a wolf's pant. She caught herself but did not retract the smile. In all her years, this might have been the most thoughtful thing anyone had done for her.

The only thoughtful thing.

It made her feel so good that she refused to taint the moment with superfluous speech or additional questions. Her eyes held his and the smile faded, replaced by something more.

Hunger.

Aetius sensed it too, lunging across the way and kissing her, tearing at her robe and massaging her breasts.

She felt the change beneath her bones but pushed it off like the first tremors of orgasm. It was not always easy to suppress the wolf, but this was a worthy effort.

Aetius tugged at his own clothes, kissing and blowing on her nipples while his fingers gave gentle pinches. He growled as a dark mane spread across his chest, then rippled up his back like porcupine needles.

Elisabeth curled her legs around his naked body. The sensation of his vibrating and shifting bones heightened her pleasure. She flexed her thighs in acceptance, but squeezed his arms and whispered in his ear to discourage the change entirely.

"You," she said. "Not the wolf."

"It is both me."

"Like this," she said.

Both wolves wanted to come out and play, but she kept hers leashed, gnashing her teeth and scraping them back and forth to keep the animal down. Aetius trembled and groaned, treading between pleasure and pain as a human on the verge. Her flesh tingled beneath his hot breath and wet licks.

Aetius stood hunched inside the coach, so large his shoulders seemed to extend from one wall to the other. His dark and swirling eyes burned with uncontrollable lust.

This was going to hurt, but how he loved having her this way.

And this was all for him.

His teeth were sharper in the moment, and his jaws came down on her shoulder, tearing her. Her nails dug into the skin behind his stretching, pulsing head, screaming out as he slipped inside. She was moist enough to take him, but cried as he thrust forward. A blood rain fell from her shoulder, painting her breasts red.

The wolf lapped it like water.

He was right, even as a human, he took her like an animal.

Her eyes swelled and tears ran down her temples, every thrust sending crippling pain through her. Each motion easier to bear until the pain was suddenly pleasure.

She ruffled his cropped hair and pulled him closer, moving her hips to match his rhythm as much as she could stand.

Maybe he is more in charge than I thought.

When he took her to orgasm and kept going, she decided she did not care.

And it was all the stuff of memories now.

A distraction while she walked.

The morning sun had not yet risen when Elisabeth was snapped from her thoughts. She tried again to encourage the wolf's return but her muscles only sputtered. Alina had been right. She could not depend on the animal for this.

It was impossible to combat three men with a dulled blade. She relied on the wolf for these things and knew little about survival otherwise.

Taking on the familiar one and his followers meant that her body would only be wrecked once more, and maybe worse, if she could not change.

In the distance, they emerged from the mine and she stole a sigh of relief. She had been so discouraged by her inability to get at her wolf that she had not realized the magic around here had faded. No more charms or wards and no lingering threat from the depths below. They were unlikely to come back this way, but she stood her ground, holding her breath as they marched in line and without words, disappearing down a stone-laid trail.

They would be easy to find.

Come on, she thought and tried the wolf again.

Her will echoed, but the wolf did not hear it.

Defeated, Elisabeth reached the cave's mouth and paused.

She felt worse about her chances. If they could defeat black magic, they were more dangerous than she wanted to admit.

Her eyes dropped to the dagger in her hand. It was so dull it would not cut wet cheese.

"Bastards," she said and took a step inside to see what could be salvaged.

THE VILLAGE
OF THE MOON

GARRICK ORDERED THEM TO STOP just before dusk, and even then, no one felt like speaking.

The forest pushed in on them from all sides as they made camp and waited for first light.

"No longer concerned that Raven is nipping at our heels?" Timothy said. He folded his legs in the dirt, cleaning the blunderbuss' barrel with a bristly rod.

"That's my *only* concern," Garrick said. "So ready yourselves. We're taking shifts."

Sebastian volunteered for first watch. He needed rest, but the possibility of sleep was tenuous. Not because of his throbbing shoulder, which continued to ache and burn with relentlessness, but because he was scared of meeting Tulcea in his dreams. He saw bursts of her whenever he closed his eyes, flashes of a nightmare that startled him like thunder in the sky.

Timothy offered the use of his blunderbuss for night's watch. Sebastian took it and circled the encampment. Without long lines of sight, the kid's scattergun was preferable to his flintlocks. He hoped he would not need it at all as he listened with envy to snoring men and inquisitive owls.

Timothy rose at some point and offered to take over. Sebastian was grateful and dropped onto his bedroll, eager for the last few swigs of gin. Blacking out from exhaustion the way to go. If he dreamt then, he was not likely to recall it.

You have no power over me.

That was a lie. A piece of him remained excited to see her. Longed for her. Tulcea did not indulge his reverie, though. Sebastian imagined her tiny frame glowing hot by torchlight. Recalled her small breasts and hard nipples gliding against his chest. Savored the memory of her intoxicating scent.

And the talons on her feet.

Don't think about that.

"Lower your weapons." Timothy's order came on full-tilt. Sebastian lunged upright at the sound. His shoulder screamed out as agitated nerves protested the unexpected movement. He was more disoriented than he realized, wondering how long he had managed to sleep.

Two men stood at the forest's edge.

Timothy held them in place, brandishing his weapon and stabbing it forward every so often to sell his seriousness.

Sebastian drew his flintlocks and rushed to join him, gnawing on his cheek to quell the beating pain.

The strangers wore nondescript tatters of clothing and their faces were bruised and bloodied. These were not hard men, but survivors. Harmless.

"We are merely passing through." The stranger's breath was tortured. "Neither of us would be foolish enough to engage the likes of you."

They brandished farmer's weapons: Wood axes that dripped with fresh blood. Their expressions were haunted, decidedly not the scowls of highwaymen.

Of that, Sebastian was certain.

"Where are you coming from?" Garrick stepped from the shadows. His six-shooter flashed against the unsteady lantern glow. "I believe you when you say that you mean us no harm, but that does not explain *those*."

The men looked at their weapons as if suddenly remembering they still carried them. "We ran into trouble, these were all we could find."

"What trouble?" Sebastian said. "Where?"

"Follow this road through the forest, you'll find out soon enough."

"I'd rather hear it from you," Garrick said.

The more talkative of the two strangers swallowed, throwing his friend a sideways glance. Sebastian read it as despair.

"Back east," he said, "caught a bunch of looters inside my family tomb. We got them before they got us."

"Try again," Garrick said.

The strangers shifted like children caught in a lie.

"And know that if I do not believe you this time, I may come to believe you *do* intend us harm."

"It's not like that…"

"Good," Garrick said. "Tell me what it *is* like, because you're not happening past a family tomb in the middle of the night. In those rags. A man lives the way you do, looks hard and worn like you do, he's got more problems than someone breaking into his ancestral crypt."

"Okay, suppose it was us doing the breaking and entering…"

"I buy that more," Garrick said.

"We're not evil men, not by a long shot, but these lands are wilting. Families back home depend on us, you know."

"Something wrong with Constanta?"

"Yes, they caught us thieving there already."

"Fugitives, then," Garrick said. "The puzzle pieces snap into place. Yet, you still neglect to mention why *those* run red."

"You already heard the truth where our axes are concerned."

"Amidst your desperation, you thought it best to visit the old family plot to pay your respects?" Garrick's gun cocked in disbelief.

"No, we were breaking in…as a last resort. I am nothing if not ashamed of our actions. But our families…tell me, why should jewelry adorn the dead when our living sons and daughters starve? Once we were inside, we found…them."

There was silence then, as if they were supposed to know what *them* meant.

"They had yellow eyes," the second stranger said. "The smallest girl reached for me like it was a game of hide and seek. I thought my eyes were playing tricks on me before I heard the laughing…"

"…laughter that surrounded us. A mother. A father. Easing off stone slabs from a fresh night's sleep. Teeth like scythes, wanting to bite us." He raised the axe on cue, finishing the story through silent gestures.

"Did they?" Garrick asked? "Bite you?"

"Of course not."

"Strip then."

The men disputed, but Garrick cut through their protests with a flash of his gun. The strangers pulled their shreds away and stood shriveled by cold air.

Sebastian and Timothy gave them a physician's attention. Save for a few surface cuts, the wayward wanderers were clean. With that established, they were then ordered to redress.

"Is there anything else you would tell us," Garrick said. "So that we do not befall the...*challenges* you faced?"

They shook their heads in unison.

"And where do you make for now?"

"Anywhere." The answer was eager.

"Away from here," said the other.

"Best you hurry then. Follow this road for as long as you can. It is long, but uneventful. You should pass without incident."

The men offered nervous thanks and hurried on their way. Once they were out of earshot Sebastian laid back down, eager to resume his search for Tulcea before he was even conscious of that desire.

"You know what you've just done," Timothy said, incredulous as always.

Garrick nestled into his bedroll without an answer, closing the lantern's airflow once he was settled.

"You sent those men to their deaths. If she really is tracking us..."

"Then I bought us some time," Garrick said and rolled onto his side.

Sebastian found sleep impossible. The forest's natural bustle brought no comfort as each noise made him suspicious of varcolac, vampires, or thieving killers.

A series of relaxed breaths gave way to a thin layer of sleep, but it was eventually severed by the desperate screams of two familiar men in the far off distance.

Then there was nothing in the night except silence.

○

Fresh blood broke across the wolf's nose. From the depths, she stirred, wanting nothing more than to surface. Her human guise wished it too, calling for her even now, as she straddled the twitching corpse, splattered with lifeblood that encouraged the change.

The wolf's stomach rumbled, her hunger great.

And yet, it was not enough.

○

Sebastian felt like he was suffering the worst drunken stupor of his life.

They marched, without food or water to supplement the grueling pace, and his mind grew more fatigued than even his body.

He kept his desire for Tulcea secret in a mixture of selfishness and shame. She had chosen *him*. And thinking about her made his stomach warmer than all the gin in London.

His arms swung like logs as he walked, his eyes rolled back in his head as the sun begun falling.

He needed sleep. Not a few hours of bedroll rest, either. Genuine respite for as long a while as he could afford.

After this journey, I'll be able to afford quite a bit, he imagined.

The day dwindled to a bleak gray sky. Ahead of him, Timothy gasped.

Sebastian shambled forward and leaned on the kid's shoulder for support.

A village sat ensconced by a crescent-circled stonewall. Pointed stakes jutted up around the perimeter, each of them capped by a slack-mouthed severed head. The heads were the color of char, scorched by the sun's errant rays, reaching through the trees whenever the wind blew just right.

A declaration for travelers to stay far, far away.

Sebastian took a seat in the dirt. His breaths were stubborn wheezes plucked from his lungs. He watched Garrick as the hunter eyed the situation.

"He will not survive without proper rest," he said and gestured for Timothy to help him up.

The town's streets were sparse. A few villagers shuffled past them as they crossed the threshold where soil became cobblestone. Faces that were so worn and tired, they continued their dead-eyed business without acknowledging the travelers. An attitude expected of a place that decorated itself with the decapitated heads of enemies.

They headed up the hill to the estate grounds. It was set against the furthest part of wall, and fenced off by an iron gate.

"Stay alert," Garrick cautioned and then headed for the door.

He was about to knock when it creaked open. An old woman offered a plump smile. She smelled of a pig's sty even from across the way.

"Been some time since we had a visitor." She spoke another tongue entirely and Timothy translated it to Sebastian in a whisper.

Garrick returned the language, offering a quick and light response.

"Considering the decorations outside your walls, it is not hard to understand why." Timothy's translation continued.

"I am sure you can understand." A voice behind them spoke in shattered English. A man emerged from an empty stable ornamented in noble riding colors. He was bacon-fed with pink jowls that swayed as he came forward—an incongruity in this part of the world. He glanced at the sky and brushed dirt off his thighs as if newly returned from a ride. "You are well-armed and outfitted. Against the evil in this land, I assume?"

"Does it pester you as well?" Timothy said.

"It *terrorizes* us."

Sebastian shoved off Timothy's support and squandered what little energy remained by crossing over with his hand outstretched. He was not just hoping for their hospitality, he needed it.

"Sebastian Miles."

"Ion Bey." The man grinned and took Sebastian's palm in his gloved hand. "Governor of this quaint village of Rodica."

"Does Moldova have a democracy?" Garrick said. "I thought we were in Ottoman territory?"

"We are," said Bey. "But their rule is a formality. We bow to the Sultan, but are little more than a tributary to his regime. A check mark on their conquest map."

"Is it customary for the Ottomans to cut the heads off their enemies and decorate village walls with them?" Garrick said

Bey was not amused by the question. "We defy the demons who affect this land."

"What demons?"

"You'll excuse me if your ignorance comes off as disingenuous. I believe you know all too well what besieges us, considering the equipment you carry. Those *are* silver sabers, yes?"

"Many things could besiege you," Garrick said. "Peter the Great and his Russian Empire push in on you from the north. We know that to be true as we have seen his destruction and the resulting scarceness every step of the way."

"Peter the Great thinks there is hope of expansion, but he is no threat to us."

"So it is not the heads of his men poking up over these walls like curious children?"

Ion Bey sighed. If Garrick's arrogance and belligerence spoiled their chances at asylum, Sebastian was likely to kill him as his last order of business. "You know those are not the heads of soldiers."

Garrick went silent and the two leaders stared at one another. Everyone knew what plagued Bey, but the truth did not spill so easily into the air.

When Garrick had no choice but to test the waters he cleared his throat and spoke with molasses. "Wolves?" he said.

"And worse," Bey added.

"I did not know their rampage extended this far east."

"All darkness converges here," Bey said. "Wolves, yes, but it is the dead that are drawn to us. Our very presence taunts their hunger, and the relentless war between rulers invites them to linger."

"We have fought the undead as well," Sebastian said.

The possibility of assistance prompted a smile from Bey. "Our requests for support have fallen on deaf ears. My people are not helpless, as the pikes attest. We've stopped a share of them and left some on display so the devils think twice before coming back. You noticed our quiet city streets?"

"Hard to miss them," Sebastian said.

"As hard as it is to live when your only thoughts are of demons that sack your livelihood."

Bey walked to the edge of the gate and peered out at the desolate street. Rodica resembled a drab oil painting in dusk light. Its charcoal color scheme was a rough sketch of a village: Blurred spaces populated with sporadic butter glow from candle-lit windows.

"We prefer the nights now," Bey said, dragging fingers across the iron-wrought bars in lament. "It is when *they* come, and we stand a better chance of being on guard if we sleep the day away."

Garrick negotiated for them to stay the night. Bey required very little convincing, even insisting that Rodica prepare a feast in their honor. Before Garrick could so much as accept, Bey added, "and we may yet request your ear for a few pressing matters as well."

The hunter had Timothy escort Sebastian to the inn. One of the villagers led the way, asking urgent-paced questions as they shuffled. Timothy answered in native tongue while Sebastian's eyes drifted and his vision blurred.

The inn was a two-story building just down the hill from Bey's estate. The rooms offered nothing beyond marginal luxury, but it was paradise to Sebastian. The beds were stuffed with assorted feathers and they embraced his back as soon as he lay across it.

Now that he was comfortable, his heart skipped and his blood thinned. In this privacy, he wished once more for Tulcea. No point in resisting, she would come whether he looked for her or not. He took some breaths, thinking he was not relaxed enough, but disappointment remained as his mistress continued to be nothing more than a wish.

And then he slipped into unconsciousness.

The room was pitch-black when he awoke, hearing Garrick and Timothy's hushed voices shushing through the night.

Sebastian stumbled into the hall like a last-call pubber, catching himself against the far wall with a propped arm. After all that rest, he felt worse than ever.

Garrick and Timothy watched him with an air of disgust, but said nothing of it. The hunter informed them they were to have a late supper in the tavern. And that Ion Bey had arranged the entire village to speak with them.

"We cannot afford to play hero to these people," Timothy said. "Sebastian is hurt, our supplies are nearly spent."

"If we flat-out refuse, it will be worse," Garrick said. "Surely, you feel the desperation here? To this town, we are a last chance. In your profession, pup, you must know all too well what happens to men when they find themselves facing death."

That halted Timothy's protest.

"Now go down there, have supper, and above all else, understand that you do not have to speak so much." They objected when Sebastian insisted on going along, suggesting that he get plenty of rest.

But Sebastian refused to hear it.

The village was scrubbed in moonlight as they headed down the street. It was almost inviting at this hour. The pikes were hardly visible from this side of the wall, and the stone-cobbled street saw shadows prancing around the torchlight that lined several windows. From an upstairs terrace, a beautiful voice sang in a language Sebastian could not understand.

When they reached the tavern, they found rows of long and wooden tables. Ion Bey waited for them upon entrance and motioned for them to join him in the corner, their backs against the wall so the entire village could be their audience.

Garrick came in a few moments behind them and stole some private words with Bey. Then he took the middle seat so that Timothy and Sebastian flanked him. Timothy lit one of the torches at their backs so they would not sup in darkness. The décor was brownstone. That, or it was lined with so much filth that it had adapted that color. Each table was bookended by unlit candles.

"It seems everyone has a story of woe," Garrick said, marveling at the amount of tattered villagers entering. His performance feigned interest, a ruse to keep Rodica's walls around them.

Dinner was a chintzy offering of potato stew and hardened loaf. The steins housed flat, dry ale, and they sipped it with polite-but-disheartened eyes.

As they ate, the town's survivors continued hobbling in and took seats wherever it was darkest. They recounted predictable stories: Wolves mauling anyone who ventured beyond the walls, emboldened creatures that soon ventured into Rodica's outskirts. Monsters were everywhere before long, hiding in the alleyways and preying on the unsuspecting by waiting inside basements. Howls ignited the streets, regardless of dusk or dawn. Rodicans became prisoners for long stretches of daylight. The wolves leaving only once they had fed, and even then, they were never gone for very long.

This was Freywald all over again—another vulnerable outpost awaiting a killing bite. Garrick had to know this as well. It was the underlying motivation for his ruse. Sell them one narrative, hope and valor, while carrying out another.

Spinelessness.

Sebastian was in the business of helping those who could not help themselves, though never at the expense of his own life. Their ability to wage another war on the scale of Freywald was long gone. Moving forward was their only hope. Moving fast.

The room of beaten eyes filled Sebastian with insurmountable pressure. His conscience responded with pangs of guilt that forced his stare to drop into the cloudy soup bowl. He kept his glance there and only listened.

When it was not the wolves, it was the undead passing through Rodica, demanding attention for their special hungers.

"We gave them our sick," a woman said upon entering. She went to the tavern's farthest table and slipped into shadows before Sebastian could get a look at her. "Thought that would make them go. Instead it created an expectation of regular feedings."

A young child came through the heavy door and sat beside her. His tearful recount was of the night his mother and sister were raped and shredded by a wolf that had hid beneath their bed until transformation.

The stories swelled as the tavern's occupancy grew to

resemble Sunday mass. Only Rodica's residents no longer dressed for the Lord, if they ever had. Tattered rags were the village's official colors now. The low light cast shadows over most faces. The ones Sebastian could see were as dirty as the tavern walls.

Defeated people, hanging on for dear life.

For some reason.

Garrick pushed his empty soup bowl toward the center of the table. He fell back against the wall and folded his arms across his chest as he listened.

"Ion Bey," Timothy said when the stories finally lulled. "Why do you rise in the evening if that is when the creatures are prone to attack?"

"Nocturnal lifestyle is a necessity. Sleeping at night, we found, led to unnatural deaths. So, we maintain our haven then, when we are best alert and can defend against invasion."

"It cannot be easy to tend chores in the dark," Timothy said.

Ion Bey shrugged. "We make do, because we must."

"I only ask because I had looked around earlier. I came across your farmland north of here. It was not entirely fallow, as I had expected in a starving and destitute village. I wonder who in Rodica performs those agricultural responsibilities, and when? If you all rise at night…"

The governor's eyes narrowed. He glared at the three men as if Timothy's interrogative curiosity had somehow insulted his honor.

Sebastian wanted an answer, too. He leaned forward eagerly awaiting one. Timothy must have cased the grounds while he slept. His was a good catch that made his paternal instinct smile.

Something was wrong. Now that Sebastian was wary, he considered something else: why had Rodica's residents not eaten so much as a crumb of food in all this time?

"I am governor here and these times are desperate," Bey held his hands up in front of them as if surrendering. "My hands wear farmer's calluses from unrelenting labor. Used to be others, you see, who helped me tend our lands. I do what I can to feed those who've survived, and sometimes that is not enough."

The village's meager hospitality came to feel like a standoff. Both sides glaring at one another as mistrust sprung up between them, filling the tavern to the ceiling.

Sebastian did not like Bey's answer, and judging from the way Garrick's body tensed beside him, the hunter was equally nonplussed. If times were so desperate, and if the governor really worked in the fields to serve his people, why did his gut move in ripples ahead of the rest of his body? His nose was as pink as those droopy mandibles dangling off his chin. He held neither the physique nor the attitude of a working man.

And he's eating better slop than this shite up at that estate.

"Good enough," Garrick said. He eased from his seat. "We should return to the inn and discuss our approach privately. We'll share our strategy with you tomorrow evening, once you have awakened and we've had a chance to strategize."

Ion Bey grinned, rising in time with the hunter.

The rest of the village followed him.

The entire tavern was on its feet now.

Yellow eyes dotted the shadows, dull glows that flickered and sputtered with just enough strength to reveal their natural forms.

Hence the trap. One way in and out of here, and a mass of vampires suddenly standing between them and it.

Garrick lifted his sword from its scabbard as he cried, "Cut their heads off!"

Timothy followed the hunter's motion without missing a beat as the room descended into chaos. The villagers set on them at once, lumbering forward wearing bladed smiles—the same kind of delight one wore when sitting down to a grilled steak.

Sebastian drew his gun on the hungry-eyed mob and fired as Garrick leapt to the tabletop, swinging at the nearest vampire before it could ascend to meet him. The blade cracked the neck, sending the vampire's head spinning through the air.

Bey slipped into the oncoming crowd, satisfaction etched across his porky features. A sea of killing hands reached for them, and Timothy recoiled. The kid was almost useless without his blunderbuss. Sebastian lost sight of him in the chaos, focusing on a screeching woman launching toward him with outstretched hands that headed straight for his neck.

They would have landed, had a blade not hacked through the air, leaving clean and bloody stumps to push against Sebastian's chest.

Garrick did not have time to acknowledge the saving blow. He hurled himself and his sword in the opposite direction, chopping another head clear.

Down in the trenches, Sebastian could not swing his sword without hitting Timothy. He blasted the amputee below her jaw with his other pistol. A cloud of brain matter rained on the ravenous crowd.

She hissed her displeasure and fell forward, flashing rotted teeth beset on both sides by jutting fangs. Sebastian put his wrist to her throat to stop the teeth from advancing, dropping his gun and taking his blade out in time to push it horizontally against her neckline. He applied pressure until the sword disappeared into her hardened flesh like butter.

Her head came free and dropped clear. As quickly as her body collapsed, more hands were already grabbing and slicing him.

"They're killing us," a broken and hoarse voice protested.

Across the way, Sebastian caught the briefest glimpse of Ion Bey. He looked on from beside the door, but some of the crowd had turned their attention on him: those who preferred a meal that would not fight back.

Bey protested as claws came from the darkness and closed around his shoulders like spiders. The smug satisfaction on his face turned to instant terror as a pale visage slipped from the obscurity of shadows, mouth agape and ready.

"There will be no one to protect you if you do this," he screamed. "Kill *them!*"

Nevertheless, the vampire dropped her mouth and Sebastian could almost hear the spurt from here. As soon as the aroma of spilt blood hit the air, several of the vampires whirled their attentions back the way they had come. The onslaught reduced.

Garrick remained overhead, hacking his blade back and forth as if he was clearing a path through overgrown fronds. Limbs spilled across the table while enemies poured in around them.

As weakened as these creatures were, there were too many of them.

The inflamed wall sconce lifted and then came free. Timothy had it in his arms like a spear. He charged the crowd, cutting a swath through now-flaming creatures, men and women burning around them.

Sebastian leapt for the table and stabbed down into the skull of an elderly man with one protruding fang. Timothy wielded the fire with a roar, sending the vampires scratching and clawing for the door.

"Don't let them escape!" Garrick's voice lorded over the commotion as he pulled the other sconce and lit it against Timothy's.

The fire bounded off the burning villagers and climbed

higher. In a moment, hot and fiery trails roared across the ceiling. Whatever was overhead was sure to come crashing down if they did not get out.

The creatures on the far side of the tavern charged, not with murder on their faces, but with fear in their eyes. Two of them had bloody chins, dragging a twitching and spurting Ion Bey behind them as they went for the door.

From the opposite side, Garrick was headed in the same direction.

The vampires reached it first and flung it wide. The feeders spilled into the streets of Rodica with Bey. Garrick severed the escape path by charging forward with angry flame. The remaining creatures slipped instinctively into the corner.

"Get the ones who've escaped," Garrick roared. Sebastian and Timothy hit the streets next, nearly tripping over Bey's discarded body. They followed the two fleeing shadows into the forest beyond the wall.

The targets flailed, glancing over their shoulders in retreat. What blood they had siphoned out of Bey had increased their speed and agility. If Timothy had not set the place aflame, these bastards would have had enough strength to charge through the commotion and kill them.

Sebastian pushed himself, determined to prove to his companions, or perhaps himself, that he was more than a dying old dog. He dove for the vampire's legs and pushed them together. They toppled and Sebastian threw himself on top of the creature while Timothy's legs whizzed past in pursuit of the other.

Sebastian's shoulder screamed in agony before his throat could. The vampire's mouth wiggled and Sebastian was not concerned with finding out if it was to bite or speak. He swatted it with his blade and took the head clean off. It rolled back down the hill toward Rodica.

He turned onto his back and gasped for air. His pain might have been dulled by waning adrenaline, but its return was a certainty. His chest was snug and his vision whitened.

The kid never knew when to quit, but Sebastian was too breathless to summon him back. There would be no finding the vampire by torchlight. Sebastian knew he should help, and wanted to, but his body was extinguished.

He attempted to call out, but his voice was a hollow echo.

His head flopped over and his cheek hit the ground. Through squinted eyes, he saw someone moving through the forest toward him.

Tulcea stepped into the path of the moon. Blonde hair covered her face as her lithe body squatted over him. He stared transfixed by the sex between her legs. How badly he wanted it. A terrifying thought, and one he could not fight. He pursed his lips as her thighs hugged his cheeks, eager for the suckling juices that would cascade down his chin like a bite from a peach.

"Come with me, Sebastian," she said. "There is nothing back there save for despair."

He would have done anything to go. His mind not so far gone that he believed this to be right, however. He remembered the talons on her feet, even if they were not there now. Yet, somehow, she was also perfection, sliding down his body so that their faces touched. Her skin was translucent, and Sebastian saw the forest through her. Timothy jogged out of it, a severed head dangling in his hand as she faded and became nothing.

The kid dropped the trophy and skidded to his knees beside his friend as the witch vanished.

"Come on, up you go. *Now.*"

"Leave me," Sebastian said. It would be easier to let go right here. Despite his mind's betrayal, its insistence that he could somehow perform sexually while struggling to breathe and move, his body demanded rest. Probably an eternal amount. Tulcea would help him have it, and he was certain he was okay with that.

"Rubbish," Timothy said and slapped his face. "Let's go, old man. You've got to prove Garrick wrong, so move!"

He pulled Sebastian into a sitting position, careful of his injury. Against his hip, the frozen, open-mouthed vampire stared indifferently. There was eventuality in that gaze. A reminder that man and monster ended up the same, no matter how one lived their life. He brushed that dour realization off and tried to stand, asking what the hell Garrick was on about.

"That witch-finder's opinion isn't any damn good to me and you know that," Timothy said as they wobbled toward the village.

Garrick stood outside the tavern, sweating against the collapsed building that continued to burn.

"Were you bit?" he asked to no one specific.

Timothy answered for both of them, but Garrick did not seem satisfied with the response. He eyed them carefully.

Sebastian sucked for air but managed very little of it. He blinked and found Tulcea, not the girlish creature that captured his sexuality, but the wrinkly hag who had bled puss. Her cadaver stench attacked, prompting a gag he could not suppress. This weakness elicited a hysterical laugh from her. A torment no one else could hear.

Sebastian was transfixed by the parade of grotesquerie that marched through his mind. Her flesh was purple and her eyes drooped. Her chin wore strands of prickly silver fuzz. When her mouth popped, he saw just two teeth.

"What needs to be done?" he said. Anything to avoid her torment.

Before Garrick could respond, Timothy stepped between them. "How could you not realize we were waltzing into a trap?

You, the great hunter, easily duped by desperate vampires."

"Did you think anything wrong of Ion Bey? They were smart enough to keep a healthy envoy in place as their figurehead. Do you wish to berate me further, or shall we cleanse this village on our way out?"

"We're not leaving yet," Timothy said. "Not until Sebastian has had some rest."

Garrick nodded. "First, we do a building-to-building search. I am certain we'll find stragglers here…ones so withdrawn from blood they're too weak to walk."

They divvied the homes and fanned out. Sebastian shambled though the few Rodican buildings he had energy enough to check, sifting through clothing and other personal belongings. He felt only despair in this. Family portraits, children's drawings and toys—lives and memories reduced to worthless junk.

In the last house, he found an elderly creature crawling out of a dirt mound in the basement, hobbling on broken hands. He circled the thing and watched its feeble, impotent advancement. Tired jaws snapped for his ankles, falling on mushy gums. A guttural noise passed its lips, suggesting long-held suffering by an unquenchable thirst.

The silver blade wound back and clipped down through its neck.

They regrouped at the inn and exchanged stories. All totaled, there had not been more than four laggards.

"I found this," Timothy said and tossed a ball of red cloth on the floor between them.

A red cloak unfurled across the stone.

Sebastian's heart lurched at the realization. Had Codrin and his followers intended to bring them here? When the three of them stood in that sun-laden field, having just repelled their vampiric captors, they stared at village rooftops in the far off distance and agreed that the vampires had planned on taking them *there*.

Now he realized that Codrin was likely steering them the long way around the mountain.

Around Tulcea.

Of all the dumb luck. All they had to do was keep going. An afternoon's walk and they could have been saved. Sebastian did not believe these sickly creatures had enough strength to overthrow two villages. Occupying Rodica made sense for them. It was shrouded almost entirely by forest—natural shielding from the sun. But the village that might have been their salvation?

"If only we had kept on the initial path…"

"We cannot know that," Timothy said. "That village might have been every bit as gone."

If Garrick dwelled on misspent opportunities, he managed to hide his regrets. He revealed that he had found a coiled map of the area in his search. He loosened it on the table in the hall and placed a few candles over the curled paper to keep it straight. He tapped his finger on a crudely stenciled forest and then slid it to the right, over a large pool of blue.

"We are closer to Constanta than I expected," he said. "No more than a few days away."

No one wanted to stay in Rodica, least of all Sebastian. The city was close by and bed rest could wait. Timothy would not hear it, though, and Garrick advocated for a night's sleep as well. As they figured out how to divide the evening into watch shifts, Sebastian protested.

"I cannot be the only one to see the danger, the stupidity, in this decision," he said. "We do not know how many more of those creatures are out there and we would be foolish to assume we got them all."

"So desperate were these vampires that they let a human

live among them," Garrick said. "Why would they do this? To rope in daytime travelers, I suppose. They were starved, many immobile, and yet Ion Bey walked free, with little slits in his arms and thighs so he could feed them *just* enough for consciousness. They raised piked heads around the wall for…well, who can say? To claim what little blood remains this far east while keeping stray vampires away in the process? You wouldn't want others looking for blood when there's none to go around. I don't understand undead logic, but I cannot imagine there are more like them out there. Not close by, at least. They would be even worse off than our charred friends below."

Sebastian gave his rented room a stranger's eye. Looking at the feather bed set his heart racing with anxiety. He preferred this reality of cunning blood drinkers and scorned wolves to what waited atop that cradle of death. Tulcea was anxious to take him, and she would do it the next time he slept. That was not paranoia or pessimism, but knowledge he simply had. The back of his eyes throbbed in time with her private laughter that echoed just for him.

Constanta was his best hope. Why could the others not see that? As soon as they secured passage to England, the hag bitch would leave him forever. He was sure of it.

He felt the familiar skirt of her smooth fingers on his softened stomach, delving beneath layers of frock and linen. Her smell returned, reviving delicious memories from that cave. Allure so powerful he floated to the bed like a magnet, unable to recall anything unpleasant there.

He pushed his arm against the wobbly dresser and turned back to the doorway. "We should march," Sebastian said. "I know I don't look like much, but I can make it." His tone would not have convinced an acolyte.

"You have no choice but to get some sleep," Garrick said.

He rummaged through his satchel and fished a tiny phial of blue liquid from it. He came into the room and put it on the end table, urging Sebastian to sit and then lie back.

"You have to take that," he said. "It's important."

Timothy popped his head in.

Sebastian knew that expression. It was one he had seen only once in their years together.

Guilt.

When he awoke earlier this evening, Sebastian knew he had not been delirious. The kid and Garrick had been discussing him in secret.

They know.

Before Sebastian could say anything, the hunter pointed at the phial.

"Drink it," he said. "Now."

"Why?"

"If you don't, you'll be dead by dawn."

THE BEYOND

GARRICK AND TIMOTHY STOOD AT the foot of the bed. They wore tribunal faces and said nothing.

Sebastian did not protest. Not when Garrick had killed Ritter for being a liability and not now. Sebastian was that and worse. That he still lived in the hunter's presence was a miracle.

"I'm afraid I knew what I was doing back there," Sebastian said. "Her magic maybe prevented me from resisting, but I wanted her. I've always appreciated our fellowship, kid, but *she* made me realize just how lonely my nights have been. Trading sloshy words with other drunks. Those misspent evenings watching the sunrise through the bottom of a dirty whiskey glass. Friendship like that is no substitute for having an angel in your bed."

"Stop speaking in past tense." Timothy forced a smile. "You are not dying, old man. That bottle can save you."

The kid's optimism was as stubborn as the rest of him. It somehow remained unblotted by months of cruelty and death. A searing mark of character, if ever there was one.

That Timothy was a pain in the ass mattered not, because he had grown into a good man in the face of a hundred reasons to be anything but. Sebastian knew the kid had always possessed these qualities, and that the late Mrs. Hackett shouldered the responsibility for this. Still, he wanted to think he deserved a sliver of credit for steering him along the straight and narrow at a time when the angry orphan might have surrendered to his bloodiest instincts. This was as close as Sebastian would come to fatherhood, and so the thought offered great comfort.

Timothy Hackett was going to be all right, even if this new dawn was darker than any before it.

Sebastian turned his attention to the rolling liquid sloshing through the phial. The miniature glass was dainty, it could break between his forefinger and thumb. Still, its presence in his fist held sway. If this bright liquid could spell salvation, what in the hell was it?

He decided not to inquire.

"You look like you're about to go tits up," Garrick said. He tapped Sebastian's ankles over the bed sheet. "Down the hatch."

Sebastian twisted his mouth as he contemplated that order. The prospect of swallowing this liquid did not make sense.

"Pup," the hunter said. "Check the streets for stragglers. I am sure you'll find none, but once this begins we cannot be disturbed."

The kid was reluctant to leave until Sebastian offered a nod of assurance.

Once his footsteps echoed directly beneath them on the way out the front door, Garrick leaned in close. "How many times have you seen her since the mine?"

The right thing to do here was confess, but shame would not allow that. Sebastian felt guiltier than all the thieves he had ever hunted. There remained in him a desire to have her no matter the cost. His thoughts were molded by her influence, but felt correct nevertheless. His heart pounded with the excited possibility of seeing her again, the forbidden aspect only heightening that desire.

These were his thoughts and wishes, but Tulcea's effect was like a drug he could never quit.

Nor do I wish to.

He chose to keep his mouth shut because he could not help himself. Seeing her meant that he was not alone, and that was all the motivation he needed. Timothy would leave thief-taking behind as soon as they reached London, and Sebastian would become a solitary man at fifty, spinning tales to drunkards who were bound to forget every word in the morning light.

Sebastian had never wanted kids, trundling through youth with notions that an adventurous life was best. Now that he was beyond the other side of middle age, he cursed his rejections. His life ended at his last breath, and there would be no one to mourn him.

Except Tulcea.

"Are you seeing her now?" Garrick reached out and touched Sebastian's shoulder. "I should've realized what she was the moment we stumbled into her lair."

"I love her," Sebastian said and clasped a hand over his mouth. That was not true. Or was it?

"She attached herself to you…sucking your soul like a leech…it is the reason for your unrest."

Sebastian closed his eyes and saw the edges of her face take shape within the vacuous nothing. Hot breath breezed across the bow of his nostrils, smelling of fresh rain.

"There is a way to come back from this, Sebastian," Garrick said. "You only have to want it."

Every syllable was more distant than the last. It was Tulcea's voice he wanted to hear. Her lips he needed to suck.

"Christ," Garrick reached for his shoulder and tugged until his eyes fell open. "If you want snatch, then take a girl for a roll in the hay once we reach Constanta. If this thing takes your body and soul, there'll be nothing left of you in this life or the next."

Sebastian remained reluctant of these words. With Tulcea, it was not too late to have the things he wanted, even as the hunter's acknowledgment of an afterlife brought relief.

"Help." It fell past his lips in a whisper that Garrick leaned in to hear.

The hunter tapped the phial.

"How?"

"In your dreams…because there's nothing left of her body. She comes at you from the beyond, and that's where we have to go."

Timothy had returned. Sebastian saw him over the hunter's shoulder. He came no further than the doorway and shuffled his weight from one foot to the other.

"This will not be easy," Garrick said. "The things you will dream are much worse than what haunts you now."

"I think I would rather wait for Constanta," Sebastian said. "That way you can leave me to recuperate while…"

"You will not see tomorrow's sun unless it is done now."

Garrick reached back across the room and beckoned for the kid.

"What do you need me to do?" Timothy asked.

"The two of us will go under," Garrick fished through his satchel and pulled another phial from it. He clasped it in his fist, obscuring its color. "We will be vulnerable to this world. You will have to guard us until I can deliver Sebastian from the beyond."

"What's in this?" Sebastian said, holding the bottle to the bedside candle.

"You'll love it. More refreshing than the *pish*-flavored gin you haul around."

"What is it, Garrick?"

"It'll make your dreams more lucid. She will be upon you as soon as you slip under so I need to be there. I will go into the next room and take this. If we do it the other way…you could be dead before I can find you."

"Okay."

Garrick nodded and hurried from the room as Sebastian took the phial to his lips and tilted the glass. It tasted sour, staining his tongue with something like acidic chalk.

He swallowed it and fell back to the pillow, looking to the kid for some last-minute assurance. Timothy's cheeks were stained beat red, his eyes swollen. It was the face of a man who had just stabbed his friend through the heart.

Sebastian knew then what they had done.

He wanted to question it. Ask why the deception. But he knew the answer. There was no way to separate the hag from his soul. He could not even feel betrayed. He only hoped it was quick.

His throat burned, and then the fire spread to his chest.

Garrick reappeared in the doorway, looking almost as solemn.

When Sebastian closed his eyes, he saw her face, lording right over his. Close enough that strands of oily hair brushed across his eyes. He opened them again and continued to feel her touch, her lips. Her tongue slithered inside his ear, whispering unholy promises he prayed would never come to pass.

The poison worked fast, but dying did not come soon enough. The men he put in early graves got off easier than this. Was this penance for deciding the fates of so many?

A coughing fit took hold and his tongue tasted blood. With speech gone, he hoped his eyes would say to Timothy what his constricting throat could not. Sebastian needed him to know that this was the right decision. In some ways, he was proud of the kid for going along with what needed to be done.

He's grown into his own, whether he knows it or not.

Tulcea wanted to use his flesh to step back into this world. Sebastian was glad they had bested her.

He tried to smile at the thought and hoped the kid would read it as shorthand for peace of mind. Only Timothy was not looking at him anymore. His neck was craned, his face registering disbelief.

Sebastian's vision was going. His eyes lost focus but they hurried across the room, reaching Garrick in time to see the hunter plop to his knees, an axe hilt embedded in his head so deep that his skull was split open like a cantaloupe.

The witch-finder's face smashed the floor and his brains skidded across it like spilt water from a mop bucket.

Behind him, the raven-haired wolf woman they had tried so hard to kill stepped into the room.

There was a witch's laughter in his head as his vision darkened and his body shook. He felt rotted hands sliding across him while her thighs tightened around his hips. He was sinking into oblivion now, and with his own personal guide to hell.

He slipped from life knowing they had failed.

○

Elisabeth could hardly believe her luck when she saw it was the familiar one on the receiving end of her axe. Finally, fate twisted in her favor. A laugh skipped from her throat, but it was more a startled reflex than anything else.

Rot, you bastard.

He goes to his grave with all the dignity of a common victim. One she might swipe out of boredom or for pleasure. She knew that every man died the same, but to see this one go so easily, with spilt bowels dampening his trousers as he crashed to the floor, was a startling reminder.

This moment did not allow her to rest on laurels. She stormed into the room as the wolf inside her growled a sudden surge of confidence. The animal was propelled outward by the murder of her deadliest foe, black fur swallowing her skin as the desire for fresh meat became too insatiable to ignore.

Elisabeth's stomach rippled, a startling, uncontrollable transformation upon her. She tried holding it back, thinking she was too vulnerable if she changed in the middle of close quarters battle. Undeterred wolf bones pushed up through her moon-kissed flesh. The time was not right, but her human protests vanished beneath commanding growls.

Two of her prey remained. One convulsed beneath bed sheets, his arms and legs lifted and fell as if controlled by marionette strings. Foam bubbled around his mouth and poured past his lips with a mixture of blood.

As good as dead.

That left only one, and not for much longer.

Survivor lifted his gun, but the space between them was short. Her hand, a contradictory menagerie of human forearm spearheaded by a wolf paw, knifed through the air and clasped around the barrel. She yanked it toward the ceiling as he squeezed off a shot. Silver shards exploded into the beams overhead and wood splinters rained down.

Elisabeth shrieked and pulled the gun away, leaving his hands open and then fumbling for another means of defense.

Survivor looked as though he were about to cry, tucking his head into his shoulder and pushing through shattering window glass. His body went horizontally through the pane and tilted toward the village street below.

The wolf lunged, attempting to catch him. His boot heels slipped through her claws. The incoming wolf filled the air with a howl of frustration as she gave pursuit, diving between the glass teeth and hurtling toward the ground.

She smashed atop him and rolled aside. Her torso stretched out, her thighs becoming muscular hinds.

Survivor stood. A rivet of blood dribbled from his hairline and streaked his face like war paint. True to his look, he unsheathed his blade and came at her. She parried his thrust but he adopted a defensive stance.

Quick for his kind!

He pivoted on his heels and turned, preparing for her counter-attack.

She barked and dropped to all fours. One final surge tore through her and chased away the last relics of humanity, leaving the wolf to circle him with ready forefeet. Her claws were prepared to lash out the moment he dropped his guard.

But he did not. He hurled the silver dagger forward, blade-first. The wolf snarled and hopped out of the way. It gave him all the time he needed to dash off down the cobblestone. Survivor could never hope to outrun her, but this was what she had expected him to do all along. They always tried running.

He ran straight for the smoldering tavern and disappeared through the smoke-filled doorframe.

The stone street was unforgiving on her claws as she skidded to a stop. Her toes swelled as her nails scraped the riveted pavement.

The fire had run its course, but lit embers remained alive on the largest pieces of broken and fallen wood. Throbbing and intense heat kept the wolf at instinctual distance. She swiveled her head one way, and then the other. Survivor was nowhere that she could see. The second story had collapsed, restricting his movements and creating a smoldering impasse.

The wolf worked up the courage to step to the fire at last,

driven by urges of hunger and retaliation. Her form was so large that squeezing through the doorframe took a swell of effort. When her shoulders got through, she searched the air for his smell.

From the darkest pool of consciousness, Elisabeth fought to get her human rationale heard. *Do not do this*, she cried, feeling as though her implorations were being offered to a brick wall. If the beast had not forced her slender human frame away, she could have followed him inside and ended this.

Let me come back. That thought reverberated through her mind as if she had shouted it from the bottom of a well.

The wolf's ears flexed, but the dwindling blaze of popping wood drowned out the other ambient noises. Her reliable snout returned charred wood, and long rotted, now burnt, flesh.

However many parasites had burned up in here, it was not enough.

The wolf pulled away from the doorframe and circled the building. A stairwell led into a cellar out back. She crawled the stone steps and took cautious sniffs. Survivor could have been waiting on the other side of the door, but his escape options were limited. She could wait him out if need be. If he opted for cowardice, he would burn to death or die by smoke. Not the most satisfying vengeance, though his death was what mattered.

Elisabeth hurried back to the street and stretched out on it. The stone was cool against her undercoat, balancing the heat from the fire. In another life, this would have been a beautiful and tranquil sight. The blaze's glow was warm and relaxing. Low, deep rumbles were the only noises filling the quiet morning sky.

The wolf yawned and dropped her muzzle between her front paws, eyeing the door with a singular recurring thought.

Food.

Elisabeth's human rationale reached out once more, but there was no reasoning to be done. The animal had been away for too long; her hunger was unrequited. She did not trust the wolf to her own devices. Not against someone who had annihilated so many of their kind.

She flashed Nightfall across the wolf's brain. How these men and their weapons had nearly taken her life.

Do you want to feel that again? She screamed out. These efforts were exhausting and the wolf grew irritated with them. It was an argument Elisabeth could not hope to win. So she changed up her thought process, accepting that Survivor would be eaten and that, yes, he would make a delectable meal.

There was no argument there. The wolf and Elisabeth had fallen out of step, and they needed to find common ground once more.

Both of them wanted this one dead. Toying with Survivor could be the best way to get back in touch with the animal. *Why rush this?* Familiar One and Old Man were gone, leaving a single boy to suffer her wrath. This was about more than flesh and blood, despite the wolf's motivation.

Hunger and vengeance did not have to be separate goals. Her thoughts and the wolf's could harmonize within this shared space.

Make him fear you, she thought. Terror was exquisite when absorbed into the flesh. Let him soak in that before moving in for the kill. Remember how much better this meat is once it has basted in panic.

The wolf considered this, along with all the examples of it that she had encountered over the years. She paused, and for a moment, Elisabeth saw an opportunity to climb out of the abyss and help steer.

Her influence over the animal was suddenly winning.

LAST MAN STANDING

TIMOTHY HEARD THE WOLF PUSHING through the warped doorframe. He crouched inside the stairwell, trapped. What should have led to a second story was now a gaping hole beneath the sky. The steps overlooked spilt rubble and broken wood spread across the first floor.

He crossed himself but chided the useless gesture as soon as he was finished. He would not go running back to the Bible now.

They won't have that satisfaction.

His mother had read that book to him when he was a boy. Regaled by nightmarish stories of avenging angels, demonic possessions, and a merciless God, there was precious little in there for him to appreciate. It was a horror show, and his impressionable mind glommed onto the death and misery of it all, leaving him worried about superstitious gestures and wrathful spirits. Looking over his proverbial shoulder each time he did anything less than pious, wondering if the holy ruler might deem his blasphemy enough for punishment.

If mother had not been murdered, she might have been able to iron those fears out, straightening his hesitation into lessons to be carried throughout his days. Then again, Timothy wanted to believe that no matter his upbringing, he would have recognized the church and its teachings for what they were: another way for society to control its people.

It was terrifying to think now that those stories, at least some of them, might have been more than that.

You cannot deny all that you've seen, as much as you would like to.

Timothy resented his logic turning against him like this.

The wolf rattled around in the doorway like a caged animal, and Timothy gripped Sebastian's flintlock pistol in his palm. Wide eyes glared down the barrel sight with itchy reflexes.

It became clear that the wolf could come no further. He followed the stone steps as high as they went, lifting his head into the naked air. When the roof had fallen, part of the outer wall had gone with it. From here, he could reach for the windowsill across the narrow alley.

Timothy had almost no energy in the reserve coming out of tonight's battle. He spent every last drop to lift his weight up onto the opposing building's window and grab for the slanted roof.

Delivered from the immediacy of harm, he lay across the sloped shingles and gasped for breath while peering over the ledge. The animal was stretched across the cobblestone in front of the tavern. Her rich black fur made her look like a gigantic pulsing shadow—a bottomless hole in the middle of Rodica's street.

The air up here stung. It was filled with cooked flesh and smoky wood, a combination that confused the wolf's sense of smell. Not to the point where Raven would think him gone, but plenty sufficient to obscure his trail.

He needed all the help he could get because he was not making it to Constanta with a varcolac nipping at his back.

How the hell am I supposed to do this?

Contemplating life without Sebastian brought no pleasure. The old man had done everything for him. He had plucked an urchin child off the street before the local orphanage could capture him and cultivate his malaise. Timothy remembered seeing the cold, iron-wrought fences on countless occasions while under Sebastian's supervision. Forsaken faces looked out on free London, defined only by the tragedies that had led them there.

Sebastian Miles had done a good bit more than rescue him from noble incarceration, though. He had afforded Timothy the opportunity to hunt the men who left Mum raped and bleeding. Presented the eleven-year-old child with a choice upon finding those butchers: kill them now, *yourself*, or risk the Queen's justice.

Even then, Timothy had never been controlled by requital. Such notions were outdated, and if society was to rise above them, he would have to practice his beliefs hard and strong. Knowing that he must lead by example if he were to change minds, he had chosen to turn those savages over to the law, hoping that a civilized world might tame even the harshest of souls.

The important thing was that Sebastian had allowed him the choice. Rather than shape his young mind into a jaded copy, the old man had demanded he remain true to himself.

That was the most generous thing anyone had ever done for him.

Timothy was not inherently violent, not when they killed Mum and seldom during the days that followed. That changed when they faced down Evan's killers. All he could think of then was the way his friend had gone to his death with a gash in his throat the size of a cannonball. In that moment, he had been glad to track the murderers, squeeze the trigger.

It was right after, when there was nothing in the air save for swirling gun smoke, while pools of blood formed around his boots, that Timothy felt corrupted.

Violence was a tool for the powerless. The real answer was to be a harbinger of change. Make the world a better place for all. If this attitude made him naive, so be it. He still believed in it, even as he glared at the wolf and felt insurmountable hatred for it, or her, whatever. The need to kill might have been worse now than on that midnight road facing down Evan's murderers, when paralyzing terror prevented action. He still resented himself for that.

Timothy swore now that he would hunt this beast to the brink of extinction. His blood became incalescent with every image that flashed into the mind's eye: her death at the tip of his blade, or her brains blown out through the top of her skull. So many possibilities, each a satisfying conclusion to this story.

Garrick might have been proud.

When the hunter had taken him aside earlier to tell him that Sebastian was already dead, and had been that way since allowing the hag to take possession of him, Timothy was appalled by his proposition.

"If we do not kill him tonight," Garrick had said. "The hag will take his body and return to this world."

There was no hope for his mentor, apparently. Garrick had asked Timothy to be complacent in Sebastian's demise, assuring him that the poison would at least set the thief-taker to rest.

"His soul was gone the second she slipped inside of him. You will not wish to see what happens if she takes him completely."

Garrick's pleas were bona fide, and Timothy knew deep down this was a merciful action. He had watched his old friend suffer, entranced during the days following the mine. That had not made the decision any easier. Fighting side-by-side with Sebastian in the tavern onslaught, Timothy had been tempted to slash his throat, ending things quickly, but he could not find the savagery within him to do it.

He could not look his friend in the eye like that, feeling too much like Marcus Brutus on the Ides of March.

Below him, the wolf stood, jostling his mind out of regret. She trotted off beyond the town's entrance, bolting into the swaying greenery as the sky took its first steps toward a bright November morning. It would have been chilly if not for the diminishing fire beside him.

Timothy followed her retreat with a twisted neck.

Raven, unlike the creatures living in Rodica, had the freedom to attack during the day, so the sun did not spell safety any more than he believed her withdrawal to be genuine.

He used caution when shimmying down the building's side, hitting the ground and sprinting for the inn to salvage whatever he could take. That was Garrick's satchel and a few weapons. In the interest of buying time, he spread a layer of silver coins across every windowsill and doorway. It would not stop the wolf, but if it brought her to even nominal pause, it was a worthy strategy.

Sebastian's hands were curled around the thin bed sheet and the foam gathered on his face was deflating one bubble burst at a time. His eyes were frozen wide and looking straight at him as he entered.

"I'm sorry." Timothy started, but swallowed the rest of the excuse whole. There was a choice here. He could succumb to the guilt and give up, meaning that Garrick and Sebastian had died in vain, or make a break for Constanta to reach the Order of Osiris.

I owe the fallen that much.

He slid Garrick's dark doublet over his own blood and sweat-mixed clothes, and took dual holsters off his old friend next. He apologized again while strapping them to his belt. Then he loaded the guns, thinking he would need every shot available to put Raven down. The blunderbuss ate the remaining shards of silver and his heart offered an excited jitter at the thought of pulling the trigger in Raven's face.

Timothy slipped Garrick's holster free and attached it across his chest. The hunter's basket-hilted blade sat on the floor beside his corpse. It would do nicely if he had the chance to go at Raven in close quarters again.

Do you truly expect to kill the one that seven of you could not?

He had not intended to disturb Garrick's body any further, but decided that he wanted the silver vambrances over his wrists in case the wolf got up close and hungry.

Among all the weapons, there was enough silver ammunition for nine shots.

They had thrown six times that amount at her on the top of that mountain and it did little more than slow her down.

From the window, Rodica was empty, only there was nothing peaceful about it. It had been a haven for the undead until last night, and the worst creature of all lay in wait in the forest beyond.

With the day wearing on, Timothy offered up a half-hearted prayer for his fallen brethren as a ceremonial goodbye. Not out of disdain, but because he did not know the right words and wished now, for the first time, that he did.

The sendoffs were quick and awkward, and Sebastian was still looking at him, through him, as he was ready to leave.

"Thank you, old friend," Timothy said.

Then he left to collect the silver coins, choking down his fear as he went.

○

The wolf was hungry.

Soon, she tried telling it. The discontented growl that shot back startled her. The animal no longer felt like part of herself, and Elisabeth was at this stranger's mercy—along for a ride she could not control. Hard to blame her bestial side for this rebellion, considering she had been deprived of food for several days. The familiar one's death delivered a catharsis that restored the animal's confidence and lured her from hiding.

Her stomach managed a harsh rumble.

The wolf controlled her as if she had never before been uncaged, running through the forest with newfound freedom. Elisabeth made assurances to the animal, hoping the beast may reconsider this hasty pursuit. She reminded herself that Survivor needed more time for his fear to set in; that they must not be too hasty in their delivery of vengeance. The wolf brushed these considerations aside, reshuffling their thoughts until there was only the hunt.

Elisabeth drowned beneath a wave of instinctual flashes: Survivor's face, her claws tearing through him, jaws closing over his neck. The wolf wanted food, was hungry for this specific kill. Those thoughts repeated in rhythm with the animal's movements as the forest blurred past. Shards of humanity managed to break through on occasion, and Elisabeth struggled to stay afloat. Each time she managed a plea for reason, the wolf snarled it away.

There was almost nothing left of her.

The wolf allowed Elisabeth a shred of humanity as long as she focused on the death of the familiar one and did not try to change the animal's mind. How could it feel so futile? Maybe vengeance always shook loose this way, but she wanted more. Killing him brought only the slightest satisfaction, an already dissipating feeling. Not enough.

She demanded revenge, not only for Aetius, but for her slain pups as well.

Elisabeth did not think herself maternal, but they had been her children still. She grieved their deaths as any mother would.

Survivor's scent was suddenly pungent. All around them, perspiration misted. The wolf fell back to follow it without arousing suspicion. Her muscles flexed in order to crawl along the forest floor, a careful predator taunted by her prey's sweltering aroma.

When Elisabeth changed her thoughts to Survivor, the wolf tensed, cautiously allowing the intrusion. Elisabeth's only reminder was that this had to be their most satisfying kill. He was the last, and every bit of this hung on ripping him to pieces. It could not be as quick and hollow as the familiar one. The wolf could not squander this.

He had to know she was here, but Elisabeth was disappointed that she could not yet feel him. His terror. It would boil over into something sweeter than the animal had ever tasted. She promised this to the wolf, thinking back on her best hunts in an effort to make the animal understand.

The wolf's tongue fell from her mouth as she skulked; drool repelled down her chin, spattering the dirt beneath her paws as she imagined feasting on those innards.

He traveled fast, always ahead of her. His agility made sense considering he was the youngest of his troop by at least ten years, though that did not explain his speed. Survivor covered a lot of ground and showed no signs of slowing after dark, his movement undaunted by the terrain.

The Black Sea's relaxing breeze closed in. Elisabeth's midnight coat rustled as she charged against it. Every so often, she smelled salty air on the insides of her nostrils, causing her heart to beat with excitement and inevitability.

Do…not…rush…this.

One last plea in the event they found him cowering. When the animal corralled that thought, unconcerned with anything else she had to say, Elisabeth changed her approach to something more forward, tired of tiptoeing.

The boy will not be granted a quick death. I will not let you do this.

But the animal was beyond reason. Just as the wolf had sprung from her bones, breaking her flesh like wet paper, she was determined to follow Survivor to his death. She carried rage in her belly, yes, but it was secondary to the hunt. The animal had not been duped by her pleas for savoring the moment, realizing that falling back had been a necessary strategy to draw him out.

Elisabeth felt less in control now. Discouraged. The animal might have allowed her to think she was getting through, but that was anything but true. This was a ride. Just a ride.

The wolf's pace became rushed again as Survivor's musk threatened to stray too far from her nose.

Elisabeth sniffed the air with desperation until her nostrils returned nearly nothing. No trace of him. The only smells were of local animals. If she flexed her ears hard enough, she heard the waves breaking against the Constanta-shore.

The boy was fast, yes, but not *that* fast.

Elisabeth's human impatience roared but the wolf ignored it. He was still here. Somewhere.

Skittering impulses pushed her onward. Her yellow-blue eyes prowled the night with swirling anger and admiration: a predatory yin and yang. How had he done it? In the distance, she heard a black bear rustling, its own instincts concerned with shelving away enough food for the impending winter.

She worried that the creature would try to kill the hunter to claim his meat, but the bear smelled far too docile to be worried about trespassers.

Elisabeth moved across the ground, her dark mane blending with the night, rendering her an anonymous visitor to this domain. Her senses continued to fail as Survivor's musk vanished entirely. She went on the move then. A graceful, yet panicked sprint. Beneath the rounded dome of her skull, the human was nearly hysterical with failure. The wolf fired back some calming urges, but it was too late for them to hold any sway.

The animal had botched the hunt, and the human was returning.

The wolf fought regression, snarling against Elisabeth's surging dominance, determined to not go quietly. Not without her hunger sated.

The wolf did not care about delicacies. She only wanted to eat, not fully understanding why she could not.

Elisabeth was out of excuses. It dawned on her that the wolf had gone scampering into retreat when wounded, and the human figured she could use that fear against the animal. It was the only thing she had not tried, and knew in that moment it would work.

Survivor knows who hunts us, she thought. *Let him lead us back to them so that we may put a face to our enemy. If not, they will continue tracking us, and the pain will come again and again.*

The wolf rescinded at this, at least momentarily. Her dominance faded, followed by her form. Elisabeth did not wish to reach the Black Sea on the soles of her anguished feet, but was relieved to see the creature go. Glad the push and pull was done— for now.

For the first time since being bitten, she feared the monster within herself.

THE CITY BY THE SEA

THE SPRAWLING CITY STOOD BEFORE him like a mirage.

When Timothy stepped from the woods, he slipped the blood-soaked bear pelt from his shoulders. He had found it in the inn's kitchen back in Rodica, freshly slain and drained. The vampires must have killed it prior to their arrival.

This trick had outwitted the wolves during the mountaintop ascension and proved just as effective a second time. Best he could tell, it did not throw his scent completely, but confused Raven just enough to send her searching for a different, more human, smell.

With any luck, the bitch was still chasing her tail.

Constanta was such a sight for weary eyes that Timothy thought he might cry.

At last, safety.

His face and hair were covered in thick layers of jellied blood as the bear pelt dropped. The Order of Osiris was here somewhere, but damn if he knew how to find them. And that was the start of his problems. There was also the issue of convincing them that *she* had killed their hunter. Not him. At present, this was a bigger worry.

Constanta stunk of fish and the city came bursting to gritty life as he entered it. Homeless persons sat lined beneath a wooden garrison, covered head to toe in ashen robes, a line of bloodshot eyes followed as he shuffled past. A row of carts padded the street's other side, stacked with fish, meats, and cheeses. Excited merchants called out as he navigated past, ignoring their fluctuating bargains.

Stray cats hissed and meowed, and Timothy wove between the creatures as he slipped into the silk and fabric district. Hookah smoke swirled and dangled overhead before dissolving in the mild bay breeze.

The sights, sounds, and smells of Constanta were so varied that he doubted Raven could find him here. Confidence heightened as some of the city's wealthiest female occupants made eyes at his passing, pretending he was not a blood-covered mess so that he may feel comfortable enough to buy something.

They stretched out varying shirts and dresses spooled from the most exotic fabrics available, and he lingered over their tables just long enough to make an impression.

His appearance would surely capture the attention of some, and that was what he banked on. This was a strange land. If he wanted to find Garrick's order, he was going to have to get noticed.

Across the street, the sweet and smoky smell of cooked sausage kicked up voracious hunger. He had not eaten anything since the greasy stew conjured by Ion Bey, so he crossed the way and asked for two. No telling what currency Constanta accepted, but the vendor's eyes popped with delight when Timothy offered him a silver coin.

The language barrier was not as problematic as he feared. He moved through throngs of people without incident, pointing and grunting his way to general understandings. When it came time to inquire about a place to sleep, he mimed his head resting on a pillow. An old woman with chin stubble and bleeding gums warmed to his mimicry and was delighted to walk him to the nearest inn. He tipped her a piece of silver for her trouble and she hurried off, mumbling appreciation underneath her breath.

The proprietor spoke English that was not so much broken as it was obliterated. This being a port town, it was probably beneficial to pick up an extra tongue or two. As close as Timothy could figure it, the silver coins were enough to secure him a room for an entire month if he wanted it.

I'll be dead if it takes that long.

Panic reared, suggesting that he use the remaining money to board whichever ship set sail tonight. He wanted to do that very much, eager to return to a life of academia.

No, you won't run. Not after Rodica.

Sebastian Miles had deserved a hero's death, something more dignified than what he got. No one should be carted off with a succubus wormed around his soul. As much as Timothy wanted to leave, as much as he knew his old mentor would *want* him to, he could not. The grudge grew inside of him like a weed, an unwanted emotion that spread until it was all he could think about.

Killing the Raven.

Looking in her eyes when she died.

That fantasy came to occupy his every thought. A repulsive reality for a pacifist who prided himself on bringing law to the lawless. Life on Garrick's road had withered him into someone he no longer recognized. The old Timothy Hackett was in here somewhere, pleading for him to do the smart thing. To leave.

He decided to compromise. Find the Order of Osiris and set them on Raven's trail. They would do what he could not. Kill her. No, that would not quench his bloodlust, but it would be enough for him to sail from here with a clear conscience. He hoped his most violent urges would abandon him then.

The inn housed a bar on the first floor. He ordered a drink and was served dark plum wine in a wooden goblet. He carried it onto the sidewalk terrace to a row of crude stools and rounded tree stump tables.

The bustle of the city hurried past, undeterred by his bloodstained attire. Dockworkers shuffled inland as the day tired. They looked like barnacles detached from the ship bows, crusted and slimed. As worn as Timothy felt, the exhaustion on their faces looked worse in the moment.

Then again, he considered how he must have looked to them.

Like a man sitting on a stool covered in blood and drinking plum wine.

He had his own problems.

A stroll around the city would help quell his nerves. Garrick's robes were understated by design, he guessed, as it was not pertinent for a secret order to advertise. If Constanta housed them, news of a bloodied man in a drab doublet would find its way to the right ears.

Or maybe they will just drag me kicking and screaming to a sanitarium.

He burned off the rest of the day walking. He collected a few odd stares, but nothing that resonated as suspicion. He stumbled across a vendor offering bloodied animal pelts and realized that plenty of tradesmen walked around with blood on their clothes. He did not stick out as much as he thought.

When the street was lit by torchlight, he made his way back to the merchant district, figuring he would have to antagonize someone publicly if he was to get noticed by the order. Call someone a varcolac, take a swing, and hope the right people heard the whole story. The risk was the city guard could arrest him first, and word might never get back to those he sought.

He spotted a painter across the courtyard packing up his stand for the night and jogged across the way to meet him. The language barrier was thick and Timothy diffused it by placing four pieces of silver in his hand. The old man clasped the money and stood back, watching Timothy take the color daubed easel in his hands. He held it outward and motioned that he was going to leave with it.

The painter looked at his coins and then up at Timothy. He nodded his approval from behind an expression of uncertainty.

"Thank you," Timothy said and trotted off, snatching the used brush from the pail of water before going.

He found his way back to the inn. The street had quieted some as Constanta wound down for the night. He wasted no time in utilizing his purchases, brushing streaks of yellow across the stone. Once he had three, he dipped the bristles into the mound of dark green and painted a line straight down through the slashes.

Garrick had described this symbol to he and Sebastian once, when the older thief-taker had asked how the order communicated while on the road. These were colors of Osiris, and to arrange them in such a way signaled to inducted travelers that an information cache was nearby. They hid it, always below ground, always across from the symbol.

Timothy went quickly up to his room and put the painting materials there. He then trotted back down to get another goblet of plum wine before going outside to take a seat directly beneath his masterpiece. Someone would undoubtedly report the hieroglyphic, but the foot traffic had dropped to almost nothing, and no one seemed to care about his crude artistry.

He sat alone, eroding his apprehension with fermentation.

Some time passed and his eyelids began dropping in time

with his lolling head. A group of drunken revelers came roaring around the corner, filling the air with shrill laughter that jerked him back to attention. The goblet tumbled from his hand and spilt purple into the street.

He bent to grab the cup as the group hurried past. His eyes found a curious pair of legs facing him from across the way: A short man wearing a golden jelick vest with a red kalpak resting atop his head. His eyes flickered and there was horror in them. Their gazes crossed and held, but then the stranger's attention was pulled back toward the wet paint overhead.

"Brother?" He seemed to mouth.

Timothy stood, the plum wine lending sluggishness to his steps.

The man's brow rose in fear as a late shift of dock men came hurrying up from the waterfront. Timothy ran headlong into the passing crowd but they refused to accommodate his direction, shuffling him back and forth, as he fought to move against the grain. The jelick's shimmering back vanished down an alley and out of sight before he could get free of the horde.

Timothy gave half-hearted chase but found no sign of the man. He sighed and headed back to the inn. Whatever had frightened his *brother* off would not stick. He would be back, and with others.

At least they knew where to find him.

The inn's room offered a bed and little else. His clothes were a mess of bodily fluids, plum wine, and oil paint. He changed out of them, happy to be free of the oppressive fabric. If Garrick's order decided not to show, he would regrettably don it again tomorrow in an effort to be fished from the crowd.

He kept the windows open and listened to the city. Merchant district bustle quelled with each deepening shade of evening black, and soon there were only bawdy sounds of tavern drunkards in the distance. Breathless laughter coughed in a language that sounded like blather to his ears.

It was comforting. There was order here. And if it was not order, it was predictable chaos. Men hurting men for the same motivations as always: jealousy, rage, and despair—all for their own gains. It could be combated and controlled. All of it preferable to what was happening outside the city. A world he wished he had never come to know, and still did not understand.

He fished for his copy of Thomas Hobbes' *Leviathan* and held it warmly. It was like visiting an old friend. The philosophies contained therein never ceased to calm him, although he felt less connected to the words tonight. They were alien to his eyes and thoughts, almost unrelatable. True, he never paid mind to Hobbes' religious proclivities. He tolerated them, however, because they were a prelude to something more. Hobbes did not believe in a greater good, but thought mankind would do well to avoid greater evil.

Greater evil was defined as the anarchy of a man outside of society. Hobbes had no knowledge of the *strigoi viu* that had dragged Sebastian's soul to damnation. She and the Raven walked among man but they were decidedly not. Beyond control or reason, they were greater evil personified.

Someone had to fight that greater evil for the good of man.

Someone will. Not I.

The air floating off the Black Sea was crisp and cold now. Timothy closed the window, but not before lining the pane with his remaining silver. The door got similar treatment and he was thankful that there were only two ways in here because there was not enough coin to cover another.

He settled into bed and imagined the closed-door deliberations occurring in another part of the city: *Is he a thief?*

Perhaps he hails from another order.

They would have no way of knowing until they asked.

Even with the window closed, he heard crashing waves from a few streets away. With so much anxiety controlling him, he half expected never to sleep again, but must have dozed anyway.

It was impossible to say how much time had passed, but hearing the words "wake up" repeated two or three times should have been enough to bolt upright. He was only half awake when the chill of cold steel stung his throat.

Timothy lifted his hand out from beneath the sheet and flashed Garrick's pistol. A hand lashed out and socked him in the eye.

"Don't be stupid." The voice was a whisper and it belonged to a shadow. "You are of great interest to us, so relax."

Timothy nodded and then the blade pulled away from his neck. "I am here on behalf of Garrick," he said.

"Garrick." The voice was not impressed by the name drop. "Those are *his* clothes, then?"

"Yes. We hunted varcolac." Even now, that word sounded absurd. It was clumsy to speak, sounding like a wad of phlegm in the throat. Seventeen years of conditioning could not be undone over the span of a few months. "I am the last one alive."

The shadow barely moved and Timothy did not intend to test it. He embraced the silence and waited.

"Get dressed and come with me."

"Where?"

"What you came here for." There was a second voice now. "Or did you paint the wall because the mood struck you?"

The sound of a match cracking flint, and then a lantern glowing at the foot of his bed.

Two men in dark vests hovered, one pointing a pistol straight at him. Timothy recognized the other from earlier.

His *brother*.

The armed man collected Garrick's bloody tatters and Brother watched Timothy dress.

"If you've been honest with us and this belongs to a fallen brother, it's important that we perform the necessary departing rituals."

This sounded to Timothy like more superstition. A parting ritual would benefit Garrick about as much as a bandage on his head. He kept this dismissal to himself, nodding and then following the men outside. Their steps echoed on the nearly vacant Constanta streets.

They walked toward the ocean to the city outskirts. A shack sat atop the docks far off the harbor. It looked brittle enough to collapse the next time the wind blew it wrong.

Timothy questioned this place as the order's stronghold as they approached, but the gunman gave his shoulder a harsh shove and forced him over the threshold.

They ushered him to a lopsided wooden table that scraped his knees and thighs as he sat down and slid beneath it. A single pathetic candle flailed atop the surface, somehow steeping the room in negative light.

The inquisitors fell in line on the table's opposite side. Their faces were cold and pale in the damp wicker glow. Brother leaned in and lifted Timothy's shirt from his chest. His breath was rum-soaked. He tossed the shirt aside and took the candle in his hand while Gunman kept his weapon drawn. The light roved his body with precision, as if looking for something.

Bites or markings, he guessed.

"Why do you seek us?" Brother asked.

"I told you…I have news of the death of one of your own."

"Stand and strip. I will not ask you a second time."

Timothy pushed the chair back and got to his feet, stepping from his breeches. The candle was at his thighs and circling him then. Once Brother was satisfied, he told him he could put the pants back on and take a seat.

"He isn't bitten. He isn't…like her," Brother said.

"And he isn't like us," Gunman countered.

"That is true," Brother agreed. He placed the candle back and folded his arms. "And Garrick didn't apparently care enough to give him a ward."

Timothy thought back to the tattoos and carvings that littered Garrick's body.

He could've protected us.

Brother smiled. "Tell us about Garrick."

Timothy obliged, beginning with Evan's murder, and how that led to Garrick's offer of an almost inconceivable sum in order to assist on his hunt.

"Of a varcolac woman?" Brother said.

Timothy nodded. "The Raven and her army."

The rest of the story did not take nearly as long to summarize.

"Quite the adventure. And Garrick was murdered by…"
"The she-wolf."

"Whom you then lost in the forest outside of Rodica?"
Timothy nodded.

Brother laughed. "This woman you call the Raven… she followed you every step of the way…and you believe that she somehow lost you because you wrapped your ass in a bear pelt?"

Timothy swallowed. Was it possible he was so daft? Elisabeth had not let him live at all. She wanted him to get away.

To see where he would go.

To find the rest of Garrick's order.

The men sensed his arrival at this conclusion. "She is a bit cleverer than you would like to admit, I think," Brother said.

"If she *is* coming," Timothy said, and then stopped when the Gunman raised a hand to cut off his words.

"We'll worry about her," he said and headed for the door.

"She'll come," Timothy said. "She intends to finish what we started."

"Perhaps," Brother said.

"And that's why you took me here, as opposed to your sanctuary?" It was beginning to make sense now.

"Yes, we've been looking for her for some time."

This was good. He was among friends who would help vanquish her. Sebastian would be avenged yet. That bitch deserved everything she got and so much worse.

I'm glad we killed your lover when we did, he thought, now that it was safe to be this cocky.

He took perverse satisfaction in this, confessing to himself now that he had enjoyed chopping the large wolf to pieces, he and Sebastian alternating hacks until the monster's appendages broke off one at a time.

"But we've also been looking for you." This voice was new, but familiar.

Timothy turned and found an upside down face dangling in the corner, rotted and scabbed. In what should have been an impossible motion, it dropped from the rafters and moved his legs so they caught the floor. Brother shuffled outside to join Gunman on the night watch as the mystery man took stage.

This creature was naked. His jawline was massive, and curved fangs fell so far past his lips they looked like walrus tusks. His head was bald and scabbed, and the last time Timothy had seen him, his facial features had been far more recessed.

Codrin was feeding.

His yellow eyes burned brighter than the candle. He was

delighted to have Timothy's recognition, eyeing him like a plate of salted beef. A bead of spit coiled around one fang and swung across the bottom of his chin while his eyes blazed.

"I'm going to devour you…in every way possible." Calloused hands rubbed Timothy's chest. The feeling was no better than being dragged across rugged terrain, stomach-down. The errant spit swayed back and connected with his forehead. "But not until *she* comes for you."

Timothy's eyes fell to the floor. After all of this, he was as good as dead. Not even a flagon's worth of plum wine could keep his terror buried.

Codrin seemed to feel it rising in him, if his satisfied face was any indication.

Without any weapons, with hardened killers just beyond the door, Timothy did the only thing helpless bait could do.

He closed his eyes and waited.

○

Elisabeth looked down at her figure and shivered. She had come the rest of the way nude. Her gooseflesh was scaly to the touch, sliced and moist with blood from a dozen branch scrapes. Perspiration was so intrusive that her own nose was nearly used to it.

She preferred this body on most days, even when it brought more pain and embarrassment than she was comfortable with.

Fingers trailed the valley between her breasts. Even the traces of scar tissue were a memory now, as if her body had never been damaged. Her spirit would take longer to heal, but that recovery was also guaranteed. A troubling thought, considering it was that pain driving these actions. There would come a day when Aetius' death no longer stung. When she was forced to leave him behind.

That scares me more than anything.

Elisabeth took cautious steps through the forest. Her muscles felt like they had been tied in knots, putting an awkward limp in her step. Her will remained steadfast, though her body begged for respite. Wrestling control away from the wolf had been draining on all fronts, but at last her curves felt natural again, her reflexes controlled.

"Nothing natural about what we are," Aetius used to say. He had never liked her overt comfort with human flesh, chiding her preference for it as some kind of varcolac blasphemy.

The power of the wolf had no equal, true, but humanity delivered the best of both worlds: The ferocity of the animal and the calculated temperament of man.

As far as Elisabeth was concerned, she was perfect in this skin.

Besides, the human was necessary tonight, and somewhere inside, the wolf knew it, too. Slipping into Constanta undetected would not be easy, not even for her. A veil of caution hung over the streets, as if its citizens recognized the malevolence lurking beyond the borders and defended them in the moonlit hours.

She sensed mass superstition here. People apt to keep silver blades by their beds and their windows littered with matching coins. This, in addition to wards and deterrents for other evils. Caution rose not only through her nose and bones, but in her gut as well. A rule of threes that should not be ignored.

She plotted her move in the darkness, occasionally huffing the air to ensure that Survivor had not yet left port. It was difficult to find his scent amidst a city of thousands but, every so often, she caught his desperation. There was just enough of it to reignite her killer instinct. She ground her jaw in anger, rubbing her shoulders to get the shiver out of her body. The real trick was keeping her thoughts straight while she figured out the best way to get at him.

The wolf, enticed by traces of Survivor, and equating him with food, returned like a spasm. It took everything Elisabeth had to keep the animal at bay. The coming was too powerful and Elisabeth doubled over in pain, a sensation worse than any debilitating stomach cramp. Her innards twisted and throbbed as she grit her teeth and pushed back.

You…will…not…come…

Each time she smelled Survivor, the animal reacted like she was being antagonized.

A troupe of guards took watch along the city's parapet. They fanned out through the front-facing streets in packs of two. Handheld torchlight enabled them to defend their immediate perimeters.

The forest held her anonymity as she studied their patterns and watched for a hole in formation. It may do to skirt around and gain entrance from either the north or the south, but the city probably held a stringent defense wherever you tried getting inside of it.

Wolf tremors took a reluctant break as Elisabeth shook them off, overwhelming her bestial half by considering several attack strategies. The animal recognized it was in her best interest to get inside the city. A horse-drawn cart approached from the heart of the forest and Elisabeth's ears perked at the sound.

A merchant making his way back home, most likely.

She plucked two scents from the sky. Perspiration nearly as severe as hers, indicating a long-walked road for two men. One of them sold wares and the other sold protection.

Her body shimmered beneath the moon and her shoulders gyrated to chase away the last few muscle cricks. She strode toward them with confidence, despite the musk beneath her arms and other crevices. It should not matter. Attracting their attention would be simple, no matter how ripe she was.

Lust had a specific smell, and it drenched most men. It was useful when determining who would be most susceptible to her charms. As soon as she swayed into the center of the dirt path, it was obvious to Elisabeth that these fools wore it like cologne.

Her appearance energized them. Desire surged. Elisabeth could not read minds but understood chemical reactions easier than words. These timid, dull-faced oxen would lick her sweat bead-by-bead if she commanded it.

"Hello," she said, instilling her voice with as much innocence as she could manage. She had never been much of an actor and did not enjoy empowering these lowly animals, even in charade.

"Miss." The bodyguard had wide shoulders and carried a rifle in his arms. He pulled the horses to a stop and jumped from the wobbly cart. He did not aim at her and seemed to forget that she had a face. His gaze was bolted to her bare breasts, better for her this way.

It would be over faster.

She came forward to greet him, refusing to yield until they stood nose-to-nose. The sellsword did not resist. She arched her back and pushed her full bosom against him.

This man, who presumably collected an honest wage by defending the still-silent merchant, had no intention of speaking. His heart thundered. Men were always so nervous in the presence of women. This was as assured as changing seasons, and she loved them dearly for their predictability.

Before he could speak, she opened wide and made for his neck, hoping she could make this kill with her human mouth. She bit through the flesh until her top and bottom teeth scraped together in a gush of blood.

The mercenary lost his balance and fell to the ground. Elisabeth dropped him like a spent newspaper and ran to the wagon, attempting a convincing performance once more.

"He gave me no choice," she said. "He tried to have me. You saw it. Say that you saw it."

She wiped the blood from her mouth and managed a single tear, an intricacy lost on the stuttering imbecile who could not see in the dark.

Elisabeth took his head in her arms as he leaned down to her. The wolf's strength surged and she snapped his neck. The merchant's body went limp and tumbled off the cart.

She slipped her shoulders into his oversized coat, pulling the large garment tight and giving her body enough warmth to chase off her goose bumps. A frayed pair of breeches was draped over the cart, along with a pile of linens. She pulled the pants up past her waist and slid into a muddy pair of boots to complete the lowly peasant costume.

Not the best choice of clothes, but she needed to be able to move through the city uncontested.

There was a hunt on, after all.

She unhitched the horses and gave each a harsh slap on the rear. They thundered off towards Constanta, stomping the mercenary's corpse into a twisted pile of pulp.

Her stomach growled but she would not allow the wolf to eat until this was over. She could not afford the animal's return if she could not control her. Even now, the wolf attempted a coup, and Elisabeth gave everything she had to keep her subdued.

The charging horses would put the guards on alert and it might not be long before they discovered these bodies. By then, she would be lost in the city's shuffle. This crime was so brutal that they would be on the hunt for a large male suspect.

Normally, Elisabeth would enjoy making them see the

error of their shortsighted ways, but there was no time for a lesson in equality.

She chose to traverse the forest from another direction. Holding her pants up with her fist, she pulled strands of nappy hair over her face and worked her most hysterical emotions to the surface in case the guards discovered her and she needed to give another performance.

With Survivor so close, she could not afford to make enemies of the city guard when all she wanted to do was kill him and find the others responsible. Drumming up a war was not the way to accomplish that.

Approaching the quiet city, she recognized something else in the air. Something worse. The same graveyard rot that had plagued her back at the mountain.

Elisabeth chewed the inside of her lip to keep her composure. The wolf's rage mounted and her nose tingled worse than ever. Both human and animal suddenly understood their error in leaving the vampire's fate to chance. That thing should have burnt up in the morning sun on the top of that mountain. It was all but guaranteed, and Elisabeth had not wished to expend the energy to finish it when daylight would do the work for her. She despised acknowledging parasites, they were so far beneath her. Somehow, though, this one had managed to get away.

And make it to Constanta.

○

"I knew we should've chased you down and killed you," Timothy growled.

The vampire sat in the corner of the room, leering.

"Make him bleed," Codrin hissed, "just a little."

Gunman had returned, keeping Brother on patrol outside.

Two humans doing a vampire's bidding. He wound back and punched Timothy in the jaw. Then he smashed him upside the head and sent another fist driving between his eyes.

"The more he bleeds, the faster she'll come. This is like chum to her." Codrin's voice was a squeal. He ran his long and brittle-looking fingers over Timothy's bare chest, massaging his pecs with a mischievous grin.

When Timothy winced, the vampire flashed his enforcer a weary look.

Gunman grunted his approval and hit Timothy so hard that his tongue swam in blood. He fought the urge to spit it out, thinking that Codrin may lose complete control once it hit the air. No sense in making his death any easier for the monster.

The vampire hovered somewhere behind him and Timothy was grateful for his broken nose. It muted the putrid stench of his permanently decaying flesh.

"Go outside and watch for her," Codrin hissed.

Gunman did exactly that. When Timothy was alone with the vampire, the creature retreated once more into to the far corner so that only his yellow, unblinking eyes remained visible. They hovered in the darkness like frozen fireflies.

A gunshot roared across the waterfront.

Good, Timothy thought. The city guard must be on the way. Surely, someone complained about a couple of men using a dock station as their after hours office.

Something hit the floor with a splat. Timothy looked down in time to catch the upper part of Gunman's head bounce across the wooden planks, leaving stamps of blood wherever it hit. When Timothy glanced up, a figure filled the doorframe—a silhouette of unkempt hair and formless clothes.

Any relief he felt was short-lived. Whoever wound up the victor would be his killer.

"Huntress," Codrin spoke like there was a grievance to settle. "If only you allowed me to help you from the start."

She stepped into the flickering candlelight. A silver ball wedged into her temple. It jutted out from the side of her face like a third eye. A trail of crimson tears scaled her cheek.

There was no killing this woman.

She smiled and flashed her growing and changing teeth. The vampire slipped behind her with incredible speed and threw skinny arms across her body. His sickly, grey tongue lashed her blood-wet cheek.

"More," he cried in between licks. "Give me more!"

Raven winced and a simple extension of her arm sent the vampire flying. She wiped spittle off her face with a wave of her elbow, looking at the creature with wide-eyed astonishment.

Timothy saw his chance and leapt from the chair. He dashed for the exit, pushing his legs as fast as they could move.

Raven did not follow.

"Enjoy your last night alive," she called.

Timothy sprinted into the night as wicked laughter filled the evening sky.

○

The vampire was a sniveling mess at her feet.

"Please," Codrin tried to say. She placed her boot on his mouth to force his silence, and his tongue lapped at her sole.

Elisabeth laughed at the pathetic sight and bent down to face him.

"Your plan was what? Draw me here? For revenge?"

The vampire snickered but said nothing.

Elisabeth retracted her foot and slammed a palm down on the table. It splintered in two. She pointed to the wood with her chin. "Somehow you survived the mountaintop. I will not leave it to chance a second time."

She reached for a piece of timber as a hand broke through the dock floor. It missed Elisabeth's foot by the length of a fingernail, just as a second hand launched upward and pulled her foot through the hole, toward the water.

Codrin's wheeze became a laugh, one that strengthened as he rose to his feet.

The ground around them exploded into splinters. More hands poked through and Elisabeth swatted away the sea of open palms. The haze cleared to reveal slimy, rotted bodies hoisting up and out of their watery graves.

"We are starving," Codrin said. "Have to be careful in a city that houses the Order of Osiris, but what else can we do in desperate times?" He dropped down and lapped Elisabeth's cheek again, running his tongue up and down like a paintbrush.

She struggled as hands clamped around her ankles and thighs, belting her to the floor.

The vampire's lips closed around the silver ball embedded in her head. He sucked so hard that it popped free, delivering a gushing drink of her. Color came back to his face while he gulped, and his hold tightened with each swallow.

"It's all about you. Kill a human in this city and you raise eyebrows, but a varcolac foreigner? I saw your lover turned to toast back on that mountain. I doubt anyone else knows you're here. When I crawled into the forest that night just ahead of the sun, holding my head to keep it attached, I promised I would see you die. The Rodican refugees who left home in search of survival have lived in shame for months, existing on scraps until I arrived. And you know why they listen to me? Because I promised them the blood of a huntress."

He kissed her full on, laughing as his mouth crushed hers.

Elisabeth only had her teeth for defense. She bit for him and his reflexes were slow, catching his bottom lip in her teeth and yanking a flap of dead flesh away with a snap.

Codrin looked as if he could not fathom this. "We were going to feast on you. Bleed you dry and have our way. But now I think that would be letting you off easy."

"I hope I give you rot gut," Elisabeth snarled.

The floor broke apart as the bodies pushed up further, dropping everyone into ocean water. A dozen hands wrapped around her, splashing and grabbing.

She fought to break free but the hands were too many. Exhausted and depleted as they were, dinner was within reach and they would fight to be fed. Sharpened nails dug in and drew blood wherever they could.

Codrin waved his creatures away as he took her in his arms.

"You may be invulnerable to many things, but what happens if you are bitten by a vampire?"

She refused him the satisfaction of an answer.

He smiled and his eyes danced with life fire that had not been there before. Her blood had rejuvenated him in the blink of an eye.

"I take it you do not know." The vampire pinched her lips together in the grasp of his clawed hand. "So what say we find out?"

His teeth came forward, prompting a reaction that surprised her.

Elisabeth screamed.

O

Constanta was built on fish. Just as its docks were held

above water by cylindrical trestles, the entire city was propped on that economy.

The streets snaked away from the waterfront, but that smell somehow followed Timothy and his busted nose as he gave chase to the bloody man that had once called him brother. The fish smell was vague and he could not be certain he really smelled it, or if he just knew it should be there. Either way, he hoped it was enough to keep Raven off his trail.

She hasn't had any problems finding me yet.

Brother ran in spastic motions, but with surprising speed. Timothy gave chase because it was his last chance to find Garrick's order. They would want to know that one of their own had been corrupted by vampires.

If Brother reached the order before Timothy could counter his lies, his fate was as good as sealed.

Footsteps echoed inland. The only other noise on the street was the two winded men sucking air. Without weapons, Timothy was not sure he could take Brother in a fight, but Raven had injured him upon her entrance, taking advantage out of the equation.

She did me a favor.

The chase curved through alleyways and, up ahead, a bustle of nondescript doublets caught Timothy's eye as they rushed past in a darkened blur, crossing the main street before either of the running men could reach it. Timothy glanced left as his pursuit intersected with the now-vacated main street, catching a glimpse of armed men rushing toward the water.

He had an idea where they were headed.

Please kill her. Finish this.

Timothy wanted to be back at the waterfront, but he could not leave Brother to the fates.

Constricting alleys spilled into a wide-open forum called

Ovidiu Square. The bloody men made feet for the church across the way—a large basilica marked by a heavily decorated steeple and topped with a golden crucifix.

They sprinted up the steps and Timothy leapt for Brother's ankles, throwing him off-balance. The traitor tumbled back with a yelp and his weight dropped onto Timothy. In a moment, they rolled down the stairs, trading fists.

Timothy saw an opportunity and pressed his fingers around his opponent's neck. Scum like this did not deserve life when a good man such as Sebastian had given his along the way. In this moment, he wanted nothing more than to snuff this bastard like a dying dog. His hands tightened and squeezed, stunned to discover how much satisfaction he found in this action.

"That'll be that." Someone said from behind them.

The words came first in a foreign tongue that Timothy refused to hear. He continued squeezing Brother's throat. The voice tried a different language that was also lost on him. Finally, there was English, and that prompted Timothy to turn and look.

A pistol hovered in his face, a flintlock that would tear half his skull off given the distance. Behind the gun, a dark and flowing robe concealed the man completely.

Timothy released his hands and lifted them toward the church steeple before standing.

"You are a most brazen thief," the man said. "Are you so desperate that you would rob holy men?"

"This isn't a robbery," Timothy said. "This man is a traitor. His allegiance is to the undead." Timothy could not quite believe the words, even as he offered them.

The traitor only wheezed. His attempted defense broke apart with hoarse crackles and he curled up to suffer a coughing fit.

"If you allow him to lie about it, he will," Timothy said.

"We come from the docks where he held me prisoner. I believe your brothers have gone there to quell the eruption of violence. Your man is more than involved."

The pistol remained fixed on him, and the man's robe bristled in the sea breeze. Timothy could hear him thinking from here. When he spoke at last, he sounded more inquisitive than angry. "You come from the waterfront? And how will you convince me that you speak the truth?"

Timothy pointed to the bloody man. "He was attacked by a varcolac. The same one your friends hunt…the Raven. I am here on behalf of your order. His name was Garrick and he fell in battle two nights ago. I was with him…we hunted a pack of her kind across the Holy Roman Empire and beyond."

"*Well* beyond if you are here," the man said.

Brother was to his feet now, hunched over with hands on his thighs. Each time he attempted breath, he coughed. Watching him suffer brought Timothy enduring satisfaction. So much of it that he wished he had hurt him more.

The arbiter kept his weapon trained and retreated up the church steps. An etching on the door labeled it St. Matthew's. He hoisted the lit torch off its bracket and came back down.

He held the light over Brother's red-drenched face, asking him to turn around, lift his chin, and show his neck. In this light, he was absolutely mangled. Deep gashes left flaps of frayed skin dangling. Timothy would have sworn him wearing a mask of fresh ground beef. When the armed man was finished surveying his brother, he offered a *tsk* with his tongue and shot him in the throat. The turncoat tumbled back across the city's street, covering his neck before dropping to the ground.

Timothy felt a smile propping up at the corners of his mouth.

"He *was* bitten by a varcolac," the arbiter said. "Clearly.

But it's up to you to sell me on the rest of the story."

He turned his back on Timothy and headed for the church in a surprising display of trust.

Timothy shrugged and followed.

○

Elisabeth's only course of action was to bite back. She thrashed while the icy arms of the hungry undead struggled to contain her. She kicked faces and swatted limbs, but her resistance only piqued their aggression.

Codrin came for her neck. He got so close she felt his fangs scrape the surface of her skin. Her elbow knocked him away followed by a scream of protest. A sign of weakness, sure, but this was desperate. If they bit her—

She decided against finishing that thought, determined to summon the wolf. It refused to come trotting.

Commotion on land was nearly as excited. Elisabeth assumed that more parasites were coming to feed and only fought harder. The vampires were concerned with tapping her wellspring, ignoring the land-locked bustle just as much.

Codrin caught another of her elbows. This one connected with the patch of skin she had yanked from his chin. Her eyes ballooned once she caught a glimpse of what was coming for them all from atop the broken dock.

Nine or ten crusaders jumped into the soggy maelstrom. Blades flashed, wooden stakes stabbed, and a volley of gunfire sparked the night. The stench of sulfur presided over the battle. This was something out of a nightmare. She hoped that the parasites and crusaders would kill each other, but they had never attacked in such overwhelming numbers. The vampires could not survive their preparedness.

When the familiar one and his band had reached her on that mountaintop, she could tell that only he had been trained to fight this way. His movements were reflected in the way these men moved, attacked, and defended.

They were good shots and the parasites scattered like cockroaches. It presented an opportunity she did not intend to squander. Codrin reached for her as she bent her knees and kicked off his chest, knifing through the water in retreat.

Elisabeth waded away as he lunged. The entitlement in his face enraged and provoked the wolf. Her legs bulged and jutting nails poked through her fingertips. A perpetual growl hung in her throat.

No…

If the wolf understood this plea, she did not appear to care. These were not ordinary men. They would hunt her to the end of their days if the inkling took them. And if they were to witness a woman become wolf in their presence, that is what they would do.

The smarter thing was to slip into the night and watch this unfold from the shadows. She had been lucky enough to make it this far amidst the chaos. The hunters were too distracted by the vampires to assess their surroundings. They were more immediately concerned with avoiding the infectious bites that chomped at them. A girl at the edge of this chaos, a possible victim, as far as they might have been concerned, was of no consequence.

Let the crusaders have their victory by stomping out a nest of parasites.

Sand sunk between Elisabeth's toes as she soft-stepped onto shore. The wolf's intensity rescinded as the sand cooled her feet, and her bones ceased stretching. She struggled to calm the muscles further as dry sand stuck to her wet soles. Then the impulse to kill barked back.

If the wolf wanted this, she was powerless to stop it. Elisabeth offered whispered pleas to the animal that only cemented her helplessness. To the wolf, turning felt like the right thing to do. Her skin would tear. Her bones would break. She would scream. The crusaders would know.

"Please," she mumbled, but the display of weakness only incentivized the beast. The animal recognized it as a way to wrestle control. A snarl followed on her lips that she did not want. An animal grunt that mocked her human weakness while reasserting dominance.

Elisabeth's legs gave next. She fell into the sand and screamed. Her groan contorted with her body. Her arms bent back and then bolted up as her spine rippled and pressed against her flesh. She used every muscle to beat the monster back, but it was almost laughing at her, stomping on her protests with confident claws.

"Not now," she cried. Pleaded. Begged. The monster was behind her eyes, no longer asking to be unleashed. She was just coming.

In between chipped breaths, Elisabeth watched the remnants of Codrin's tribe slip beneath the water. The hunters stood in the distance, waist-deep in their own befuddlement. Amid her convulsions, she almost laughed. Parasites did not draw breath and could easily hike the Black Sea's floor, rising off the coast of a desolate village whenever they felt safe enough to do so.

If Codrin had been smart, that would have been *his* approach, too. But his grudge for her had rendered him careless. The extermination and scattering of his brethren was on his head, though he was certain to blame her for all that had happened.

Elisabeth was not so blind to miss the lesson in his fate. She threw this logic at the wolf, arguing that the animal would destroy her by forcing this change. The wolf responded by forcing

Elisabeth's head to look once more at the waterlogged crusaders. This was the time to fight. Here they were. And perhaps their numbers were greater, with weapons that would sting like the Nightfall ambush, only worse because of the number of them, but there was one difference: She was ready and had nothing left to lose.

The tightening pain around her skull reminded her that there were other things to worry about. She pleaded with the wolf, forcing the animal to recall every injury atop that mountain, reiterating that she had been lucky to get away and may not be that way again.

They'll run me through and then do so much worse.

The wolf hesitated.

"Hold it." Elisabeth did not hear the voice until arms curled around her shoulders and, with a harsh grunt, lifted her off her feet. "What are you doing out here?"

Elisabeth thrashed and flailed her arms against the thick fabric pressing against her back.

"This one escapes," he called.

Some of the warriors in the water already trudged toward them.

"Your skin…" He flung her back to the dirt and Elisabeth found herself staring down the barrel of a gun. The wolf sent another convulsion through her, and then animal teeth shredded her gums and forced open her mouth.

No, she thought, but had no time to finish it. Her body tensed, every muscle tightening at once. The wolf stormed her bones in a single burst. They broke in unison, shuffling and chasing away the form of a skittish and frightened woman.

Leaving a huffing black monster behind.

The man on the beach took a startled step back as his compatriots reached the shore.

Elisabeth's jaws shot outward. She rose onto her haunches, staring at him from down an eager snout.

A howl careened through the desolate Constanta streets.

Then she attacked.

O

Just like that, his dream was over.

Codrin watched from the reeds like a frightened victim. The Order of Osiris lorded above his tribe. They stabbed and hacked the waters with diligence, killing vampires that crawled through the shallows as they struggled to escape onto shore.

He might have held out hope if not for the wooden stakes in their fists. They used them to stab through the water. Strained hands launched to the surface, the few who had been smart enough to make for deeper waters. Fingers stretched wide in death twinges before falling back with one final splash.

It was not supposed to happen this way.

Codrin was not greedy, just hungry. Leaving Rodica was always going to be a risky proposition but someone had to shepherd the blood back home. He volunteered then because he was destined for something better. Something dignified. Yet he crouched here, a failure.

Now the battle was over, except for the erupting howl from the shore. The Order of Osiris waded that way with weapons still in hand.

Codrin had not intended to cower like this, but the huntress had pushed him out beyond the action during their struggle. In the time it would have taken him to rejoin the fray, most of the vampires had already been exterminated.

Because of that, slipping away was the only reasonable option.

I could've led them.

He felt nothing but regret over the way this had played out. Greatness was within his reach. Not an hour ago, he had been supremely confident in his plan. He was so close to making the huntress suffer for her betrayal. Now, his dreams were buried deeper than his tribe beneath the Black Sea.

He swam around to an inland rivet, leaving the wolf to be hunted like the bitch she was. As much as he wanted to see her die, escape was more important. He climbed through loose stalks, away from the action. His ongoing existence felt more like a curse. Every aspiration was stomped out, even when he tried placing the needs of the many high above his own.

Codrin really had wanted to feed his people.

If he was being honest, however, he had to admit that his desire to help did not stem from a place of selflessness. It was rooted in his craving to be worshiped and adored. To *matter*. Because of that, he had been driven to make the huntress pay for her warped conceit. What a hero he would have been if he had managed to kill her and deliver her blood. Above all else, he still wanted to hurt her.

I have never tasted blood that sweet.

He should have been drinking it now.

He ran from the city and his mind folded over how the order had arrived so fast. It must have been the discharging pistols that had triggered their attention. Codrin had told his human servants that the huntress could not die by conventional weapons, but that had not stopped them from trying.

Was it delusions of grandeur that had forced them to act with such impatience? Kill the huntress to service their order *and* his tribe? Recruiting some of Osiris had not been easy. The things he had to promise those degenerates. It also had not been worth his time, as it turned out.

We should've taken the city by force.

That would not have been any easier. So dilapidated was the tribe that the first few kills would have posed a genuine struggle. Once they got their tongues wet, maybe. The countryside was in drought and Osiris knew it, realizing full well that desperate *demons* would make their way here. Hence their high numbers and immediate response.

Codrin had been clever, though, setting a trap for the bitch where his kind could lie in wait. When she came inside the shack, bleeding, it had driven them all to the brink of madness. She had served herself on a platter, but even that had not been enough.

Everything undone because of a couple of ill-timed gunshots delivered in haste.

The few drops of huntress that he had managed to steal gave him enough energy to navigate the dark morning with heightened senses. As he distanced himself from Constanta, his frustrations grew into obsessions.

So close to killing her!

So close to delivering a varcolac feast to what remained of my people!

So close to being king!

His name would have been legendary.

Now, it was scantly a footnote.

A cemetery sat at the top of a hill, enclosed by a stonewall of varying rocks and held together by gypsum. Elisabeth's blood granted enough agility to hop it. Gargoyles took perch on each corner. Gravestones poked from the earth like crooked teeth. The further back he went, he found a village of mausoleums.

It would be daybreak before he knew it and there was no reason to get caught in the forest once more. He approached the nearest crypt, elongated fingers curling around the metal door handle. Spending more energy than he might have liked, he lifted the latch and forced it outward with a grunt.

The door shrieked and swiveled. A cobweb thicker than cotton stretched out and finally tore as he stepped inside.

Codrin closed the door and pulled it tight until it came scraping against the stone jamb, deeper than it was intended to go. This way, no human could disturb his sleep. He hopped onto the stone slab at the center of the room and tried to shut his eyes.

He contemplated his options for a long while before realizing he had none.

His dream of leadership was finished. It was twice that the huntress had prevented it.

Whore.

His fingertips rubbed his torn chin where the wolf woman had chomped through. The protruding jawbone was coarse to touch. Something to remember her by.

"You don't want me to remember you," he whispered, and stretched out on the cold slab. The silence in here soothed him. The outside world did not exist and would not intrude.

I think I'll just lie here a while.

With his thoughts.

They were dedicated to the wolf woman.

◯

Timothy was ushered into a pew and told to sit. His warder sidled in beside him and jammed the pistol against his ribs.

"Say nothing until I ask you to."

Timothy nodded without eye contact. In his experience, men like this wanted an excuse to perform violence. Often times it was for as simple a reason as *'he looked at me funny.'* This situation was already sensitive, with his accusations and implications driving the order to an uncomfortable place. No point in agitating it further.

They sat without speaking for so long that Timothy drifted

into sleep. He dreamt of life as a university professor, where he stood behind a wobbly podium delivering a *Hobbes-ian* lecture. A blinding light shaped like the Star of Bethlehem radiated outward from the middle of the room, its points reached floor-to-ceiling and stretched wall-to-wall. There were students in here but he could not see them. Only the light.

He delivered discourse on Leviathan's third section, *Of a Christian commonwealth*, reiterating Hobbes' philosophy on devils and demons as duplicitous notions. While he spoke, he wondered what right he had to stain the minds of those more impressionable. It was his own upbringing that had pushed him away from God, more so once Mum was murdered. But could these concepts not offer salvation in trying times?

No. I know best.

His voice was full of fervor as he pleaded with learned ears. The Bible's institution of evil spirits kept the world ignorant and submissive, governed by fear of an afterlife that did not exist. He implored them to place their faith in the sovereign and in tangible concepts of salvation. Thinking that faith could do the same would only lead them to confusion.

Double vision, he and Hobbes called it.

A voice rose in interruption to challenge his concepts.

"If the Kingdom of God exists, but only takes significance at the end of all things, why not offer our allegiance to Him as opposed to the sovereign? His embrace is eternal, yes? Following the sovereign may pit us against Him in instances of war and atrocity. What good is blind loyalty to a ruling body when mutual benefit is merely an illusion?"

Timothy could not see the speaker, but the star's glow had waned a little. Its pointed tips no longer touched wall or floor. He hated being challenged, especially by one of these *know nothings*. Garrick and Sebastian had scolded his inexperience. He took it from them because his dogma had been untested then.

Now, though, he was a survivor.

And a liar. You deny them the truth in spite of the things you've seen. You can never go home again. The way things were in your mind never existed anyway.

As soon as he thought it, the dissenting voice said the same aloud, demanding to know how he could sermonize opposition to the truth.

"Vampires, witches, varcolac…you name it. They're as real as the rising sun. Yet, you insist on keeping us ignorant? Vulnerable. Tell us how to defeat such evils. Give us something that will save our lives!"

Timothy stammered to find an answer. The truth had flustered him, in part because he knew better. He wanted to forget such horrors, not revel in them. Each time he closed his eyes he remembered everything when all he wanted to do was forget.

I wanted to absolve them of my burden. Save them from learning what no man should have to know.

The voice stood prominently against the fading light. Timothy's fingers curled defensively around the podium, transfixed by the transference of energy from the starlight to the speaker. A silhouette stepped through the star's heart, stomping it out as he came forward. The room plunged into black, save for a band of shimmering light around the shadow's outline.

It approached with familiarity, speaking with the same passion that had defined his earlier words. This one knew his secrets, and called upon him to remember them all.

The wolves they slaughtered.

The witch they destroyed.

The vampires they fought.

"And the huntress that killed you."

A mirror image stood before Timothy. A once fresh-faced

boy whose dark eyes had been deadened by a world of violence, and worse. Timothy touched his fingers to his own face and rubbed his chin. Surely, this sight had to be wrong. But his reflection did the same. Signs of his youth remained in the doppelganger, but they receded until the likeness was no longer recognizable.

Harsh talon gashes emblazoned the face, running diagonally and mangling his features. One eye was broken and cloudy—a runny egg with a drippy yolk. When he smiled, his teeth were missing, his gum line completely shredded.

Timothy screamed—

And opened his eyes. Sunlight blared through the stained glass windows of St. Matthew's, scorching his eyelids.

He was alone, at least where the living was concerned. The blood-faced traitor from last night, *Brother*, had been laid across the altar up front. His body stripped of Osiris' robes and replaced by an all-white cloth that wrapped him head-to-toe like an Egyptian mummy.

His killer walked through a doorway at the far left of the altar. He approached the corpse, but stopped when he found Timothy awake and watching. Rather than continue, he nodded and flashed what must have been his attempt at a disarming smile.

"I have pleaded your case, thief-taker. One of our brothers has already departed for Vatican City. He is to confirm the existence of this Garrick you speak of."

"Good news," Timothy said.

"Certainly? If they have no record of that brother…"

"I haven't deceived you." He only hoped that Garrick had not been the deceptive one. What if the hunter had not actually been among this order?

Sebastian's cynicism seeps in. Timothy decided it was not worth it. He figured the hunter had known too much about this world and the order to be an impostor.

"Good to hear," the arbiter said. "I'm not in the habit of trusting strangers, believe me. If your story wasn't so…unique, I would've sentenced you to die. But liars are not often capable of spiels such as yours. If you are as honest as you say, it will make the next step much easier."

"Which is?"

Beneath the stained and sun-soaked glass, Timothy got his first good look at the guy. They were roughly the same age, only arbiter's skin was darker, his features unmistakably from this region, even further east, perhaps. His English was good but he spoke it loud, and with a thick accent that did not always settle on the ears.

He extended his hand and Timothy shook it, happy for any display of camaraderie, no matter how tiny.

"Salih," he said.

"Timothy."

"The commotion at the docks has Constanta on edge. My brothers are not yet back, even as daylight rises. So rare to find vampires in populated areas such as this."

"One of them comes from a band that abducted us a few days back…they were worse off than plague carriers."

Salih nodded. "They grow bolder each night. Skirmish with the Russian Empire has left much of the countryside devastated. Survivors flocked here, and many have gone beyond the sea already. We knew it was only a matter of time before the vampires came to where their food is."

"Is that why there are so many of you here? Garrick didn't speak of your practices, though he implied you didn't work in large groups."

"Our order is small and our work expansive. It calls us to every continent of the world. The men here are not all…*hunters*, as you call them."

"I called Garrick witch-finder once and he threatened to burn me to death."

Salih laughed. A jolly, infectious sound. "Yes, I suppose that is an insult. We do not force ourselves on farmer's daughters once the nights get cold and lonely. Officially, we are Warders of the Dead. Put another way, keepers of the gate. Warders guard the abyss and ensure the dead stay where they belong. Those who escape the *Duat*, the beyond, are hunted and returned by necessary means."

"Warders," Timothy said, turning the concept over in his mind. It made him uneasy. It was more real than he wanted to imagine, meaning it would be harder to forget.

"Sometimes my kind is required to fight alongside the warders, though our concentrations are off-battlefield. Some of us design weapons…you might have noticed that we only carry the best into combat, for example. Others, such as I, find demonic patterns and ensure that information flows to all our outposts."

"Chroniclers?"

"Labels are not consequential." Salih did not sound anxious to offer anything else, so long as Timothy knew he did more than tell stories.

"What of the Raven? She is in Constanta." He recalled her terrible laughter from last night and shivered. "She is the one you must worry about."

Salih spread his arm outward and made a *follow me* motion. Timothy rose and walked alongside him toward the altar. They stared at Brother's body while a man in priest robes shuffled in, his eyes staring daggers.

Timothy might have been intimidated by this sudden appearance, but Salih offered a reassuring nod.

"Our brother goes to his rest," he said, watching Timothy. "Because of your accusations, we deny him assured passage to Duat, his final resting within the Realm of the Dead. If his betrayal is genuine…and let it be said that I believe it is…then it is our Father who determines his fate in the next world."

Timothy felt those daggers turn to ice. The priest might have been a friend of the traitor. He could not know for sure and would never ask. Not while he was a prisoner in this place. It was clear not everyone had Salih's open mind when it came to dead brothers. Sebastian's cynicism returned once more as Timothy wondered about other turncoats housed here, sitting secretly in Codrin's employ.

"He was marked by varcolac," Salih said. "As good as dead."

"The varcolac are not dumb enough to come to Constanta," the priest said.

"This one is different," Timothy said. "She's here because of me."

"Salih told me of your assassination gone wrong." There was arrogance there, as if the accuser would not have made such a thoughtless mistake.

"Perhaps Garrick should've recruited you then," Timothy said, "instead of relying on a bunch of peasants to get the job done."

"That wouldn't be possible," Salih said.

"Enough," the priest said. "You would tell him more when he already knows too much?"

Salih ceased speaking and peeled back the traitor's bandages, revealing that Brother was covered in symbols that had been tattooed on his chest and arms. He unsheathed a garroted blade and carved the markings away like turkey slices. He flayed the strips of protected flesh and tossed them to the altar's floor.

"He is no longer entitled to our refuge on his journey."

That *protection* was how Garrick had been able to avoid the necromancer's spell in the salt mine. It could have been Timothy that the *strigoi viu* had fixated on, but Sebastian's injuries must have made him a more susceptible target.

That memory, less than seven days old, felt like it belonged in another life.

"Today," Salih said, "you are witnesses as our brother takes the void."

The priest offered a miserable grumble. Timothy supposed he understood. The mark of the wolf stained this brother, and no one could understand what part he had truly played in that.

Salih walked around the altar and stood beside him, a buffer from the hostility. "You and I depart the city at first light. We make haste for the village of Rodica."

Timothy's mouth dropped as the priest covered the slain man in white fabric once more while offering a mumbled prayer.

"You didn't expect us to take what you had to say at face value, did you?"

Timothy shrugged. He should have been glad for the chance to leave this judgment chamber. How long until the order returned and one of the accusatory faces shivved him to death when he least expected it? But the prospect of going back through Devil's Row loaded him with dread. He could not know the future, but recalled his mutilated face from the dream and had a pretty good idea how this ended.

"You remain our guest tonight," Salih said. Timothy thought the word guest sounded a lot like prisoner. "Rodica is a two-day ride. If we can corroborate your story, and the Vatican confirms the existence of a warder called Garrick, you will be compensated for the part you played in this."

Timothy obsessed over everything that could go wrong. In a heavily forested town like Rodica, woodland animals had likely made meals of the corpses already. If the evidence has been disposed of and things got really desperate, could he kill Salih in a fight? What if Raven picked them both off along the way?

Timothy tried hiding his anxiety with a miserable sounding, "Of course." What else was he supposed to say? Resist now and they would assume him a liar, sentencing him to die without the benefit of a civilized trial.

"This way then," Salih said.

Timothy followed him and the priest trailed behind, making sure he did not escape. He knew the unspoken drill. They went into the hallway off the altar and ducked immediately down a winding stairwell.

The air cooled as they slipped beneath the ground. The bottom was a chamber of wooden tables and chairs. Along the left wall were rows of doors that extended all the way down its length.

Salih cut across the opened space and walked to the last of those doors. He pulled it open and stepped aside. "Please," he said.

Timothy glanced inside and refused to go any further.

It was a cell.

○

The wolf ran and the men followed.

She did not fear the fight, but knew it was best to take them separately. These were humans, and humans got tired. Vulnerable. Fatigue chomped away at her, too, but it was secondary to hatred. These were the ones who could hurt her, and if she did not kill them, they would do it again.

Elisabeth was through being weak.

The wolf led them into the city, her shoulders scuffed the alley sides as she twisted and turned through brick corridors. A peasant curled against the wall in front of her, blanketed by a threadbare cloth. He noticed her charge but shuffled too late to avoid it.

Realizing there was no time to dodge, he kicked the sheet free and curled up to shield the stampede. She did not bother navigating around, mauling his body beneath her muscular legs. Claws pierced and tore, leaving him mortally maimed and run red.

The crusaders continued their chase in the face of fading diligence, banging into one another and grunting hoarsely as they funneled into the alley in pursuit. The disorganized mob dashed with desperation, stumbling forward. Their clumsiness made her contemplate a final stand, but the alley offered limited maneuverability and had the potential for flanking.

Best to get away from here. If she hovered any longer, the fresh-spilt beggar would prove too much of a distraction for what had become tormented hunger. She had gone days without eating, and here lay a fresh carcass topped by a bared neck and running blood. An irresistible meal any other time. Now, her blood had thinned to the point where rage guided her, demanding she finish this tonight. Food was of no concern. It could not be.

Once this was over, there would be plenty of time for that.

She knew that she could take these men. They were brash and arrogant, as most were, and the waterfront battle had sapped all of their will. Even now, their stride slackened. Their hearts roused with a final burst of excitement, but they could not keep pace forever. Just as she would not surrender hers. She had to get behind them and pick off the stragglers.

At the next street, she banked a left and trotted toward the docks once more. A gunshot tore the sky apart, and she knew they had shot the vagrant dead. Maybe a mercy killing, though more likely they could not be bothered to check for a bite, and had assumed the worst.

Behind wolfen eyes, Elisabeth was amused. Nobility was a convenience, a façade that masked selfishness and fear. She wanted this city to see the truth about its protectors, and feel afraid of them.

She twisted through the terrain until her hunters had no line of sight to her. She scampered back over her steps, her nose following the spilt beggar blood. The mauled body was there, leaking from a single bullet through the eye.

She ignored this to focus on the figure standing just beyond it.

One of them.

His back was to her, looking out at the barren street, posed with his rifle at the ready.

The wolf's first instinct was to charge, but human Elisabeth reined in that urge. The creature let it go and rose to her haunches. Her nails clacked across the stone-laid street, and her front arms flexed to strike.

Her claws cut straight through the back of his neck. The sound was a crack, like an axe on wood, and the creature moved with grace, sliding her arm from the body cavity and pushing her mouth against his neck. She ripped it clear with a simple tear, and then dropped the gargling mess.

Next, she headed to the merchant quarters, hugging wall-thrown shadows while moving low against the ground. Her underbelly dragged against the cool street as she crawled, frustrated that her nose could not sniff out the rest of them. These men were not so stupid to split up entirely. Her nose puffed the ground as she searched out the soldiers, wondering why there was no sign of their perspiration.

It was likely they moved in smaller groups. The loose soldier back there assigned clean up, making sure the wolf-mauled body did not change. But why leave him on guard alone?

Her nose stole another sniff, returning only caged dogs somewhere close by. In that moment, she knew that they had not abandoned one of their own.

Before she could turn, she realized why she had not picked up on the presence of others. Barking dogs wiggled her ears, creatures offering hesitant growls at her back. Three of them stood in the alley mouth across from where her victims lay splattered. They bared their teeth, snarling displeasure over her intrusion on their turf.

Behind them, a dark-skinned man clutched an axe in one hand and held a leash in the other.

Elisabeth admired his quick thinking. The dogs could overpower and mask a human scent. Breaking three of them from their alley pen had been enough to fool her.

They were all bark, though. The wolf stood firm. She puffed the fur on her face to inflate her size, summoning her best roar to assert her dominance. The dogs whimpered in response and their terrified steps floundered in all directions, overwhelming their master, who dropped the leash and made a few indecisive motions of his own. Whether he ran or stood his ground, it did not matter. He was as good as dead.

He chose to try to live.

The wolf read his sudden retreat as a taunt. She snarled and darted after him, closing the gap with just a few quick bounds. He did not fight, despite the weapon. She leapt through the air and her front paws pierced his shoulders, knocking him headfirst to the ground, his axe tumbling beneath his chest. The curved silver blade burst through his back and scraped against her chin. Then death throes took him.

Elisabeth felt mild disappointment in seeing him killed by his own clumsiness. She left him thrashing and continued her search of Constanta's back alleys, rushing to beat the rising sun. It would not be long now.

She found them once more on the water and was insulted by how foolish they thought her. The entire order lined the wooden dock as far as it would go, silver weapons glinting in their hands. Two men stood atop the largest ship in the harbor, rifles slung across their chests. Their vantage point afforded a clear line of her only possible approach.

Once they saw her coming, they would retreat until they were all aboard the ship. They would trap her there or do something more destructive, like set it ablaze and watch her burn. Either way, she would not indulge their ambush. Atop *Nightfall*, contentment had dulled her edge, making that trap possible. She had not been content since, and would never be again.

Putting this waylay attempt out of her mind, she set off to find the Survivor. It was better if they stood out there a while longer, wondering about every passing shadow. This while Elisabeth employed her cunning to do what she had come here to finish. The wolf liked the strategy, too. For the first time in what felt like forever, their thoughts were synchronized, welded together by the beauty of this evening's carnage.

The wolf dashed against dwindling night, heading inland. Survivor's week-old stench made him easy to follow. Little nuggets of sweat took her right to the church doorstep, where human Elisabeth felt like laughing.

Of course, they would hide here.

The wolf had no interest in stealth, considering the majority of her enemies were still waiting for her at the water. She smashed her fists through the wooden entrance, and stepped into the narthex. Wood-chipped haze swirled around her as she stepped through the hole, offering a growl that signaled her arrival and carried her inside without fear.

Kill Survivor, and then wait for the order's defeated return.

Take them here, by surprise. She would have all the time necessary to create an appropriate offense against them, and asked the wolf if she could regress so that her human hands could perform the tasks necessary to do this.

The creature did not protest the suggestion.

"She is here," a voice called from across the nave. Disbelief mixed with hopelessness. She never tired of that melody.

Elisabeth froze, but the time for caution had passed. A priest pointed at the fast-galloping wolf. He was undeterred by the unholy sight and refused to surrender his movement. He ran across the altar, ducking beneath an arched doorframe.

The wolf squeezed through. Overhead, rickety stairs creaked and groaned beneath the holy man's weight.

She tilted her head to the side and watched. He moved with more speed than she would have thought possible, considering his age. The stairway was cramped for the wolf and her feet were too large for the treads. Her movement was steady, but slower than she liked.

The confined space gave way to the human's heavy breath. It echoed throughout the tower like a heartbeat, antagonizing the wolf as she climbed.

Pushing against the stairs gave her muscles a workout, and her ascent hastened as she reached the first landing. Somewhere overhead, the priest showed no such slowdown. He moved as if his life depended on it.

A bell started to ring and Elisabeth knew why the rush.

She dropped onto all fours and scrambled for the top, her nails carving grooves into the stairs as she went.

The priest stood at the top, a blade tucked into his fist. With his other hand, he made the sign of the cross and spoke frantic, dribbling Latin.

The wolf cocked her head as human Elisabeth tried

processing the order's arrangement. They wore the dress of several different faiths. It might have been confusing if she did not understand the bottom line: the world had united against her kind.

The Latin grew louder until the priest raised the dagger high and descended. Behind him, the bell continued ringing, even as its momentum slowed.

The others would be on her in a few minutes and then it would be Elisabeth who was trapped.

She tucked her shoulders and kept her snout low as she took steps to meet the full-on charge. The knife stabbed down with surprising force, eliciting a *whoosh*. Before it could land, she pushed her shoulders high and lifted her snout, knocking the priest off balance. He dropped the blade and smashed his back against the stairs. The constricted space stunk of blood then, but the priest refused to be dazed. He kicked at her with fury, screaming in his foreign tongue, words so desperate they were almost hateful.

Elisabeth wound her neck and watched his feet flail. The wolf was like a dog captivated by torchlight shadows. Her jaws reached apart and darted out, catching a leg. With a snap, her teeth took it off, and then she dodged spurting blood.

Even so, the father would not be incapacitated. He pulled along the railing, attempting to stand on his good foot. It was tiresome. Elisabeth took that ankle in her claws and twisted. The skin rolled up onto itself looking like a corkscrew. With a yank, it popped free. A human whimper boomed as she tossed the foot off the rail.

A deterrent for those coming to challenge her.

"Up there!"

Voices from below.

The wolf glanced over the ledge. If she could have smiled, she would have. The stairwell was much too narrow for them to traverse it any way other than single file. At first, she thought they were going to be foolish enough to do that.

"Light it, brother."

Another command from the darkness. This as five men wound their way up to face her. Elisabeth was about to start down to greet them when she saw a series of dancing flames reach through the arched doorway. She flexed her eyes to see one of the warriors holding two torches. He lit the stairwell, but the fire was slow to catch.

Those rushing headfirst were guaranteed death.

Elisabeth loved it when men threw their lives away for the greater good. Though she supposed she might have to rethink her claims of insincere nobility. If she did not want these bastards dead so badly, she might have been impressed.

Her growl fell down the belfry with enough acoustic force to sound like twenty wolves. Her steps dropped like thunder. The impending battle dominated her focus. All that mattered was getting the first strike. Get that, kill the first, and the others would die without challenge.

The bottom stairs caught flame, and it looked as if the men were charging from the fires of hell. She hit the landing as the first man reached it. A saber rattled through the air and caught her between two claws, cleaving inward through her paw. Elisabeth had another hand though, and her nails dove through the warrior's armor and lifted upward.

His innards rushed to escape the vertical splits and they plopped across the stairs. Elisabeth took the sword in her hand and yanked it free. Just in time to stab it straight through the nose of the next in line.

The wolf had never taken a life with a weapon before. She watched the blade with curiosity as the head tipped back and the body became an obstruction to the advancing men. She wasted no time in diving for them with her mouth wide. Her teeth shredded the neck of number three, tearing ligaments and muscles free as a patch of blood slapped her across her nose and eyes. She swallowed the unpleasant tissues as two bullets fired off and struck her, one in the shoulder and the other in the neck.

Elisabeth slipped and fell against the stairs.

There was commotion and screaming, but nothing was as loud as the roaring flames. Two crusaders came forward, one holding a smoking single-shot gun, while the other balled a six-shooter in his fist. She rolled to her side, shielding her face from the inevitable sting. Three shots boomed and her ribs erupted in pain.

The wolf clawed her way up to the next landing, over the blood-run bodies that clogged the steps. Her claws closed around the embedded silver blade and yanked it from the demolished face with a slurp.

She braced herself for two more stings of silver as she spun back around, but they never came. The wolf kipped, lunging forward with the sword and plunging it through the heart of the eager gunman, whose reflexes had failed him in the end.

The last of the assassins dropped his spent pistol, choosing to wield a cleaver because there was no time to reload. The blade chopped her limb, leaving a runny hole the size of a mouth on her forearm. Her newfound sword dropped from her claw with shock.

A whimper slipped from Elisabeth as she reached out for his weapon hand. She took a step and flashed her teeth. They stretched and dripped with eager saliva as she pulled wide. In her outlying vision, he fumbled for something else. Another weapon.

Elisabeth howled and then chomped down on his face. His bones cracked as she opened her mouth and swung them shut once more. One of his eyeballs broke in her mouth, but the awful taste of puss did not deter. Her jaws opened and shut until there was nothing but a stump of broken, mealy bone and runny pulp.

The fire approached and threatened to take the landing upon arrival. She let him drop from her relaxed grip. The only escape was back up, although it was hard to tell what good that would do. These fools had given their lives to trap her here.

Blood ran from her gashed appendage and she whirled on her feet to start another awkward climb. When she reached the next landing, she saw two vertical openings in the tower, but the wolf was far too large to get through them.

Then she saw the grappling hooks wedged into the stone ledges and realized that she had not yet won.

Death bellowed from above, coming in the guise of an axe blade slicing through her shoulder. The crusader's feet hit the wooden landing just after she felt the pain, but there was no time to face him. Another one rushed down the stairs and shot her. The silver pellet missed her eye and broke through her cheek, decimating her vision. Her eye dimmed and barely saw.

She took him in her fist and lifted him off the floor. His gun fired again and the silver landed directly beneath the first shot. Blood splattered across her rippled snout and stung her good eye. The wolf roared her displeasure as he shot again, screaming as he pulled the trigger. The next pellet hit her mouth, exiting through the back of it.

The sound of a body dropping from behind them—

She could not afford to look any more than she could suffer another shot, pulling the trigger-happy assassin against her shoulder with such force that the jutting, embedded blade broke through his forehead. He dangled off her like a fleshy piece of armor, and she whirled to face the last of them.

He was sprawled across the ground, a silver pellet blown through the top of his head, taken by friendly fire.

Elisabeth dropped, exhausted. The fire had not yet eaten its way up here, though it gained momentum. She could hurl herself over the railing and hope the drop did not cripple her, only there was no water to break her fall this time.

She could not say for certain what would happen to an immune wolf if she spattered, and did not wish to find out.

Let me return, Elisabeth thought, calling her attention to the grappling hooks. She expected the wolf to balk at this suggestion, but it was embraced, almost immediately.

The beast pushed the dangling human shield from her body and lifted the axe free. Then she closed her good eye and looked to her human form to finish this.

○

It was hard to feel hopeful about anything.

Timothy's head thumped from being smashed—the only way they had been able to get him inside this cell. The back of his cranium swelled. A tender mound grew beneath his hair, raw to the touch. It prompted the kind of pain that ignited whenever he moved his head or rolled his eyes. If he did anything besides stare whichever way his head was already aimed, it was a crippling migraine.

It was also the least of his problems.

The cell was a closet. His legs were tight and he was desperate to stretch them. The space was so confined that he could not move but a sliver's length in any direction. Because he could not do it, he suddenly *needed* to do it. It was like standing in an upright coffin. Maybe it was just as well that he got a head start on his fate. He was tired of running.

Salih looked at him through the tiny window of grey bars. His voice talked tough, but there was remorse in his eyes. He took no pleasure in this interrogation. "If you have nothing to hide, we'll discover the truth soon enough."

"It happened as I said!" Timothy's voice was a roar. The wrong move, he knew. Salih would read it as desperation and think that captivity was getting to him. The truth was that Sebastian had taught him to withstand worse than this. The only thing bothering him was the idea of being caged when an unstoppable wolf ran loose.

Timothy's heart pounded as he thought of Raven, but Salih seemed tired of his pleas.

"Look," the scribe snapped. "No one wants to travel to Rodica, but that was all I could arrange to prevent your execution. The warders will not believe your story. Many of them have killed for less. Understand where I am coming from."

Timothy did. He hated it, but the position was clear. He had to remain cramped in here until daybreak. He tried relaxing, somewhat encouraged by the positive side of Salih's words. The man had apparently stuck his neck out beyond what was customary. If the roles were reversed, Timothy wondered if he would have done the same and gave the thought a toss when the answer depressed him. He pleaded with Salih to keep careful watch. "Because the Raven will come," he said.

Someone's entrance to the cellar chamber was signaled by a thunderous slam of the door. Timothy could not see the new arrival from where he stood, but Salih, who leaned against a table across the way, leapt to his feet with startled reflexes. His body language was rigid as he looked toward the stairs, but his shoulders soon relaxed and his weapon hand fell with them.

"The wolf is here. The belfry burns but she refuses to die!"

Salih threw Timothy a revelatory glance that might have been validating any other time. He shuffled against the wall on worn legs, too nervous to speak. Once the words found the courage, he blurted, "I can help."

The scribe fumbled with the locking mechanism while the

warder hurried past, moving into a different room. "I am going to open this," Salih whispered.

Timothy nodded with so much eagerness that it was nearly a seizure.

"But you will not help us. You will run."

"How can I run if she is upstairs?"

The warder returned with a pile of weaponry in his arms, a mixture of long and short ranges. The things they had thrown at her on that mountain. Garrick's plan had only made her angry.

"He doesn't run," the warder said in an accent nearly as thick as Salih's. "He fights beside us."

"This is not his fight," Salih said. "Someone must know what happened here." He edged the cell door open. It creaked and Timothy nearly tumbled from the crevice.

The scribe was wrong about this not being his fight, it was his more than theirs, but Timothy would not argue this time. Long gone was the inclination to do so. If there was a chance he could get away from this mess, he was taking it. His mind was a canal floating that single concern. This was not yet over. The bitch had not yet won. The maimed vision of his future did not have to come to pass—

The warder's hand trembled as he loaded a pistol with silver pellets. He might have taken an oath on behalf of his order, but his robes, perhaps dignified on their best day, were lathered in soot and accented with crimson lashes. His eyes were soaked and his lip quivered. A man who did not want to die, but whose pledge held greater sway than his survival.

Salih slipped a gun into Timothy's hand and helped him across the room. He opened a wooden door and they overlooked a descending stairwell.

"Go," Salih said. "Now."

Timothy took a few steps and then recalled the last time

this man had opened a door for him.

Sensing his reluctance, Salih came onto the landing with him and closed the door.

"They would've killed you if not for her," he said. "Your trust could never be proven to their satisfaction. I'm sorry I lied, but the order was never going to allow you to leave here."

Timothy had questions, but none were as pressing as the need to defend his life. He thought about urging these men to come along. Surely, they were stronger in a group of three, although it had not helped Sebastian and Garrick. He started down the stairs and looked back once more. Salih was about to turn, but caught Timothy's motion and froze.

"You will die," Timothy said. He had meant this as a question, though it sounded a declaration. Probably more accurate.

Salih nodded. His forced smile could not hide the horror in his eyes—a man walking willingly to his grave. "If we must die, then we do it while upholding the order, so that we may go to the next life in honor."

For a moment, Timothy was compelled to hold his ground and fight. He owed these men nothing, and did not mourn their fallen, but this would never end while Raven lived.

"No," Salih said, sensing his reconsideration. "You don't understand. No one can know we exist. If Garrick truly drafted you for help, know that he intended to kill you at the end of it."

Garrick's frosty demeanor and silver-bladed cruelty made sense at last. Sebastian told him once of the things he had caught the warder doing to the prisoner wolves inside Freywald. A few weeks later came Ritter's cold-blooded murder, and then Sebastian's poisoning.

To which you agreed.

"He will die humanely," Garrick had said in the hallway of that inn. "Without pain."

So the witch-finder had wanted Sebastian to die there. Less of a mess to clean up later. He must have figured that Constanta was close enough to reach with just one man, saving at least one bullet for Timothy's skull.

Sebastian could've been saved, then.

He wanted to ask Salih for confirmation, but now was not the time for a discussion of alchemy. The answer was known in his gut, and Timothy would go to his grave knowing that he could have prevented his friend's death.

That thought stuck him like a blade to the heart.

He took a few more steps until he was far outside the cone of torchlight, eager to leave these fools to their crumbling crusade.

I hope she kills you both.

Then he was moving through the dark.

Alone again.

○

Elisabeth came into the church, stepping over the splintered door that the wolf had earlier smashed. She was so broken and torn that she could only shuffle her feet in the slightest forward motion. Anything more and her body threatened to stop then and there.

She dug silver pellets from her face with cracked nails as she staggered past the pews. Her body was ripped, painted red with still-spilling blood. The palms of her hands bled from rope burns accrued from her tower descent.

Somehow, those hurt the most.

The curved bell tower entrance looked like a roaring fireplace. The heat tickled her from here and she sauntered away from it, shambling beneath the Stations of the Cross to avoid it. The back of her throat burned where a silver pellet had torn a hole, though every shot had missed her vitals. She tried to laugh but her damaged tongue made a mushy noise much closer to a chicken's cluck.

The hallway off from the altar led to the priest's bedchamber. She dragged her feet inside, searching for unwanted surprises, such as additional bodies that could flank her as she entered the down chamber.

The room was sparsely decorated. A bed tucked into the corner wearing a tangled sheet, with a small crucifix nailed into the wall beam above. His dresser housed different vestments and cassocks, and was devoid of any personality.

A bottle of alcohol sat on the floor near the bed. It took every bit of strength to reach it. Its pointed stench stabbed upward through her nostrils. Very assuring. This would do nicely. She lifted it to her face and let the contents bathe her.

Every cut and wound cried out at once, but relief quickly washed the irritation away.

She then passed through the stone hallway's other ingress, finding the winding stairwell she knew would be here. Every rat had a hole. It descended into cool, musty confines and she stopped at the bottom, in front of the wooden entrance. Her heart trundled, a feeling that she resented, as she stared at the door with hazy vision. She struggled with clipped breaths and tried summoning her senses to understand what waited beyond it.

She pushed in and her eyes struggled to adjust to the darkness. The torches had only now been extinguished. They were still smoky and cooling as she shut the door behind her. Her pupils enlarged in the blackness to cover the front of her eyes. Without ambient light, her vision was as useless as theirs, or nearly so.

Her wolf's ears would lead her right to them, though there was no trouble finding their shallow breaths in this plunging blackness. Two men, both positioned at the back of the room, tried their best at silence, despite tense bodies and terror spilling off them like sweat.

Elisabeth guessed they were counting on her advance. Her knees bumped against a table and her hands fell atop it. She traced the length while moving, searching for its edge. Once her fingers dropped off the side, she ran her toes along the floor until they brushed against steel.

A leg-hold trap.

It prompted a smile. This was cunning, almost commendable. The fools had chosen to make their final stand. They might have snared her if she had been just a little less hurt and a little more eager.

She went to her right and found another table that extended across the middle of the room and to the wall. Their hope was to funnel her right through the center, but Elisabeth got to her knees and crawled beneath the blockade.

The back of the room rustled, knowing now their trap had not worked.

Chairs were pushed in against the table, barring her exit. If she moved any of them, she was tipping them to her approach. She could not sustain any more damage without losing consciousness, and that could not happen while she was in the belly of the beast. They surely had the means to lock her away forever, and would do much worse to her body in the process.

Elisabeth considered those atrocities. It would not be the first time supposedly good men harbored more cruelty than the allegedly evil ones. The memories returned to her without warning, as they were wont to do. The way sick men, crusaders, struck her mother down with sadistic laughter. How they took pleasure in eradicating her village, burning away lives like they were nothing more than piles of dried brush.

How they had orated their pent lusts in her ear while

forcing her to march—too stunned to understand what was happening.

A burst of strength from the wolf took her. It came as simply as a flexing muscle, and Elisabeth pushed upward with a growl. Her back rippled and the table rushed up to greet the ceiling. It smashed and tumbled somewhere behind her. The wolf's snarl pulled from her damaged throat and was somewhat hollow as she strode forward in the chaos, sending the chairs scattering in every direction so her approach could not be pinpointed.

Her body was stuffed with too much silver for anything beyond a momentary surge, and the wolf went whimpering into her subconscious once more.

But it was enough. She had managed to breach their last-ditch blockade, catching a whiff of Survivor as she stomped forward with one of the chairs in hand. He was not among those here, but close by. Her booze-drenched nostrils burned with him as her arms wound back, raking the chair legs along the ceiling.

She hoped the noise was unexpected enough to startle them.

Elisabeth caught a shifting shadow, and she moved wide with the chair while his outline craned to follow the sound. With a roar, she slammed it down and dropped him chin first. She fell onto his back as the chair broke apart, and she was tugging and twisting his hair and then his head, searching for that satisfying crack. It finally came, signaling that he would bother her no more.

This caused the other man to retreat against the wall, his fear leading her straight to him. Dark skinned and drenched in panic, his face broke into tears as she shoved her now ghastly visage into his.

"Shhhhh," she whispered. Her fingers slid down the length of his arm to his wrist, and finally, his hand. She slipped the dagger from his grip, closing her hand around it, pushing inward, through his soft belly where the skin broke without effort.

The blade cut into him and he crashed against her, his stomach splitting and then spilling. The center of his sternum broke and cracked like a walnut. He slipped down her blood-wet body until he was motionless on the floor.

Elisabeth took the time to recover her breath. It was no less labored, although she felt relieved to be rid of these men, even if satisfaction continued to elude her.

After some fumbling, she found a plate of matches on a table and used them to reignite a few of the torches.

The opposite end of the hall housed a small antechamber. Torch in hand, she stepped inside. An iron door sat on the wall beyond it. A planning room with a row of empty seats.

She shrugged it off and returned her attention to the corner desk. It housed several rolls of parchment, many scribbled in an unintelligible language she had never seen. A few bound books offered the same language, and a map of the Carpathian Mountains was stained heavily with black ink.

These men were searching for something and eliminating areas where it was not by marking them off with a black x.

Castle Daciana.

The implication made her nervous. How could they know of its existence? What other knowledge did they possess? There was no time to find out. The church was burning by now, and others would be here soon. She held the torch to the books and papers so that they would join the bell tower in flames.

Elisabeth stepped back into the main hall. The door beside her was an empty cell, and she stared at it in disbelief. *His* overpowering scent broke on her again and again.

He was here. Now, gone.

Beneath her, the dark-skinned man groaned. His will to live was impressive.

Anger and frustration filled her. The joy of murder, of painting this bloody masterpiece, was offset by Survivor's evasion. She knelt beside the wounded man and her muscles shifted. Something about this easy kill goaded the wolf. She loosened her body and the sensation went away. As much as it hurt to do so, she was going to have to speak to this one.

"Where?" Her words were quiet and jagged.

The man tried to speak but a glob of red came bubbling past his lips.

"I will end your suffering if you tell me."

He was only capable of more gurgles.

His organs were coiled on the floor between his legs. Elisabeth stirred them with her hand. In a better mood, she might have giggled while doing so, because the look on his face was so stupid, helpless and pathetic. She watched his eyes tilt toward the back of his head. The noise that followed was a death rattle.

"Not yet." She gave him a harsh slap across his face. It was enough to make his eyes flip back to normal, though any ability to focus was long gone. Her hand moved inside the runny moisture of his opened cavity.

His insides were warm against her wrist and her eyes refused to waver. Every exploratory motion made him wince in a different way, an amazing, empowering sight.

"Be my instrument," she whispered, elbow-deep in him. Her fingers closed around his spine. "Give me this." Her elbow jerked, trying to obtain a sense of how to remove it. "And I will use it to claim the lives of good people. The innocents you sought to defend."

His eyes were dull, the light all but extinguished. A shame he could not comprehend this more fully.

"Accompany me in destruction. *That* will be your legacy."

With a snap, his spine broke free from his head, killing

him at last.

Elisabeth wrestled the bone through the cavity and took it in her hand, holding it along with the dagger as she rushed into the crypts below, following the familiar scent.

She closed her eyes and breathed a sigh of relief. Survivor had not gotten far.

And soon he would go no further.

It was impossible to mask her joy as she hurried down the stairs, eager to make another kill.

O

Timothy moved through the dark with a stiff arm extended out before him. He stepped fast, trying to ignore the sleeping dead on either side. Even in the blackness, he felt their permanent gawks. *What's your hurry?* They seemed to be asking.

The tunnel carried him inland. Occasionally, the direction shifted and his fingers tapped against the open remains of those buried here. A hardened rib cage or a frozen grin. Each was provocation to move faster. Each was a reminder that he was about to join them in permanent slumber.

Timothy remembered that he carried a pistol. It was not much, but could serve him well. Every so often, a shadow scuttled through the gloom and encouraged him to fire it. Probably at nothing more than a rat, though, and he had come too far to surrender to gullibility. After what he had seen, it was beneficial to believe there were worse things down here.

That thought put more speed into his stride. He pushed on, thinking this tunnel had to end sometime. Dying down here was not how this ended. Coming to Constanta suddenly felt like a strategic disaster. Had he truly believed it was going to be as simple as finding the order and telling them about the Raven? Was he expecting a pat on the back and a *we'll take it from here* assurance?

I think I was.

For all his trouble, there was imprisonment and a conspiracy to murder him. Hardly worth his efforts.

And Garrick had been planning to do the same?

He felt ill. Bile rose in this throat like high tide. He had wanted to find and kill Raven, but that courage was dissipating. The Order of Osiris was no better than she. Maybe they hunted varcolac and other abominations, but they were prone to murder innocents for no crime beyond learning of their existence.

For what?

Timothy regretted this peek behind the curtain. Sebastian was dead, same as Evan before, and Mum before that. Striking back against Evan's killers had done nothing for his emotions, except render him morally suspect.

If Garrick had not deceived them in Rodica, they could have faced the wolf together. He put his duty ahead of his need for immediate vengeance, perhaps knowing that Raven would have hunted him to Constanta regardless. If she did not know about the order and their outpost, he might have been able to lure her into another trap.

That was his backup plan all along, the rotten bastard. Had to be. After the mountaintop debacle, he must have figured this was the only way. Drag them through living nightmares, keeping them naïve and loaded with hopefulness—all of it a charade for the werewolf bitch chomping at their boot heels. Garrick wanted Raven to think they were fleeing her when in reality he dangled them like carrots just beyond her reach.

Raven had been smarter than that, however, and now it was Timothy's mess.

His shoulder smacked against something and the ground overhead shook. It pelted him with dirt and light debris. He lifted his jousting arm and his hand skittered across earthen ceiling.

His feet found a bottom tread. He carefully ascended the stairs, counting sixteen of them. Soon his caution arm was burnishing a stone slab.

Why had Salih bothered sending him down a dead end? And if it was not, how was he supposed to find the way out in the dark?

Timothy put his shoulder to the wall and pushed. The soles of his boots stuttered. The slab cracked against his weight and the sound of rock grating against rock led to a shaving of dampened light.

He grunted and pushed harder until the stone came away from the hole with a slow and grumbling *whoosh*.

The room beyond was nearly as dark as the catacombs. There remained little slats of light shining through the tiny windows near the ceiling, just enough to make the décor pop with vague outlines. The dead surrounded him; wall slabs masked what must have been five generations of family. He stumbled inside and dropped to his knees as the door swung back and closed. Timothy turned to find a lever, but there was only a flat wall. No access from this side.

He could shoot his way out of this place if need be, and crossed the room to reach what looked like the entrance. It would not move when he tried budging it, and readied the flintlock.

Maybe it was best that he called off the hunt. No reason to play the hero when everyone who would care was dead. Ignoring the Raven meant stripping her of power. One way to win. She may perceive this as cowardice, and search him out. Nevertheless, the world was big and there were plenty of places to hide.

He took aim at the door but froze.

There was another sound in here.

The sound of hushed laugher—a deranged soul who

could not believe his dumb luck.

The sound of feet falling on the floor.

The sound of excited teeth chattering.

Yellow and familiar eyes lifted out of the darkness.

O

Elisabeth raced through the tunnel, ignoring the pain as it attacked. She followed Survivor's smell like a trail of breadcrumbs. She shifted her ears periodically, hoping to find his precise location.

Up ahead, his heart raged with newfound fear. The *thump thump* was obvious and distinct. The otherwise arid chamber suddenly moist. He was not scared of her but something else.

Something close.

She pushed her feet harder than before, disturbed by the infringing reek of decayed flesh.

O

The vampire came out of the shadows and Timothy was helpless to defend against it. He heard the swoop of raking claws but saw nothing. His chest struck hot, and fresh trails of blood rained off his body.

The evil eyes disappeared, but Timothy lifted the gun anyway. One shot was all he had. It was not enough to put a vampire down, but if the damned creature opened its eyes once more, he could hope to shoot one out and use that time to escape.

It might have been smarter to shoot the door, though there was no time to consider it.

Somewhere close, the vampire's mouth popped. Its tongue slurped off the roof of its mouth. The yellow eyes reappeared, glowing like midday suns.

Timothy winced as the orbs hovered near. Retreating steps afforded him some distance until the crypt's wall scraped his back.

His gun hand trembled as the menacing eyes narrowed, the devilish glare ushering in a sense of inevitability.

Timothy did the only thing he could. The shot rang out and his ears wrenched beneath the boom.

The vampire did not flinch. Sadistic laughter grew. Icy fingers coiled around Timothy's neck, colder than the surrounding stone slabs. Thin, frosty lips followed and Timothy's body froze solid at the monster's touch.

A stinging sensation heralded by two sharp thrusts dove into his jugular. Timothy winced and gasped.

Then he felt his blood dribble to the floor.

THE KINGDOM OF DARKNESS

ELISABETH WATCHED THE VAMPIRE. THE wolf's strength held the one-way slab open, but what she saw made her feel helpless.

In this moment, she realized she had lost.

The parasite seemed stunned by her presence. He released his grip on the Survivor. The bloody boy crumpled as the vampire turned to greet her.

Survivor, pale and stagnant, could hardly be called that anymore, even if he looked like a harder man today. It could have been the death on his face, specifically his acceptance of it, but his features were chiseled now where there had once been doughy innocence. Whatever happened beneath St. Matthew's had changed him.

And he *was* dying. The air in here was stained with spilling life, an admittedly welcome respite from the vampire's odor.

"I did this for you, huntress." Codrin stepped forward in a laconic offering of submission. "You wanted him, and I got him… for *you*."

Elisabeth felt leering eyes once more, his audacity the

ultimate insult. He had cheated death so many times that he took each day for granted, no longer aware that it was luck guiding his continued existence.

Instead of acknowledging, she went to the bleeding boy and studied him.

Meek eyes glanced up.

Their stares held.

Her heart skipped a beat.

There was no hatred there. Elisabeth had watched countless faces die and the look was always a dependable combination of shock and disdain.

This one had every reason to loathe her, almost as much as she loathed him, and yet the flicker of life that remained inside of him was calm.

Peaceful.

He wheezed for air while she chewed the inside of her lip. He had accepted his fate, depriving her of what little satisfaction might have been taken. Killing him now, like this, afforded no closure. There were countless dead men in Constanta, each one taken in Aetius' name. And yet, her pain was worse than ever. She had not been healing, but rather digging at her wound so that it would never close.

Elisabeth could count on the wolf to ensure her physical wounds would, again, heal. In return, the animal depended on her to fill the void spreading in her soul. But Elisabeth could not. There was no peace to be had when all she could think about was death, and never of living.

The realization made her feel ill.

It's pointless now.

"I got him for you," Codrin said again. Perhaps if he repeated the lie a few more times, he would begin to believe it, though she would never.

Elisabeth turned to the crypt door and went toward it in a daze, feeling lost and rudderless.

The vampire growled, incensed by her refusal to acknowledge his lies. He lunged and pinned himself against her back with the full of his body, licking blood off her without a modicum of control. His weight knocked them forward and they smashed the metal entrance.

"Not even a thank you," he said in between licks. "What do I have to do for your thanks? After everything that you took from me?"

Elisabeth thought about sticking the silver blade in his face, but he deserved worse than inconvenience. Her anger brought the wolf bounding. The vampire wrapped his arms around her, squeezing her breasts for grip, as she wobbled and changed. Her increased mass pressed against the door. Her muscles stretched, allocating additional strength through her body. Her fingers curled around the circular latch, and with a growl, she threw herself forward.

It sent them spilling into the earliest rays of morning light.

Codrin shrieked and released her. Elisabeth's reflexes were better now; the wolf spun on her still-human feet, dashing after the sizzling vampire.

Her claws boxed the sides of his head, penetrating flesh and cheekbone as if he were a rotten pumpkin. The severed spine and dagger fell to the grass but she did not need them. She threw her knee against his back and pulled, the two of them tumbling. The vampire screamed. Her hands remained in the parasite's soft and cracking skull.

Codrin's throat bubbled like rising dough. He struggled to say something but it was too late for that. His bursting skin disappeared beneath the angry blaze. She yanked her talons free and pushed him aside, rolling away from the singeing flames.

The wolf, quelled by fire, allowed Elisabeth to return once more. She was beginning to feel as she once had. In control.

Toggling back and forth could be exhausting. It was an ability many varcolac never mastered, and those who did continued suffering from the physical toll it brought.

The wolf would come no further until she got the silver ammunition out of her body. That had to be done soon, but the grass felt cool against her cheek. Her eyes fell shut as somewhere behind her, the long-dead vampire turned to scattering ash.

With a host of corpses inside St. Matthew's, and another soon-to-be dying man inside the crypt, she would have a lot to answer for if she lost consciousness now.

"Help her!" A child's voice jolted Elisabeth. At the bottom of the hill, a young girl held her mother's hand. They watched with reasonable anxiety.

"Help me," Elisabeth slurred, well out of their earshot.

She writhed with as much energy as she had to show them that she was alive.

"She's moving," the mother said. In a moment, approaching steps.

Elisabeth buried her head in the grass to stop them from seeing her smile.

○

Timothy slid against the crypt's farthest wall, recoiling from the sun that reached through the door.

He shivered and rubbed beads of sweat from his forehead. Inbound change tugged from within. For all his efforts, everything he had survived and all of the creatures he had destroyed, he was becoming that which should not exist.

His fingertips tapped the vampire's bite. Pierced holes

were raw to the touch and his neck was sticky hot. It was a twist of fate he could only laugh at. At least Sebastian and Garrick had died fighting *against* these elements. Beaten, yes, but unjoined.

The invading presence demanded his surrender. Focus was a luxury he no longer possessed, feeling only a cursory awareness of his surroundings. His soul was in the process of being reshaped, as if molded from wet clay. The change facilitated a thirst that was difficult to understand. How could he crave something so unnatural?

So demonic…

His morals went next. Right and wrong becoming secondary concepts without meaning, slaves to the thirst.

Puddles of previously spilt blood called to him. Timothy wanted to think that he would crawl into the sun before fulfilling that urge.

Yet you crawled away from it.

He stared out at the greenery, mourning a world that was already unfamiliar. Or fleeting. Bright and lively, something about that orange-kissed aesthetic made his eyes hurt and his stomach nauseous. Beyond the door, the Raven crawled on her belly just out of sight as dark splotches of ash fluttered through the sky around her.

Timothy shriveled into the fetal position. Cloudy eyesight became a gradient of solid yellows and reds. This thirst was an angry infection, constantly throbbing.

Outside, a woman screamed. Her hysteria was severed by a sloppy babble, then her smell drifted inside the crypt like sizzling bacon. Timothy got to his knees, driven by it. A much younger voice screeched next; a high-pitched squeal. The worst he had ever heard.

Even that was not enough to make him stop thinking about fresh blood.

I need it.

He did not yet. His tongue traced the bottoms of his teeth to check and there was nothing abnormal about them. But it was coming. People with amputated legs could feel a rainstorm's approach from a few days out, just as Timothy sensed phantom fangs already crowding his mouth.

The crypt's entrance went dark as the Raven filled the frame, a sobbing child standing perfectly still in front of her. The she-wolf's bloody hands rested on her shoulders, her fingers tapping the fabric of her tiny coat.

It was dark, but Timothy's augmented vision caught sight of the evil grin splashed across her disfigured face. One of her eyes was chalk-white, and two scabrous holes in her cheek were ever wet. The red and yellow hues of Timothy's newfound eyesight rendered her features appropriately demonic.

The bawling child drew no empathy from him and he was stunned by how fast this metamorphosis had taken place. He watched the girl with a predator's stare, thinking about how pleasurable it would be to slice her open and feast.

"You wasted no time embracing it," Raven said. Her tone was jovial, despite its soft raspiness.

"I wish we killed you."

"Stop it," she said. "You tried your best." This time, she coughed and looked annoyed by her forced display of vulnerability.

Timothy's heart raced, energized by the prospect of feeding. He was not supposed to want this. That it was forbidden suddenly excited him.

She nudged the sniffling child forward. "This is yours."

He would not allow Raven to have this satisfaction. To see him shred the last of his humanity. However, the child was fresh and soft, a hot loaf from a baker's oven. Timothy cupped a hand over his damaged chest to discover that his heart no longer pounded. His breastbone was as unresponsive as a slab of beef, but he swore that he felt it all the same. He was certain that it pumped with excitement as he got to his knees and crawled.

"Your change was immediate." The she-wolf sounded dismayed. "If the vampire had not drained you so during his feeding, it would've taken you days to turn."

He got to his feet in defiance and met Raven head on.

"Sorry that Codrin got to me first?" His smile was more triumphant than it should have been, but this was the last weapon he had and he intended to wield it.

He saw faltering composure beneath her mask of arrogance. A flash of annoyance that maybe said, *you've beaten me.*

There was satisfaction in knowing that he *could* trump her somehow. Show that he rejected bloodlust in both his thirst and his compulsion for vengeance. He might even take a bow before stepping into the sun, one final act of defiance.

To think, your greatest contribution to this world will be taking yourself out of it.

Raven was fast. Her hand was like a mallet to his stomach. There was no wind to knock from his lungs, but he still doubled over. His back hit the floor and she splayed her legs over him. Timothy stole an instinctive glance at her sex before she collapsed onto his torso.

Her eyes sparkled with renewed amusement, a maddening sight to behold.

What did it take to humble her?

The child whimpered and crawled off to the side, too terrified to move any further.

"Know what I like most about my kind?" Her voice was thin, but she pushed it above a whisper.

He hated her one blue eye and wanted badly to gouge them both. When he did not speak, drowning instead in revenge fantasies, she continued.

"You never know how the animal will affect you during the Turning. In some cases, our hunger prevails. That would be best for our little friend over there. She has already suffered so much…"

She lifted his hand along the lines of her slender stomach and guided his middle finger to the bloody rivet above her breast, circling the wound.

His finger was thick with crimson and he salivated at the touch. Tunnel vision took over. He needed that blood and pushed himself up, moving closer to it.

She shook her head like a scolding mother and urged him back onto the floor. "No, no, no." She gave a slap to his cheek that was somewhere between playful and insidious—just enough to snap him from the trance.

Timothy opened his mouth and pushed his tongue out, hoping to catch a bead of the blood that dripped sporadically off her.

"Will *you* give her a quick death?" She asked. The child's wails beat his ears like drums. "When your instinct takes over, you'll do anything to sate your hunger. Anything."

Timothy was like a puppy desperate for table scraps. Every thought dropped off until a singular compulsion remained. Blood. He no longer drew breath, but gasped for air anyway. It was a nervous tick that pronounced his anxiety.

"Fine," she said and allowed him to suck his finger clean. Then she touched two of her fingers to her wound and traced one of them around his lips, laughing as he lapped the remnant blood.

It was degrading but he did not care. He tasted the drops with eagerness, nabbing every last bit from the sides of his mouth. The flavor was suddenly sweet, no sign of the bitterness that had dominated this taste when he had been human.

Timothy was reminded of sipping his father's ale as a boy, pretending to like it because that was what men drank. As a teenager, he learned to savor it for real, washing down every meal with a frosty mug.

He had grown to like this as well.

"Please," he said and reached for her middle finger. It was daubed in shimmering ruby blood. His mouth dangled like a hungry newborn eager for a nipple.

"Okay," she purred and placed the wet finger against his tongue. He closed his lips around it and sucked, fellating it up and down until the hunger receded. She wiggled it in mockery and her laughter was precision cruel as he got every last drop off her.

"More," he said. "Please."

Elisabeth nodded and slid off his hips and onto his torso. Her buttocks glided across his abdomen and warmed his cold flesh through his shredded shirt. She leaned in so that her wound ran directly into his mouth.

He took her in his hands. The folds of her flesh were soft, pleasing to touch even for his deadened senses. It was almost arousing as his mouth rubbed against her toned belly on the way to the feeding. The smell of spilled blood was an aphrodisiac that ignited his senses.

His tongue slipped into the creased cut and he slurped it. His strength grew and soon he lapped the errant trails that spilled down her body. He would loathe himself once these desires had been serviced, but he did not care about that now.

Her hand ruffled his hair, a touch that was almost caressing. Her moan grew into more snickers as she came forward to show her killing face, signaled by a serrated smile. Inhuman eyes swirled blue and yellow, bursting and crazed. Teeth resembled incongruous spikes, slicing through runny gums and raining blood all over. His appetite shriveled as tufts of matching black hair burst from her smooth-as-silk skin.

The wolf attacked his neck, stealing a hunk from it. She shifted and wavered again, trading the animal's features for chiseled human cheekbones. She chewed his meat, swallowing with a look of discomfort.

"For you, maybe other urges will win out," she said with another hard swallow and deep breath. "You struggle to repress certain desires as all men do. Whatever your fantasy, you may feel compelled to act on it now."

"Kill me," Timothy's voice was barely there.

"Oh, no. Never." She laughed again. "I needed you to be strong. That is the only reason you fed from me, parasite. Without my blood for reinforcement, your undead flesh would've buckled. Your head would've been torn completely off and that would never do. Trust me, crusader, I *want* you to survive my bite."

Timothy tried pushing her off but she was stronger. No matter how impossible it seemed, her sleek frame belied her might. Her arms tightened and kept him pinned.

"Maybe you're already one of…*them*, but do you want to know what happens to a parasite after he's bitten by a varcolac? You inherit our strengths and weaknesses…and that's double the ways for you to die. Try harming yourself, and you'll succeed only until the wolf sets in and heals you. Suicide is not something that we understand."

Raven took Timothy's chin and guided it in the direction of the child. The kid looked on with miserable eyes.

"No matter what you do to her, you *will* become a far greater monster than I ever was. And you'll have no choice but to live with it. Hero."

Timothy scrambled out from underneath her, standing. Raven was faster, delivering a shove that hurled him across the room. His head bounced against a stone slab. Heightened vision wobbled and dimmed; then darkness.

A child screaming in it.

Hurried feet rushing off.

He picked his head up and sprung forward without a plan as the door swung closed in his face.

Balled fists rained against it but the wolf woman was powerful enough to resist. The door came pushing back, bouncing against his chin as it scraped alongside the stone jamb. A mist of shaved grit kicked up and clouded his eyes as it wedged shut.

There was no way to get it open while he was this weak.

A sweeping panic attack took firm and he came away from the door a defeated man. The wolf's bite had not, as of yet, affected him as it had others he had seen. Throughout the earliest wing of their journey, they had found several wearing it and the symptoms were constant: terrible infection, attached to a domineering fever that prompted maddening and incoherent hallucinations.

He felt nothing of that sort and was glad for small favors.

Until he realized it was because he was already dead.

Timothy's hands fumbled for the secret entrance that had delivered him to this demise. It was so obscured from this side that he wondered if it had ever been there at all. He pushed against the masonry and hoped the wall would depress and slide open. No use.

What other purpose did this passageway serve if not a secret entrance back beneath ground? There had to be an access panel in here somewhere, some way to get it open.

He carried out a whirlwind search, burning through his energy as he explored every possible cranny. Pried sarcophagi gave way to skeletons spun in cobwebs. They greeted him with toothy smiles as he spread their bones in frantic exploration.

Once the crypt was ransacked, and evidence of their

entrapment was apparent, stomach acid sprayed past his lips as he dropped to the floor and groaned.

Across the room, the little girl lifted her head and stole a slight peek. Tiny eyes glistened in the space between her knees and arms. Fear governed her.

Timothy's immediate instinct was to offer comfort but he resisted. Comfort would inevitably bleed into something worse, and there would be no stopping it.

He could not muster empty assurances when the worst was yet to happen, so he rocked back and forth, hoping to stave off the gnawing intrusion until he thought of a way out. The vampire's thirst was present, but its demand lacked prominence, temporarily stunted by the wolf's bite. His innards shifted once more, creating a monster beholden to two sets of rules.

The delayed thirst was certain to return, and it would be on top of something else.

The hunger.

Just a few drops of blood off the wolf's fingers had been invigorating. A little more would give him the necessary strength to un-wedge the crypt door. A child's blood would not pack the same punch, though, and he realized he would need to drink a lot more of it.

He felt his features blacken and was glad the child could not see him leering at her from between the cracks of his fingers. His sharpened teeth were little more than protruding nubs as his thoughts stretched into the unholiest places he had ever gone.

How much can I drink without killing her? Without turning her? I just need strength.

This consideration killed any altruism he still had, eroding the person Timothy Hackett once was. His thirst grew in the face of her tears, taunting him. Sapping her was the only way they could get free before the wolf took hold and ripped her to shreds.

Maybe she died beneath his bite, but there was no alternative where she was not at risk.

"I wish there was another way," he said. It was more for his benefit. But he rejected the thought as soon as he had decided upon it. His hand slammed against the floor and he cursed his misery aloud. It spooked the child into screaming. He sprung up in frenzy provoked by her wail.

"I'm trying to help you," he screamed.

Her pitch wrapped around him and squeezed. He did not think voices could carry beyond that door, but her hysteria was potent enough that he considered it.

Someone may come looking for her. If they got close enough, they would hear something, surely.

"We'll just wait," he said and leaned against the center slab. "How does that sound? You go ahead and cry as loud as you have to."

She did. He shut his eyes and tried to think. Could not focus on anything but her agony, though. He stood reborn, a resident of waking nightmares. Satanic images tunneled endlessly through his consciousness.

These desires were intruders on the brain, startling enough that he nearly joined her in screaming. But that horror faded as he slipped away from the crypt's realities, his mind crafting a comfortable world of classroom lectures to inhabit. His old friend Thomas Hobbes had labeled this type of willful ignorance the kingdom of darkness, cautioning against what Timothy now craved. It was the only state-of-mind that offered asylum.

His humanity would hold out for as long as it could, but resistance felt like a fairy tale, unattainable comfort that would not spare the girl in the end.

She cried louder, as if sensing the only thing left for her to do was die.

This was Timothy Hackett's life now.

He took an instinctive breath and sighed.

This was hell on earth.

○

Elisabeth slipped into the dead mother's clothes. The corpse looked like chewed paper and she discarded it as such, kicking it from her path. Even that was a struggle. Blood-seeped and tattered ribbons covered her body with enough modesty to help her reach Constanta without suspicion.

She did not walk as much as wobble toward it.

There should have been something more than what she felt. Ambling away from the graveyard, wondering about all she had accomplished.

Thinking that she had not accomplished very much.

Survivor would be a wolf in a matter of days, and the child would most likely be dead before sunrise, a victim of parasitic thirst. That was the preferred outcome, because he would not be able to blame the animal for it.

If a hypothetical rescue were to occur before then, it was merely a prelude to a massacre. The details of whom he might kill and why did not matter, just as long as Survivor found it impossible to live with the aftermath.

Condemning him to an eternity of torment had been her masterstroke. As with any art, improvisation was often the catalyst for pure inspiration.

She smiled at that thought, but the gesture was empty and forced.

Was this the smartest course? Allowing him to have a life of any kind guaranteed that his bloodlust would eventually catch back up to her. As had been the case with the vampire, and even the familiar one before him, it was something that would bite her when she least expected. A vicious circle with a closed, binding loop.

Elisabeth was willing to take that chance when it was the only way left to hurt him.

Her ratted hair hung in her face and her arm crossed against her chest, keeping pressure on her runny shoulder while holding the torn clothes in check. She laced through a host of early morning crowds, unable to focus on anything. The dagger and spine hung in her hand and she was much too tired to care about how this looked to the bustling masses.

Unsurprisingly, most of them were happy to avoid her completely, crossing to the other side of the street, or averting their eyes as they feigned sudden interest in the ground.

She evaded whatever eye contact happened to drift her way. The St. Matthew's steeple reached up over the cityscape in the distance, still smoking, but without flame. How great it would have been if the order's final defense had set the city ablaze.

This was her thought as she knocked against the wall. Her head swiveled and sleep became an irresistible lure. The ground at her feet swayed and the contents of her hand spilled.

"Are you okay?" A young woman burst from the crowd and knelt in front of her. Samaritan hands inspected her bloody and torn rags with a gasp. The touch was appropriately gentle, as only a woman's could be. Elisabeth felt warm fingers tilt her head back. She spoke quickly in her native tongue, allowing Elisabeth to catch only a few words.

The woman tried a few more questions. When Elisabeth did not answer a single one, she took matters into her own hands. Samaritan guided her upright and Elisabeth snatched for her discarded belongings. Even in this sudden haze, the spine was important. She called it a "trophy," hoping to alleviate any suspicion.

The Samaritan took it in between two fingers and wretched. Elisabeth grabbed it from her and then dropped all of her weight against the girl as they shuffled on.

"We don't have far to go," Samaritan said.

They disappeared into one of Constanta's many alleys. A back door creaked after several knocks and they were inside a house. Another pair of hands lifted part of her weight and Elisabeth's toes brushed along the floor and then scraped against stair treads on the way up.

Female voices spoke, but remained hollow.

Awareness came and went as cool water cascaded down her body. Cloth daubs refreshed her wounds. They might have dressed them, too, though her eyes did not feel like opening to confirm the sensations.

At last, things were quiet and she slept.

Until the moon glow came through the window and roused her. Her legs were restless and she kicked them to vanquish the stir. A woman in a white bodice rose from her chair and rushed bedside. She took a glass of ice water from the night table and tilted it against Elisabeth's lips. It was revitalizing, and she smiled at the stranger's unnecessary display of care.

"Here, drink it all." Her voice was comforting. "I cannot imagine how thirsty you must be."

"How long," Elisabeth paused mid-question to cough. Her throat still burned, even though the water temporarily cooled it.

"Three days," the woman said. "We thought you were dead. Do you remember who did these things to you?"

Elisabeth wanted to laugh at the question. To mock the conclusion that some boorish drunkard or repressed politician could have done this to her. But she did not feel the mood was right for antagonism and let it slide.

She searched for the native tongue she had long abandoned, dusting off its syllables with hesitation. She took the thick and comfortable blanket off her legs and found that they had slipped a light blue gown over her. She pulled the V-neck away from her chest and found that all of her wounds had, in fact, been bandaged.

Her shoulder ached from where the axe had struck, but if three days had passed, then it was surely healed and she was grateful they had wrapped it. It spared awkward conversation in the event they checked again and discovered it had vanished. Her eye was also confident once more. She pushed up on the mattress and rearranged into a sitting position, touching her cheek and smiling as she felt only faint scars where bullet holes had been.

"We have never seen you before," the girl said. "Emilia knows all of us…tradeswomen."

"It is a big city," Elisabeth said and took another drink of water.

"Which is why your presence is surprising. I mean, the bathhouses are one thing. Massage boys selling sex behind those walls, little girls brought in to relax the men who crave them. Disgusting. But outside those terrible places? I assumed that everyone worked for Emilia."

"Not everyone does."

"But everyone should," this was another voice. Elisabeth turned as the Samaritan entered the room. Her features were less kind in the moonlit glow. She offered Elisabeth a cursory glance before joining her on the featherbed, pressing her palm against her forehead as she sat. "Lest you find yourself on the receiving end of another animal who does not wish to pay for his urges."

"I can handle myself."

"I have no doubt about that. You clearly know what you're doing, which again, is why you should work for me. My services extend to every part of this city, even beyond it if the price is right."

Elisabeth tipped her head and stared at the moon. "I think it's best that I leave this life behind."

Emilia tsked her tongue. "Shame. I could make a lot of coin for you. And these girls are under *my* protection. What happened to you will never happen again."

"You're right about that."

"Think on it, then?"

"I already have."

"Better to spread your legs than work your fingers to the nub hauling fish from the ocean."

Elisabeth considered this and decided that she agreed, if forced to choose between the two extremes. But only if a woman was free to select her patrons by hand. Emilia might have been offering asylum, but the immediacy of her proposal illustrated how she viewed Elisabeth: an investment opportunity, and probably nothing more.

Maybe she cared for her women, but Elisabeth guessed they still had to bring home coin at the end of each day. By any means necessary.

"Thank you," Elisabeth said, the sincerity in her own voice was surprising. "But I should go."

"Is nothing. It's best that we take care of each other. No one else will, yes? And no, you will not leave yet. Your fever may be gone, but you must sup with us and have another good night's rest. I insist."

Dinner was served downstairs. Sarmale, which was minced meat wrapped in cabbage leaves. Elisabeth was not hungry for it, though she quickly ate her share, swallowing red wine by the goblet and listening to the evening woman swap trade stories. They were impressed by their perception of Elisabeth as a rogue nightcaller, and accepted her presence by looking to her for approval at the end of each anecdote. She smiled and nodded, laughed when it was appropriate, and feigned disgust when she was supposed to. She felt welcome here, and it warmed her, even if she could not wait to leave.

The conversation circled the table until Elisabeth's mysterious arrival could no longer be ignored. The women wanted to know more about her, threading their inquiries through regular dinnertime chatter until their curiosity brimmed.

Emilia was careful not to pry, always respectful of her guest's privacy. "If she does not wish…"

"It's fine," Elisabeth said and polished off her fourth glass of the night. The girl beside her refilled the goblet and pushed it close, eager for an overshare. "I paid a debt, and nearly died while doing it, as you saw."

"I hope you made him suffer." One of the women brushed her hair behind her ear to reveal a small piece of it missing. There were teeth marks on the lobe.

"Me too," Elisabeth said.

"It will be safer for you here, you know," Emilia said. "I offer protection, nothing more. You pay me a pittance for your room in this house, and for the food you eat. Otherwise, it's your living to earn. The Ottoman rule may be ceremonial for the time being, but what happens when Constanta must do more than simply bow to the Sultan?"

"Well," Elisabeth said, considering her next words with precision. "Then you'd do well to consider leaving. You can only protect your girls from so much. And never from warlords. This house will be the first to fall, your women conquered and passed around like trophies."

"Experience is the cruelest teacher, I suppose." Emilia flashed a smile that suggested understanding. "But of course

I agree with you. None of this would be necessary if these girls could earn a safe living on their own. That's important to me, you know. Them *living*."

Elisabeth smiled. "I don't need your help to do that."

Emilia's next glance lasted an eternity. It caused each of Elisabeth's injuries to throb once more, as if accenting her point.

The front door swung open and a man spilled into the firelight. Emilia rose to meet him head-on, resolute in her motion with a pistol tucked into her hand.

"Huntress," he said, and bent a knee.

Elisabeth took her place beside Emilia, watching as if this could not be real. "Claude?"

The young pup looked up and smiled. "Nothing has ever filled me with more relief," he said. "When I found the mountain site…discovered Aetius…"

Elisabeth went to him. He pointed his head back to the floor, maintaining his gesture of servitude. The boy looked good. His dress was crisp, his face clean-shaven. No older than Survivor, she recalled finding him on a battlefield in the stickiest summer months. He had been quick to accept his Turning for reasons he kept to himself, even when asked.

Those who passed through the bite became a slave to their instincts, and Elisabeth had assumed that Claude was too ashamed to fess up to his. Their animal urges were often guided by human impulses.

Aetius had gone on to enjoy the boy's enthusiasm so much that he had tasked him with an important errand.

One that he had finally returned from, apparently.

"We should leave, my huntress." Claude growled, the change eminent.

"No," Elisabeth said and motioned for him to stand. "You mustn't."

The young man's features moved, his brow wobbled and his arms trembled.

Elisabeth took his hand in hers and shook her head with vigor. "They *saved* me." She could not say why she suddenly cared about that. Only that she did.

The boy could not shake the wolf like Elisabeth. She put her head to his and whispered, "We leave without doing this…just this once, this is how it must be."

What she wanted was to leave everything. Reach Paris, spend an obscene amount on a luxurious silk mantua, and find a beautiful aristocratic apartment in which to weather the coldest months. All so she could lose herself in the culture there. All so she could forget she was alone.

The void that ate her soul was irreparable, yes. But maybe with time—

No. She did not think so. Never again. The pain was too great. The loss, crippling. The hunters *had* killed a piece of her after all.

"We really must go," Claude suggested once more, his eyes lost in hers. It was wrong for Elisabeth to suggest there could be something between them, but there was no other way to send his wolf scurrying.

"I was going to ask about this," Emilia handed her a sack. "But I think it's best you leave now and not return."

Elisabeth peered inside and saw the crusader's spine as Emilia's eyes blazed with superstitious knowledge she would not dare speak aloud. Elisabeth wished her no harm and knew the only way to ensure that was to go.

"Your kindness," Elisabeth said. "I won't forget it."

Claude put his coat around her shoulders as they stepped into the chilly night. "We are in the process of securing passage on the next ship out of harbor. It wasn't hard to track you here, but your scent is all over these streets."

Elisabeth did not feel like talking about it. She had to picture Survivor draining every drop from the orphan girl in order to remind herself that Aetius had, in fact, been avenged. The feeling of triumph was so slight that it had already faded completely.

She had planned to return to Nightfall one last time. To see her lover as she had left him: mutilated parts charred beyond recognition. But that was already a memory she wished to forget. Aetius was long departed, and she had only stared indifferently at his pieces. She did not wish to be this cold, but her attachment was no longer to those broken and burnt vestiges.

Nostalgia was tied to memories of their life, but even those would fade in time.

"I wanted to bring these to you," Claude said. He reached into his satchel and dropped some unbroken fangs into her palm.

Elisabeth held them tight, not yet ready to abandon her lover completely.

This was more loyalty than she deserved in the wake of what she had done to his brothers. They went in silence toward the water, and were almost there before Elisabeth remembered she did not know where Aetius had sent him.

"Rome," he said as they stepped onto the docks, far away from Codrin's decrepit shack that had fallen into the Black Sea nights ago.

Claude led her to a large cargo ship. The man standing in front of the ramp smiled at their approach. "This is her?" He sounded excited.

"It is," he said. "Huntress, meet Luca."

Elisabeth lifted her eyebrow, looked at Claude and sighed. Luca was human, and the tension that lined his body language hinted that he had been promised something.

"Are we all set?" Claude said.

"Right this way." Luca nodded and started up the ramp. "We were able to secure two quarters. Of course, Elisabeth Luna will have her own, and the cargo has already been placed there."

"Good," Claude said. "Please, huntress, there is something in there you'll want to see."

They went below deck and Luca pushed open the first door on the right. "This is yours," he said. "And I do hope you'll indulge me in conversation while we are at sea. I have so many questions."

Elisabeth did not know what to make of Luca's persistence and admiration. She only knew that she wanted him out of her sight. Her response was a stubborn smile that lasted just a moment. Then she brushed her arm against Claude's elbow. "Where does this ship go?"

"France, my huntress," Claude said.

"It's Elisabeth now. Just Elisabeth."

Claude nodded as he and Luca went into the room across the way. Before shutting the door, he turned to her. "Luca was very helpful in retrieving it."

"Retrieving what?"

"You'll see. Get some rest, my hunt…Elisabeth."

The quarters were not all that extravagant, but cozy enough. The featherbed was currently more inviting than Alina's throne room, and the breakfast table had a spread of fruit laid out, along with an unopened bottle of wine. Elisabeth looked at the teeth in her hand until she felt tears dribbling off her chin.

"Goodbye," she said.

Those words were colder now than they should have been, obligatory and almost meaningless.

She put the teeth inside the sack with the spine and left them on the floor. Before she could even consider getting out of this stupid gown and climbing into bed, a knock rapped against the door.

Claude hovered in the crevice. He had looked less terrified while dying on the battlefield.

"How are your, uh…"

"Accommodations?"

"Exactly! Those…if the bed is too small I can…"

"Thank you, Claude." She smiled, and for the second time tonight she had been grateful for help. These dormant feelings had been gone for so long she had forgotten they existed, and was glad to have them back. Elisabeth wished she had been able to do more to repay Emilia's kindness, and was surprised to discover she was still thinking about those women.

"I didn't do much. It was Luca who tracked it down. You really must talk to him. If you want to, of course. But he has more."

"More of what?"

"You haven't looked yet?"

"No, I'm in no rush. It's a long way to France, yes?"

"Oh, most certainly. I only…"

"I know. Thank you again, Claude." She of course would have made it out of Constanta on her own, but it was comforting to be able to depend on others.

"I am honored, *Elisabeth.*"

"I think I'll get some more rest."

"Then I shall leave you, but when you are ready…" He pointed to the tarp-draped object leaning against the wall. "Take a look. The crew offered to have it secured below deck, but that is for you to decide."

Elisabeth closed the door and locked it, anxious to get off her feet. She shoved the clumsy gown off her shoulders and kicked it to the corner. Then she yanked the oilcloth down.

Impossible…

A hundred memories returned: the terrace overlooking Piazza in Avone where she sat for an entire summer, sketching her vision with charcoal sticks before applying paint, the swirling oil colors that followed, experimentation with perspective that brought richness and depth to her work for the first time.

The personal demons that inspired its creation…

The longer she stared the more she recalled the night she was pulled away from her dying mother, the sphere the laughing men had plunged through her throat. Armored crusaders so large they looked like moving fortresses. This was over two hundred years ago, but the nightmares got her every now and again.

The men who took her in the name of God were long dead, but their cruelty haunted the shadows of her mind.

Elisabeth had begged for just one more night with her mother. The sick old woman was not destined to last much longer, but they had refused to listen. The decision had already been made: murder her and steal her only possession. A twenty-four year old daughter.

The nomadic Inquisition traveled across Europe, striking without fear or repercussion. Their atrocities fell far beyond the church's borders whenever foreign rulers had use of their services. Road-weary men were enlisted to perform certain tasks, and were in exchange gifted with the freedom to pillage isolated estate grounds as payment.

Elisabeth had been one such form of currency. A young girl who went by Elisabeta then, she became their prisoner and suffered a host of horrors as bad as anything her wolf had instilled upon the innocent. They whisked her to a nearby church where the utmost priority became educating her in the ways of Christ.

This painting had only partially succeeded in exorcising those demons. Gazing at it now, while watery and weak, she realized they were the type of monsters that could never fully be exorcised.

Back then, she had been too scared to fight, incurring punishment and violation out of timidity, and because resistance only guaranteed more mutilation. She could not say how she survived it, but no one else from her village had.

This piece depicted a forced march through her homeland. It had been hell on earth: women impaled on their sexes and hoisted onto pikes, sharpened tips tearing from their throats, all because they had lain with the devil.

According to the men who had raped them first, of course.

Elisabeth remembered how badly she wanted to kill them all. She passed the nights forming such fantasies in her mind, picturing the different ways she was going to do it. Plotting vengeance every moment of the day, more intently while in the throes of sexual violence.

So badly had they hurt her, she should never have been able to enjoy pleasures of the flesh again.

Years later, a psychiatrist had told Elisabeth that she was attempting to screw her way out of the self-loathing. She did not know what she expected from a man whose profession analyzed sanity through methods the Inquisition would have favored. Chaining patients to walls and whipping impure thoughts from their minds as if that could cure any mental ailment.

Elisabeth had not cared for that diagnosis, or the vulnerable light it cast her in. As such, she had waited outside his home one evening, tearing him and his family to pieces. She had wanted to do more, castrate him to remove *his* ailment, for example, but Aetius had convinced her that simplicity would suffice. His persuasion always could shy her away from her cruelest impulses.

On her final night of Inquisition imprisonment, a varcolac called Scythe had happened into the stronghold and *saved* her while doing what she could not. His actions were not heroic, but her enemies died anyway, allowing Elisabeth to witness retribution through the feverish haze prompted by the wolf's bite.

Not unlike the one affecting Survivor right now.

That she had to be rescued at all conjured feelings of lingering inadequacy. For two hundred years, she wondered what it would have been like to take her own revenge that night.

To this day, she resented her sire for denying that privilege.

"What would it matter," Scythe had said. "They're dead, same as if you'd done it. All that remains of them is mixed with wolf shit."

Maybe Scythe had understood her predicament all to well, speaking from experience. She did not care, because she needed to find out herself.

And she finally knew.

The mere thought of Scythe churned her stomach now. He had wanted a whore by his side then—his only reason for turning her. Elisabeth stayed with him just long enough to accept the wolf, to learn how to cope with the animal within. Then she fled far.

Distance from Scythe that she continued to keep.

Although she realized now, quite begrudgingly, that he had been right about revenge. All who were responsible for the Nightfall ambush were gone, and yet her hostility had never been greater.

Deep down, Elisabeth understood the only one left to blame was herself.

She tilted her head and chased sleep. In the next room, Claude's heart pounded so hard she heard it from here. It was oddly soothing and she counted the thumps while attempting to drift off. His desire for her was so desperate that she pitied him.

It was amazing to think that Aetius had sent him to Rome to find whatever work of hers remained, and that he had somehow succeeded. After all this time, here was an original Elisabeth Luna.

Tomorrow, she would have to hear the whole story. How Claude had managed to find it. Her name had not been *Luna* back then, and she imagined that's where Luca's expertise probably came in. Why Claude had brought him along, though, was anyone's guess.

She would not be siring him in exchange for his help, because, well, the huntress had died for good somewhere over these last few days.

Elisabeth. Just Elisabeth. Elisabeth Luna.

The Luna surname was given to her years ago, after spending four seasons whittling down the residents of a tiny fishing village back west. She claimed a life each night, and her arrival was soon associated with the rising moon. The monster attacking the village came to be known as 'the Luna.'

She had loved how it sounded and quickly adopted it, wondering now if she should not have kept her real surname. That life was long gone, though. No point in disgracing her mother by stomping the family name through puddles of innocent blood.

She kept her eyes closed, tossing and turning atop the bed, pushing her head deeper into the pillow. Deep breaths searched out calming memories, but they were impossible to find.

Sleep came at last and much darkness greeted her there.

There was no comfort in it.

AFTERWORD & ACKNOWLEDGEMENTS

This book wouldn't have been possible without some truly special people: My friend Quinn Korzeniecki, the first person to lay eyes on this manuscript and who helped get it into fighting shape. From there it became my wife Michelle Serafini's responsibility to smooth out all the rough edges. And I can't thank her enough for all those late night read-throughs. There were a lot of them.

Both *Feral* and *Devil's Row* were originally published by Severed Press, and I'll always owe one to Gary Lucas and the rest of the gang for that first opportunity to get these werewolves out into the world.

Feral helped me pick up a few loyal readers early in the game but, three years later, *Devil's Row* had the misfortune of being released about a week before the birth of my first child. They say parents don't have favorites when it comes to their kids, but *Devil's Row* admittedly played second fiddle to our real life bundle of joy. I was smack-dab in the middle of a baby daze when I should've been promoting the hell out of this sucker. It's life. That happens.

But that's why I consider this Black T-Shirt Books edition of *Devil's Row* to be its true debut. And I'm excited to see how people react to it. When I initially floated news of a follow-up to *Feral*, as a prequel, the reaction startled me. More than one reader took the opportunity to remind me that I had ended that book on a cliffhanger, and the wait to discover the fates of those survivors had already been a bit on the long side.

Here's a little secret about *Devil's Row*: It was originally an extended flashback sequence within *Feral*. I cut it for pacing with the intention of adding it back into an eventual sequel.

In the years leading up to *Feral*'s publication, I'd done so much world building that I wasn't ready to put these characters and their universe behind me. *Devil's Row* became an opportunity to pull back the proverbial curtain and explore some of the stuff that had previously only existed on character sheets. As such, this historical horror fantasy remains something I'm incredibly proud of.

So if you liked *Feral* and/or *Devil's Row*, please let me know by taking two minutes to leave some quick Amazon reviews. I intend to use this book's performance to gauge interest in a potential Feral sequel.

Thanks for supporting the story so far.

—Matt 12/15/2017

ABOUT THE AUTHOR

Matt Serafini is the author of *Feral*, *Under the Blade*, and *Island Red*. He also co-authored a collection of short stories with Adam Cesare called *All-Night Terror*.

He has written extensively on the subjects of film and literature for numerous websites including *Dread Central* and *Shock Till You Drop*. His nonfiction has also appeared in *Fangoria* and *HorrorHound*. He spends a significant portion of his free time tracking down obscure slasher films, and hopes one day to parlay that knowledge into a definitive history book on the subject.

His novels are available in ebook and paperback from Amazon, Barnes & Noble, and all other fine retailers.

Matt lives in Massachusetts with his wife and children.

Please visit mattserafini.com to learn more.